the perfect deceit

(a jessie hunt psychological suspense—book 14)

blake pierce

Blake Pierce

Blake Pierce is the USA Today bestselling author of the RILEY PAGE mystery series, which includes seventeen books. Blake Pierce is also the author of the MACKENZIE WHITE mystery series, comprising fourteen books; of the AVERY BLACK mystery series, comprising six books; of the KERI LOCKE mystery series, comprising five books; of the MAKING OF RILEY PAIGE mystery series, comprising six books; of the KATE WISE mystery series, comprising seven books; of the CHLOE FINE psychological suspense mystery, comprising six books; of the JESSE HUNT psychological suspense thriller series, comprising nineteen books; of the AU PAIR psychological suspense thriller series, comprising three books; of the ZOE PRIME mystery series, comprising six books; of the ADELE SHARP mystery series, comprising thirteen books, of the EUROPEAN VOYAGE cozy mystery series, comprising six books (and counting); of the new LAURA FROST FBI suspense thriller, comprising three books (and counting); of the new ELLA DARK FBI suspense thriller, comprising six books (and counting); of the A YEAR IN EUROPE cozy mystery series, comprising nine books, of the AVA GOLD mystery series, comprising three books (and counting); and of the RACHEL GIFT mystery series, comprising three books (and counting).

An avid reader and lifelong fan of the mystery and thriller genres, Blake loves to hear from you, so please feel free to visit www.blakepierceauthor.com to learn more and stay in touch.

BOOKS BY BLAKE PIERCE

RACHEL GIFT MYSTERY SERIES
HER LAST WISH (Book #1)
HER LAST CHANCE (Book #2)
HER LAST HOPE (Book #3)

AVA GOLD MYSTERY SERIES
CITY OF PREY (Book #1)
CITY OF FEAR (Book #2)
CITY OF BONES (Book #3)

A YEAR IN EUROPE
A MURDER IN PARIS (Book #1)
DEATH IN FLORENCE (Book #2)
VENGEANCE IN VIENNA (Book #3)
A FATALITY IN SPAIN (Book #4)
SCANDAL IN LONDON (Book #5)
AN IMPOSTOR IN DUBLIN (Book #6)
SEDUCTION IN BORDEAUX (Book #7)
JEALOUSY IN SWITZERLAND (Book #8)
A DEBACLE IN PRAGUE (Book #9)

ELLA DARK FBI SUSPENSE THRILLER
GIRL, ALONE (Book #1)
GIRL, TAKEN (Book #2)
GIRL, HUNTED (Book #3)
GIRL, SILENCED (Book #4)
GIRL, VANISHED (Book 5)
GIRL ERASED (Book #6)

LAURA FROST FBI SUSPENSE THRILLER
ALREADY GONE (Book #1)
ALREADY SEEN (Book #2)
ALREADY TRAPPED (Book #3)

EUROPEAN VOYAGE COZY MYSTERY SERIES
MURDER (AND BAKLAVA) (Book #1)
DEATH (AND APPLE STRUDEL) (Book #2)

CRIME (AND LAGER) (Book #3)
MISFORTUNE (AND GOUDA) (Book #4)
CALAMITY (AND A DANISH) (Book #5)
MAYHEM (AND HERRING) (Book #6)

ADELE SHARP MYSTERY SERIES
LEFT TO DIE (Book #1)
LEFT TO RUN (Book #2)
LEFT TO HIDE (Book #3)
LEFT TO KILL (Book #4)
LEFT TO MURDER (Book #5)
LEFT TO ENVY (Book #6)
LEFT TO LAPSE (Book #7)
LEFT TO VANISH (Book #8)
LEFT TO HUNT (Book #9)
LEFT TO FEAR (Book #10)
LEFT TO PREY (Book #11)
LEFT TO LURE (Book #12)
LEFT TO CRAVE (Book #13)

THE AU PAIR SERIES
ALMOST GONE (Book#1)
ALMOST LOST (Book #2)
ALMOST DEAD (Book #3)

ZOE PRIME MYSTERY SERIES
FACE OF DEATH (Book#1)
FACE OF MURDER (Book #2)
FACE OF FEAR (Book #3)
FACE OF MADNESS (Book #4)
FACE OF FURY (Book #5)
FACE OF DARKNESS (Book #6)

A JESSIE HUNT PSYCHOLOGICAL SUSPENSE SERIES
THE PERFECT WIFE (Book #1)
THE PERFECT BLOCK (Book #2)
THE PERFECT HOUSE (Book #3)
THE PERFECT SMILE (Book #4)
THE PERFECT LIE (Book #5)
THE PERFECT LOOK (Book #6)
THE PERFECT AFFAIR (Book #7)

PROLOGUE

Jax tried to act jaded but it was hard.

This was the culmination of her professional career so far and she was having real trouble pretending it was just another night out on the town. This had been her dream ever since she'd left tiny Vinton, Louisiana, seven years ago with little more than a bus ticket, a duffel bag filled with Goodwill clothes, her cell phone, and the $600 she'd saved working as a waitress at a bar where bare midriffs were required attire.

Now she was living in Los Angeles, engaged to a super-hot film production executive, wealthy beyond her wildest dreams, and more famous than most movie stars. And tonight, she was at the famed Pacific Design Center, basking in the glow of being named among the top fashion influencers of the year.

She had walked the red carpet, posed for the paparazzi, and done the interviews. She had been invited onstage to collect a trophy and sat in on a panel with people she'd only imagined meeting a few years prior. Maintaining the bored, "earn my interest" expression that was so much a part of her appeal was especially challenging when surrounded by so much glitz and glamour.

Hell, the queen bee of social media fashion influencers, Monay Money, who had over 20 million followers, had even given her a kiss on the cheek. Jax had smiled warmly as she returned it. But inside, despite all the giddiness, she was thinking something else.

I have one tenth of your following today but give me another year and I'll be nipping at your heels.

As she swigged her last bit of champagne, Jax stepped outside and looked for her limo. Suddenly, despite all the other people milling about waiting for their rides, she felt very alone. The solitude hit her unexpectedly, as did the painful recollection that her close friend, Claire, had died around this time just last night. She pushed the thought out of her head as quickly as it had entered.

If only she had someone to distract her. Titus, her fiancé, had joined her for the red-carpet portion of the evening. But he had to leave the event early to help wrap up negotiations with a director that the studio

1

was hoping would take over the next installment in their biggest money-making action franchise. Talks were at a delicate point and his absence would be noted. Jax was bummed but understood. She'd had to miss some of his events too. Their lives were a Jenga tower of scheduling.

Her car pulled up and she hopped in. The champagne bottle from the drive that brought her here earlier that night was still resting on ice, but she had no desire for any more. After the long evening, she was ready for some sleep.

After all, it was a Sunday night and she had to be back at it tomorrow. This was no time to rest on her laurels. She'd be turning 26 next month, which meant she'd be in the back half of her twenties, just a stone's throw from thirty. With a few exceptions like Monay Money, the big 3-0 was the kiss of death in this industry, so there was no time to waste.

With thoughts of kicking Monay off her pedestal and stepping into her place, Jax drifted off.

*

"Ms. Coopersmith, we're here," Paul, the chauffeur, said gently after opening the door and finding her slumped over to the side.

She didn't respond. He debated how to proceed and finally decided a gentle nudge on the shoulder wasn't out of line.

"Ms. Coopersmith, we've arrived at your house," he said a little louder, leaning into the vehicle and tapping her delicately with his forefinger.

She immediately popped up and he had to dart back so their heads wouldn't collide.

"We're here?" she asked, slurring her words a bit. "It feels like we just left a few seconds ago."

"Yes, ma'am," he said noncommittally, apparently not wanting to alienate or embarrass his client in his last moments with her.

"Thanks a lot," she said, grabbing her shoes, plaque, and handbag and pulling out two one-hundred-dollar bills, which she pressed clumsily into his hand.

"Thank you very much, Ms. Coopersmith," he said, taking her hand and helping her out of the limo. "Do you need an escort to the door?"

"No, I'm good," she assured him. "You have a nice night."

2

Paul nodded, got in the vehicle, and pulled out of the large circular driveway as Jax walked up the long path that led to the Los Feliz neighborhood home she shared with Titus. They were renting for now, until after the wedding when they planned to move slightly up the hill. They wanted a more modern house with an enclosed gate and had their eyes on a few places they heard might go on the market soon.

But for now, this would do. With its plantation-style architecture, it appealed to a yearning from her youth, when she and her single mother would drive by Lake Charles area homes like this, knowing they could never enter one unless wearing some kind of apron. Titus, for reasons he'd made clear on more than one occasion, felt deeply uncomfortable living in a home that seemed to enshrine the old South, and was ready to move the second they locked in a new place.

Jax opened the door and picked up the mail that had been dropped through the slot. Much of it was for Jacqueline Cooper, Jax's name from a lifetime ago, and the one she still used for correspondence and legal documents. She dropped it on the foyer table, tossed her high heels in a corner and made her way to the kitchen.

She opened the fridge, looking for a light snack. She'd barely had anything at the gala and her stomach was growling fiercely. But with a photo shoot tomorrow for a new line of bikinis, she couldn't afford any unwanted bumps. So she sliced six thin discs of banana, put them on a cinnamon rice cake, and noshed on it as she made her way up the winding staircase to the bedroom.

She undressed as she passed through on the way to the bathroom, tossing the plaque, her purse, and her slinky gown on the bed for now. As she stared at herself in the bathroom mirror, looking back into the deep blue eyes that so many followers loved to praise, part of her wanted to just flop down next to the dress and be done with the day.

But she still had a whole regimen to go through if she wanted to look good for tomorrow. Her long black hair looked tired and stringy and her tanned, toned body appeared borderline gaunt under the bright bathroom lights. She couldn't deal with all of that now, but she could get a head start.

Sighing, she went back out to the bedroom to grab the dress and hang it up in her closet. Again, her thoughts went to Claire, and again, she forced them down, despite the guilt at blocking her dead friend out of her mind. If she allowed herself to think about Claire, she knew she'd never fall asleep. There would be time to mourn properly tomorrow, after the shoot was over.

She smoothed the dress out and hung it next to the other outfits in the eveningwear section of the massive walk-in closet. Even bone-tired, she took a moment to appreciate that it wasn't that long ago that "eveningwear" meant a sweatshirt and pajama pants. Now it meant a wall of sparkly, clingy outfits, not a single one of which she'd paid for. She smiled to herself.

You've come a long way, baby.

Jax flicked off the light and turned back toward the bedroom to finish the work of the evening. A sudden spray of liquid splashed her face,, and she was consumed by pain. Adrenaline shot through her body.

She knew her eyes were open but she couldn't see. It felt like the skin on her face was melting and she thought she could hear it sizzle. She opened her mouth to scream but her lips were slick and loose.

Her heart thumped nearly out of her chest. Panic rose in her throat but only a moan came out as she dropped to her knees and reached her hands to her face. As she did, she felt a sharp cold prick in the side of her neck, followed by an unrelenting, burning sensation, as if she was being consumed from the inside out.

It took several more excruciating minutes for her to die, and when death did finally come, it was a relief.

CHAPTER ONE

Jessie Hunt was freaking out.

While her boyfriend, Detective Ryan Hernandez, called for backup from inside the house, she'd hopped in the car and started searching the neighborhood. Neither had any idea how long ago Hannah had snuck out the window or how far she might have gotten. But with a serial killer on the loose, one that Jessie had just learned minutes earlier was delighting in playing games with her, she knew this wasn't the time for her little sister to decide to run away.

She looked at the dashboard clock again. It read 10:48 p.m. She'd been driving around for nearly a half hour when she came across a neighbor, a retired history professor named Delia Morris who lived a few doors down, walking her white poodle, Grant (named after the president), and waving at her.

"Is everything okay, dear?" the older woman asked, her shock of unruly white hair getting tossed about by the late-night January winds. "This is the fifth time I've seen you drive down the street."

"Have you seen my sister, Hannah, out this evening?" Jessie asked, trying to keep the panic out of her voice.

The woman searched her memory, which was notorious for its gaps.

"Now that you mention it, I think I may have. I thought it was last night but perhaps it was this evening. I saw her help an older gentleman into the back of a car and then drive off. He looked to be unwell."

Jessie felt a cold, invisible fist tighten around her spine.

"Could you describe the man or the car?" she asked as if everything was completely normal. She didn't want to upset Delia and have any useful memories disappear.

"I'm afraid not, dear. It was too far away to see much other than your sweet sister helping an elderly man—older than me I'd say—into the car. It might have been black or blue and it was on the smaller side but that's I can seem to recall. My mind isn't what it used to be. Is that at all helpful?"

"Very helpful, Delia; thanks so much," Jessie said, praying the woman was mistaken. She texted the description to Ryan.

The serial killer who had her heart racing—the Night Hunter—was elderly and liked to use his seeming frailty to bait people into underestimating him before he made his move. If he'd done that with Hannah, there was no telling where they might be now.

It was hard to believe that less than an hour ago, Jessie's primary concern had been trying to get Hannah to take responsibility for dangerous, risk-taking behavior over the last few months, behavior that Jessie had only discovered the extent of today.

But in a sudden tidal wave of horribles, she'd learned several things in just a few minutes. First, that the Night Hunter, a legendary serial killer who'd tussled with her mentor decades ago but had subsequently gone silent for twenty years, was back in business here in Los Angeles.

Next, she had to process that while investigating the case with Ryan, the sweet, baby-faced Detective Alan Trembley had been ambushed and murdered by the killer. Finally, she'd figured out that in a twisted game, the Night Hunter had been murdering people with her own initials, "J.H.," as a way to communicate with her.

It was that last realization, along with police researcher Jamil Winslow's discovery that the Night Hunter had been staking out her home, that made her rush to Hannah's room to warn her of the new danger in their lives. But instead of finding a brooding teenager, she'd discovered an open window and a missing sister.

Jessie had no idea how long Hannah had been gone or how long ago she'd gotten in the old man's car. She found it hard to believe that her sister, even feeling petulant and wronged, would take such a risk. It was unfathomable that a girl who'd been kidnapped, tortured and nearly killed, all in the last year, would have willingly gotten into a vehicle with a stranger, no matter how harmless he seemed.

Her phone rang. It was Ryan. She pulled over and picked up, terrified at what news he might have.

"What is it?" she asked without preamble.

He didn't waste any time either.

"Her phone is turned off," he said crisply. "She must have done it herself because the last signal was from inside the house. Jamil is at the station now, logging any vehicles in a three-mile radius from the last hour that match the description of a dark-colored vehicle, sedan or smaller with a female driver. The system is also searching facial recognition for a match to her. What about you?"

6

"I've been doing an expanding grid search," Jessie told him. "I'm at the outer limit of the neighborhood now, incorporating major cross streets, but so far, nothing."

Ryan was quiet for a moment and she feared what he might say next.

"Captain Decker has closed off all roads in the same three-mile radius that Jamil is searching," he finally said. "Roadblocks are being established. Patrols are already out there, circling the restricted zone, but—."

"But by now, any car she was in would be far outside that zone," Jessie said, finishing his thought.

"Right," Ryan replied, making no attempt to sugar-coat the facts.

They were both silent for several seconds before Jessie regrouped enough to assess the situation.

"So to be clear," she said, as much to herself as to Ryan, "my sister is missing after likely having run away. She was seen getting into a vehicle with an old man and driving off. And we know that a serial killer who happens to be an old man has been murdering people with my initials for months and stalking our family for days. Does that sound about right?"

Before he could reply, her phone buzzed, indicating that she had another call. It was from a number she didn't recognize.

"I'll call you back," she told Ryan, switching over before he could answer.

*

Thirty-three minutes earlier, Hannah was tearing down Olympic Boulevard, dodging cars and intermittently looking in the backseat. The old guy seemed legitimately in distress but after everything she'd been through, part of her feared it was ruse and that he might jump up and attack her at any moment.

But every time she checked him, he looked worse than the last time. She pulled into the emergency room driveway of Olympia Medical Center, just a couple of miles west of where she'd found an old man, only a block from her house, clutching his chest and gasping for air.

Swerving past an ambulance, she parked in a loading spot and hopped out. There was no one outside so she ran in through the main entrance, where a security guard sat by the door. A sad collection of people dotted the waiting area, most with their heads slumped in pain or exhaustion.

Finally, her eyes fell on a receiving window. A youngish guy with a bloody dish towel wrapped around his thumb was talking to a bored-looking woman wearing bifocals on a chain. She didn't even look up.

"There's a guy having a heart attack outside!" Hannah shouted to her and anyone else who would listen. "He needs help."

The bifocaled woman glanced up at her, unimpressed.

"What makes you think it's a heart attack?" she asked.

Hannah fought the urge to cuss the woman out and answered the question as directly as possible, trying her best to reign in the sarcasm.

"I found him lying on the street beside his car. He was having trouble breathing, clutching his chest and drooling. He was sweating and his lips were bluish. Also, he *said* he thought he was having a heart attack. I drove him here in his car. He's lying in the back seat. He's got to be at least seventy. Do you think you could send someone out there to, you know, help him?"

The woman, suddenly alert, hit a button on her desk and within twenty seconds two younger men shot out of a pair of swinging doors with a stretcher. One of them made eye contact with Hannah.

"Follow me," she said, leading them out to the car, where the old man was lying on his back. As they moved him from the back seat to the stretcher, one of the guys began peppering the man with questions. But his eyes were clenched shut and he shook his head slightly, as if the idea of speaking was too much for him. The guy turned his questions on her: "When did you find him? How long had he been there? What did he say? Had he vomited? Did he seem coherent? What was his name?"

She joined them as they went back through the swinging doors, doing her best to answer him, though she could only offer responses to about every other question: I found him lying in the street. He said he thought he was having a heart attack. I don't know his name.

Once they had the man in a slot in the ER, two nurses came in as well. One pulled a curtain across while the other started an IV. One of the stretcher guys pulled out what looked like an EKG machine, cut open the man's shirt and started attaching electrodes to his chest. A doctor joined them in the increasingly crowded space. One of the nurses looked at Hannah and she knew what the woman was thinking.

"Why don't I step out...?" she started to offer, backing away.

As she did, she realized the old man was clutching her hand tightly. She had no idea how long that had been going on. She didn't even remember him grabbing it.

"No. Stay," he muttered through gritted teeth, then surprised her with a question. "Why were you in the street?"

The medical personnel exchanged worried glances.

"She's going to leave the room for a few minutes, sir," the nurse said, trying to help extricate Hannah.

"No," he groaned.

"If it keeps him calm, let her stay a bit longer," the doctor said. "We have another minute before we're fully up and running here. Maybe she can get some more information from the gentleman."

He nodded at Hannah, silently telling her to try. She gulped, trying to remember what the stretcher guy had asked her earlier.

"When did you first start feeling bad, sir?" she asked softly.

The doctor smiled, seeming to approve of the question. But the old guy didn't agree.

"Why were you in the street so late?" he demanded, fixated on getting his own answers.

Hannah debated how to respond. She didn't owe this old guy anything. She could give him any answer and he'd never know the difference. But a tiny bit of her wondered if telling him a lie might make things worse and if being honest could somehow help him, reduce his stress, and get him to start answering some questions of her own.

"I was thinking of running away," she finally said, surprising herself. "I was out walking, debating where to go."

He nodded, his eyes still closed. Electrodes were being attached to his body at lightning speed. Liquid was dripping from the IV bag. One of the nurses drew blood from his non-IV arm. He swallowed hard, trying to find his breath. The other nurse slipped an oxygen mask over his face.

"But why?" he asked hoarsely through the mask.

"It's my sister," Hannah replied quietly. "She's my guardian. I know she loves me, but sometimes she's just too much. She's incredibly overprotective."

The old man opened his eyes. They were a deep green, just like her own. His grip softened slightly.

"Why?"

"I've had some stuff happen," Hannah admitted, shrugging. "Parents murdered; I was kidnapped; nearly stabbed to death. I guess she's a little on edge after all that."

The room, which had been a volley of cross-cutting conversations among the medical professionals, went briefly silent. Several people stared at her with wide eyes. To their credit the pause lasted only a couple of seconds and the unintelligible terminology quickly resumed. The man rasped under his breath. It took Hannah a second to realize he was chuckling.

"I'm sorry you went through that," he said slowly, gasping for breath. It was hard to hear him with the mask on and so much noise all around them. "It sounds like you got a raw deal. And I'll bet your sister is a real handful. But she doesn't sound like the worst ever. It's your life so you should do what you want. But maybe give her a call if you get a second. Even a frustrating family is better than no family at all."

His grip on her fingers got even looser, which Hannah took as a sign that he might finally be relaxing a bit. But then he let go completely and his hand fell to his side, limp. Suddenly multiple monitor warnings began going off simultaneously. She looked up and saw that the man's face had gone slack. He seemed to have lost consciousness.

"Please step out, ma'am," one of the nurses said calmly, though there was a definite edge underneath.

Hannah did exactly that, taking one last look back at the man. His eyes were closed again but not tightly. His teeth were no longer gritted. In fact, his mouth was open. The doctor was reaching for a pair of defibrillating paddles. The last thing she saw before pulling the curtain closed was the man's hand slide off the gurney and dangle listlessly in the air.

She walked out to the waiting area. For several seconds, she stared at her reflection in the ER waiting room window. Her sandy blonde hair dangled lifelessly just past her shoulders. She thought that she looked skinnier and weaker than usual. There was really no reason for her to stick around but she sat down anyway. About ten minutes later one of the nurses came out and told her what she already knew.

"I'm afraid he passed away."

Hannah nodded.

"Here are his keys," she said, pulling them out of her pocket and handing them over. "I don't want his car to get towed."

"Are you okay, sweetie?" The nurse asked, taking them. "That was a lot back there."

"I'll be fine," Hannah assured her. "I've been through worse. I didn't even know his name."

"We found his wallet. His name was Edward Wexler. He was 80 years old."

"The name doesn't mean anything to me," Hannah told her.

"Maybe not," the nurse replied. "But it seemed like you meant something to him. Because of you, he died holding someone's hand, knowing people were trying to help him, instead of alone on the side of a road. I think talking to you at the end—I think it was a blessing for him. He was lucky to have you there."

"Thanks," Hannah said, not sure if any of that was true.

"Do you want me to call someone for you, sweetie?" the nurse asked, careful not to push.

"No thank you," Hannah said.

The nurse nodded and stood up. Hannah wondered if she would make a call of her own the second she was out of sight.

"I have to get back in there," she said. "But you take care."

Hannah nodded. She sat there for a bit, unmoving. No security guard approached her. No uniformed officer charged in. If the nurse had reported her, someone would have been here by now.

She was still free to run away. She could walk out the emergency room doors now. The nearest metro station was close by. In half an hour she could be anywhere in the city. She'd already checked online and knew there was bus leaving for Phoenix in two hours. Another headed to Las Vegas would pull out in three.

Finally, she stood up and walked over to the twenty-something guy with the towel around his thumb. He'd been waiting around for over thirty minutes and the thing was sopping wet. It occurred to Hannah that maybe *he* should have claimed he was having a heart attack.

Despite his injury, he'd been giving her sideways glances that suggested his physical pain wasn't overwhelming whatever other natural feelings were coursing through his system. She batted her eyes sweetly and, in a voice she knew would have the desired effect, asked a question.

"Could I borrow your phone?"

CHAPTER TWO

They barely spoke on the ride home.

Hannah hopped out the second the car pulled into the garage and was inside the house before Jessie had even opened her own door. Rather than storm in after her, she lowered the garage door and stayed in the car, trying to let the stew of anger, anxiety, and relief settle a little.

Whether Hannah realized it or not, this was a make-or-break moment. Things simply couldn't continue this way. Even if there wasn't a serial killer out there who seemed to have his sights set on them, her sister's behavior would be dangerous.

Jessie shook her head, trying to wrap her mind around this latest escalation in the ongoing challenges with Hannah. As she just learned earlier today, last summer her sister had confronted a drug dealer, seemingly just for kicks. Then, barely a month ago, she had broken into the home of a violent pedophile to entrap him for a crime it turned out he hadn't committed. Last fall, she'd used herself as bait to break up a sexual slavery ring. Who knows what else she'd done that Jessie would never know about?

As she got out of the car and walked into the house, she wondered if this was perhaps some warped, unhealthy way of Hannah following in her own footsteps. Jessie was a criminal profiler after all. And each of these incidents seemed to involve pursuing a criminal who was taking advantage of the vulnerable. There was probably some truth to the theory.

But as she turned on the security system and wandered down the darkened hallway, Jessie knew that wasn't the only explanation. Hannah seemed to be willfully putting herself at risk, taking wild chances that would invariably end badly, all just for the thrill of it. It was like she was some sort of danger junkie who needed to constantly up the ante to get that high.

It wasn't a shock that the girl was going through stuff. In the last year alone she'd been through more horrors than most adults could pack into multiple lifetimes. Her adoptive parents had been murdered by her—and Jessie's— own father, a serial killer who wanted to either reunite his family or destroy it. She'd been abducted by another murderer who tried to convince her that killing people was her birthright. Her big sister's ex-husband went on a rampage that ended with one profiler dead, Ryan stabbed in the chest, and both sisters nearly killed as well. It would actually be weird if she was well-adjusted.

But this was a different level of messed up. Jessie put her keys in a bowl on the kitchen counter and sat down at the breakfast table, wondering how next to proceed. She knew Ryan was in the bedroom, waiting for her. He might even be asleep already.

She could see a dim light coming from under Hannah's door. Fighting the urge to walk over and knock, she put her head in her hands and rubbed her temples. She'd been awake for almost forty hours straight and she was feeling it.

Earlier this evening, she fought off a killer who'd nearly choked her to death and her throat still ached horribly. Then she'd learned that a friend and colleague had been murdered by the Night Hunter. Plus, her boyfriend, one of the most celebrated detectives in recent LAPD history, had confided that he froze when he had the chance to take down the killer. It was too much for any one brain to process.

She knew she should just call it a night, get some sleep, and regroup for whatever tomorrow held in store. And yet she found herself mentally crafting the best way to propose that Hannah go see Dr. Lemmon, their shared therapist, tomorrow. But there was no way to suggest that without sounding condescending or controlling. With everything so volatile, it seemed particularly unwise.

She considered mentioning the Night Hunter threat, so that Hannah would know exactly how risky running off was at this moment. But whatever good that might do, it would surely be subverted by giving a traumatized teenage girl more material for her nightmares. She already had enough for now.

In the end, Jessie decided to do nothing, at least for tonight. She couldn't think of a magic phrase that would make everything better. And as much as she might like, she couldn't tie a monitor to Hannah's ankle and put her on home confinement.

Besides, Hannah *had* called her, eventually. She could have hopped a bus to Mexico and been halfway there by now if she really wanted. Instead, she apparently tried to save an elderly man who was having a heart attack and, belatedly, called her from the hospital to come get her. On a night without much hope, that was something to hold onto.

13

Jessie decided to embrace it. She got up and trudged to bed. She was already mostly asleep by the time she got under the covers next to Ryan, whose soft snores served as the gentle metronome that finally gave her some peace.

CHAPTER THREE

The Night Hunter was in a new car.

He'd bought several, all clunkers from the last century, just in case. And it turned out to be a good move, because somehow Detective Hernandez had tracked his previous vehicle all the way to the hostel where he'd been sleeping. Of course, all that effort had only led to the death of the man's partner and a moment of self-doubt that was delicious to watch in real time.

Now he was parked a block down the street from Jessie's house in an old station wagon that he could crawl into the back of if he needed a nap. But right now, he was wide awake, just as he had been when he watched young Hannah Dorsey assist the old man having the health crisis on the street.

He could have taken her then if he wanted. Prior to the man's heart attack interruption, he could have easily driven up next to the girl who was clearly running away, hit her with his dart gun, and with some effort, dragged her into the back of the wagon. Alternately, he could have driven by and tranqed Hunt while she was talking to the white-haired lady walking her dog.

But it was too early for any of that. There was still work to be done. After all, he hadn't come out of forced retirement after two decades to rush into anything. He'd come to Los Angeles to test the mettle of a young woman named Jessie Hunt. She was the protégé of his long-time nemesis, criminal profiler Garland Moses, the only person who'd ever come close to catching him.

When he'd learned of Moses's murder last summer at the hands of Hunt's ex-husband, the juiciness of the scenario was just too wonderful to ignore. He had to come out west to learn about this woman who Moses thought was worthy of his tutelage. He wanted to watch her process the grief and guilt she surely felt at having her own former husband murder her mentor.

And then to learn that Hunt's detective boyfriend had nearly died in the attack and was now just a shell of his former strapping self—it made his mouth water. The coup de grace was discovering that Hunt was the guardian for her half-sister, a teenager who'd been through a

15

funhouse of horrors herself. Part of him thought it would be entertaining enough to just settle back and watch this "family" self-immolate all on its own.

But that wasn't his style. He liked to give a little push now and then, but not too hard and not too early. One thing about being older was that, unlike some of the younger gentlemen into the old ultra-violence, he could control his urges, at least for a while. Once he'd even come up with a joke about it: he considered himself to be the Sting of tantric murder. Of course, there was no one to tell the joke to, but he thought it was a good one.

He'd be sending Moses's protégé another message soon, one he hoped she'd understand. It was so much more fun when the opponent knew the game being played. Otherwise it was just too easy. So he would wait just a little longer. But the time would soon come when he'd explode Jessie Hunt's world, if she didn't beat him to it.

CHAPTER FOUR

"What do you mean you're going in?" Jessie demanded.

"I told you—I have to," Ryan replied emphatically as he sat across the breakfast table from her.

"I get that you don't want to take a break, but you can still work from here."

"No," he insisted, clearly struggling to keep his frustration in check. "This is on me. Trembley is dead because of me. The Night Hunter got away because of me. Can't you see? I need to be in the office, working with Jamil, sending resources where they're most useful. If I'm not in the mix, I'll go crazy."

Jessie was quiet. More than anyone, she understood what he was feeling, and she didn't want to upset him more. But she was concerned at how much blame he was piling on himself. She saw that he seemed to get that he'd come on too strong and backtracked slightly.

"Hell, I'm still on desk duty, remember," he said. "I'm not allowed to leave the station. I won't go in the field."

"You promise?" Jessie demanded more than asked, as she slid a couple of pancakes onto Ryan's plate.

"I promise," he assured her as took another sip of coffee.

Jessie wasn't totally convinced but she didn't want to push any harder. After a decent night's sleep, they'd had a relaxed Monday morning breakfast up until two minutes ago. She didn't want to mess up the vibe any further by revisiting it all again. She'd just have to trust that Ryan would only work from the police station today, no matter what leads might make him want to go in the field.

"Good," she said, glad the matter was settled. "With the Catalina case resolved and school not starting up again for me until Wednesday, I can help out some on this Night Hunter thing. Now that we know this guy has been killing people with my initials as a message to me, at least we can start to develop a profile for him."

"How sick must the man be to kill people just because they share your initials?" Ryan wondered, shaking his head.

"No kidding," Jessie agreed. "After all, there are other forms of communication. What happened to just sending a threatening letter?"

After such a long, painful day and night, Jessie thought a little gallows humor was in order. But Ryan didn't seem to appreciate it and simply shook his head.

"I'm not really in the mood," he muttered.

"Fair enough," she replied. "But let's not wallow in the man's madness, Ryan." She was still concerned about how much guilt he was taking on.

"What do you mean?"

"I mean, I think the days of us being repulsed by this man's level of sickness are in the past," she said as she flipped through the file Ryan had assembled on the murders, "In the last thirty-five some years, the Night Hunter killed at least eighty people that we know of, and probably multiple times that. He's used machetes and exacto knives. He's come at his victims head-on, chopping their bodies up. He's also used subterfuge to wheedle his way into their homes, where he's incapacitated them with paralyzing injections while he skins them alive. And in all that time, only one law enforcement official—Garland Moses—ever got close enough to bring him down. That was twenty years ago, and it nearly ended in Garland's death."

"Two law enforcement officials," Ryan reminded her quietly, his shoulders sagging.

Jessie nodded, ashamed that she'd forgotten. Eager, goofy Detective Alan Trembley, who had joined the force around the same time as Jessie, had also gotten close—too close. Trembley had bled out last night, alone in a hostel bedroom, after taking an exacto blade to the carotid. The circumstances of the murder were still muddy, though it seemed he may have inadvertently stumbled on the Night Hunter, not realizing the threat right in front of him until it was too late.

"We'll get this guy," Jessie said with as much reassurance as she could offer under the situation. But Ryan clearly wasn't convinced.

"It's not just Trembley," he said, his voice dropping to a whisper so that Hannah, who was still asleep in the other bedroom, couldn't possibly hear. "It's also us. Jamil said the guy had been surveilling this house. He knows where we live. He's been tracking our movements. What's to stop him from just walking up to the front door?"

Jessie understood his concerns. She felt them too. This was far from the first time that she felt like a prisoner in her own home. She had more experience than she liked to admit supervising the set-up of advanced security systems. And even in this house, gifted to her by Garland Moses and equipped with the most state-of-the-art system of protection she'd ever encountered in a residence, she was apprehensive. But she also knew that giving in to those worries was a recipe for dysfunction.

"Walking up to the front door wouldn't do him much good," she noted, "considering that you saw him last night and can identify him. The description you gave the sketch artist has already been provided to every law enforcement agency in Southern California. If someone sees anyone who looks even remotely like him, they're bringing the guy in."

"You know what I mean, Jessie," Ryan said, his warm, brown eyes locking in on hers. "We're vulnerable."

She understood what he was saying, as well as what he wasn't. He feared that they were vulnerable because *he* was vulnerable. Before the attack, he'd been a six-foot tall, 200 pound muscular specimen. But that man was a distant memory. Still unable to walk more than a step or two without a cane, about twenty pounds below his normal weight, and quick to tire, he considered himself a liability. And based on what he'd ashamedly told her about last night's events when he froze during a near-confrontation with the Night Hunter, he seemed to judge himself a coward too.

"We'll up the safeguards," she said, not wanting to let him simmer in his self-disgust. "Jamil has promised to run a diagnostic on all our security systems and recommend any upgrades, though I think we're already top of the line on everything. I'm looking into some additional measures that always struck my fancy but that I never pulled the trigger on. We're talking heat sensors, an external laser grid, and a second panic room."

That at least made him crack a smile.

"You just love the idea of panic rooms. I think all this is just an excuse to build another one. How many do we actually need?"

"By my count, two," she answered, kissing him on the forehead. "The bigger issue is that none of those measures do much good if Hannah is wandering about the neighborhood, oblivious to, or potentially even courting a threat she doesn't take seriously."

"So what do you want to do?" Ryan asked. "Should we tell her everything?"

Jessie sat down across from him and took a big bite of pancake, chewing slowly to allow herself time to think.

"I'd like to avoid it for the moment if we can," she finally said. "As frustrated as I am with her right now, I'm trying to remember that she's

19

going through a lot. Even setting aside all the terrible things she's been through lately, she's on eggshells now that her secret is out."

"Good point," Ryan said.

"Plus," Jessie went on, "she only has a few more months of school left. Worrying about her future has to be weighing on her. We need to remember that she's not just a survivor of unspeakable violence; she's a teenager just trying to get by. I kind of want to give her a day where she doesn't have to think about any of that. With winter break, school doesn't start back up until tomorrow. Maybe we just give her a free day."

"But then how do we make sure she's free while still staying safe?" Ryan wanted to know.

"I don't know how we handle that, long-term," Jessie admitted. "But at least for today, with neither of us having school, I can keep an eye on her. Maybe I'll suggest she talk to Dr. Lemmon, although I worry that my mentioning it will make it unappealing to her. Hell, she can spend the whole day pouting in her room if she wants. At least I'll know where she is."

Jessie's phone rang before they came to any final resolution. She looked at it and felt her shoulders slump involuntarily.

"What?" Ryan asked, seeing that she wasn't excited.

"It's Captain Decker," she said. "It's getting to the point where my blood pressure rises just seeing his name on the screen."

"Do you want me to answer it?" Ryan offered.

She shook her head.

"No. Whatever it is, I'd rather just face it head on," she said, picking up. "Hello, Captain."

"Hello Hunt," Decker said, his voice raspy and even more tired sounding than usual. "How are you feeling after your extracurricular activities last night? I hear your neck got a rough going over."

"Yes, sir, it's quite sore. But I've been through worse. And considering the other guy's cheek looks like ground beef, I think I got the better of it."

"Well, I'm glad you're doing okay," Decker replied with an unusual hint of nervousness. "Is Detective Hernandez with you?"

"Yes, he's right here," she told him. "Shall I put you on speaker?"

"Yes please."

"Go ahead," she said after hitting the button.

20

"I just wanted to let you both know that I've been helping coordinate Alan Trembley's funeral plans. The service will be on Saturday. I'm hoping both of you can make it."

"Of course, Captain," Ryan assured him, his voice choked with emotion.

"We'll be there," Jessie agreed quickly, hoping Decker hadn't picked up on how hard this was hitting him.

"Thank you. He admired both of you greatly, but I think he'd be happy knowing he was the main attraction for once."

The clumsy attempt to lighten the mood felt hollow. Jessie had a feeling she knew why: there was another reason Decker had called. She waited patiently for him to get around to it.

"Anyway," he continued after an awkward pause. "As much as I would like for the whole week to be about Trembley, crime doesn't stop. I was hoping to discuss developments with both of you."

"Yes, Captain," Ryan said. "Jessie and I have actually been discussing the Night Hunter case already this morning. We figured that with her not back teaching at UCLA until Wednesday, if we put out heads together today and tomorrow, we could make some real progress, especially since it's obvious the killer has been trying to get her attention."

"I appreciate your shared commitment to resolving this," Decker replied. "And under normal circumstances, I'd love to take advantage of Hunt's help, even on a consulting basis. But I anticipate that the Night Hunter will want to keep a low profile for a little bit after killing a police detective. Hernandez, I think that you, with Jamil Winslow's assistance, can keep on top of developments from the office. Besides, after what happened to Trembley, we'll have all the human resources we need at our disposal."

Unlike Jessie, Ryan hadn't yet picked up on Decker's real motivation for the call. Before she could stop him, he launched into a counter argument with the captain.

"With all due respect sir," he said, "I'm not sure I agree. This guy isn't a normal killer. Yes, he might go underground for another month, but he might hit again tonight. Plus, he's focused on Jessie. I can't think of anyone more equipped to get into his head than her."

"I suspect that you're probably right, Hernandez, at least about the second part. Hunt would be a tremendous asset. But I need to hope this man holds off at least few days, because I need her for something else."

"What?" Jessie asked with trepidation.

"I have another case I was hoping you'd take, Hunt," Decker said, addressing her directly now.

"But why?" she wanted to know. "Surely the Night Hunter case is high profile enough for Headquarters to let us focus on it exclusively. If we can solve it, that should secure the future of Homicide Special Section. I know you've been concerned that they're going to shut it down."

It was true. The last few months had been bad for HSS, which specialized in cases that had high profiles or intense media scrutiny, often involving multiple victims or serial killers. First, celebrated profiler Garland Moses had been murdered. Then Ryan, the unit's lead detective, was stabbed in the chest. After nearly dying, he still wasn't ready to resume full, active duty over six months later. Jessie, the only other profiler dedicated to HSS, had left to take care of Ryan and teach at UCLA, where her life wasn't in constant danger. And just last night, the youngest detective in the unit, Trembley, had been murdered too.

"Unfortunately, it's not that simple," Decker said. "Because we lost one of our own during the Night Hunter investigation, the heat on the unit is even worse. If we solve the case, it's a big win. But right now, it's a black eye. And the folks at HQ only think in the 'right now,' so I have to also. And right now, a case fell into our lap that could help keep the wolves at bay. If we solve it, we could get the undying support of millions of social media fanatics, all of whom would go ballistic if the unit that got justice for one of their own was shut down."

"What are you talking about, Captain?" Ryan asked, perplexed.

"You haven't seen the news this morning?"

"We've been on an intentional all-media blackout," Jessie said. "I think we've earned it."

"You have," Decker agreed. "But that means you missed news about the murder of a woman named Jacqueline Cooper, better known as Jax Coopersmith."

"Are we supposed to know who that is?" Ryan asked. Clearly, he didn't.

"I'd never heard of her until this morning either," Decker confessed. "Apparently she's—"

"I know who she is," Jessie interrupted. "Living with an eighteen-year-old, I have no choice. I guess all that rehab you've been doing with your ear buds in saved you from the constant mentions."

"This is a famous person?" Ryan asked, truly befuddled.

"She's a social media influencer," Jessie explained. "According to Hannah, she's an up and comer, big in the fashion world. She's going to be devastated when she finds out about this. What happened, Captain?"

"Apparently she had recently returned from some ritzy gala where she won an award. Someone got into her house and injected her with what the coroner believes was drain cleaner. She also had acid thrown in her face. By the time her fiancé arrived home, she was dead. The body's been taken to the medical examiner's office already but that hasn't stopped fans and paparazzi from surrounding the house. There are even news helicopters circling overhead."

"Where did she live?" Jessie asked.

"In Los Feliz, just at the base of the Griffith Park Hills in Vermont Canyon. Detective Reid is already en route. I was hoping you could meet him there."

Jessie sighed deeply.

"Captain," she said, unable to keep the reluctance out of her voice, "I know I agreed to consult for you from time to time but this is becoming…a lot. I'm still recovering from the case you asked me to handle less than 36 hours ago, one that sent me to an isolated island and nearly got me choked to death. Plus, I was hoping to focus my attention on, you know, the elderly, prolific serial killer who seems to have fixated on me. Isn't there someone else who can handle this one?"

"That's the thing, Hunt: the well is pretty dry right now. Your beau there is still confined to desk duty. Hell, right now, he's officially still a consultant himself. Besides, he's working the Night Hunter case. And with Trembley's death, the team has been hollowed out. We have Detective Reid, as I mentioned. There's also Nettles. He's experienced, with over fifteen years on the street, but he's only had his detective's shield for a few months. Gaylene Parker from Vice has agreed to help in a pinch. But she's not going to give up running her own unit to help us out except on occasion. She can tell we're a sinking ship. And I can only rearrange so many deck chairs. We need a break, a big one. And this might be it. So I'm asking for your help."

Decker left something else unsaid, though it was foremost in Jessie's mind. If HSS collapsed, then there was no longer any single unit dedicated to investigating the Night Hunter. That put her and Hannah at greater risk. She needed their resources and their support. She realized that she had to save Homicide Special Section so it could help save her.

23

Jessie looked over at Ryan, who shrugged. She knew that HSS was just as important to him as it was to Decker. But he clearly didn't want to put any pressure on her. She wasn't even sure that, despite his affection for the unit, he thought this was a good idea. She sighed again, equally frustrated and exhausted.

"I start teaching again on Wednesday," she finally said to Decker. "That's my out date, no matter what. I've got a lot on my plate right now, as you well know. If doing this helps keep HSS intact, as in the unit that's searching for the serial killer who's toying with me, I'm in for now. But there's a limit."

"Thank you, Hunt," Decker said, sounding genuinely relieved. "I'm texting you the address. Detective Reid will meet you there."

He hung up quickly, as if worried that she'd change her mind if he stayed on the line. She turned back to Ryan, who hadn't touched his pancakes. He was staring off into the distance. She could guess what he was thinking about.

"What do we do about Hannah?" she asked, trying to snap him out of it. "I'll be out in Los Feliz. You'll be downtown at the station. I don't want to leave her unsupervised after last night."

Ryan swallowed his food and offered a suggestion that nearly made her leap out of her seat in anger.

"What about Kat?"

CHAPTER FIVE

"Are you kidding me?" she demanded, in a whispered yell, trying not to wake Hannah. She was stunned that he'd even broach the idea.

Kat was part of the reason they were in this predicament. Katherine "Kat" Gentry was Jessie's best friend, or at least had been until the revelations of yesterday. The woman was a badass— a former Army Ranger injured in Afghanistan who had gone on to run security at a lockdown facility for the criminally insane. When an unstable co-worker helped break the prisoners out, including a notorious serial killer, she'd lost her job, but managed to rebound by taking up work as a private investigator. She'd been a loyal, devoted friend to Jessie.

Unfortunately, Kat had also learned that Hannah was putting herself in increasingly dangerous situations and, rather than ratting her out, kept it a secret. She obviously felt guilty that some of Hannah's behavior had occurred on her watch. Maybe staying quiet was part of some ill-fated effort to turn Hannah around without worrying her big sister. Whatever the reason, the situation had escalated and for over six months, Jessie had no idea that Hannah had been playing with metaphorical fire. She felt wounded and betrayed.

"What other choice do we have?" Ryan asked, pulling her back into the moment. "I know she let you down. But who else do you trust to keep an eye on her? Kat's incredibly capable, and these days she's extremely motivated to do right by you. Seems like a good combination of qualities under the current circumstances."

Jessie shook her head vigorously.

"I'm not about to call her up and ask her to do me a solid just because we're under the gun. That would give her impression that we're all good now. And we most definitely are *not*."

"Jessie," Ryan pleaded, "she wouldn't look at it that way. She's probably desperate to hear from you, to make this better somehow. She's not going to think that just because she spends the day with Hannah, that everything has gone back to normal."

Jessie could feel the aggravation rising in her chest.

"That's not the point," she told him. "I don't want the woman who enabled Hannah's behavior for months to be the same person she hangs out with the day after we learned the depth of the dissembling. It's a hard pass. Any other ideas?"

Ryan stopped talking. Jessie could see that he was toggling between frustration and an honest desire to find a solution. After about ten seconds, his face broke into a grin.

"What about Brady?" he asked.

"Brady Bowen?" Jessie asked, perplexed. "Your old partner from when you were stationed on the Westside? Isn't he kind of busy detecting stuff?"

"Actually, no," Ryan replied. "He's on paid leave while they investigate a shooting he was involved in."

"What? I didn't hear anything about that."

"It was related to that armed robbery in Pacific Palisades last week. He and his partner tracked down a suspect and went to question him. But while they were in the apartment, the guy pulled out a shotgun from under a couch cushion. Brady's partner shot him before he got a round off. Brady never even fired, although he did trip over a shoe and tweak his ankle. But until the investigation is complete, he's not even on desk duty. He's basically got vacation all week."

Jessie was dubious about involving him and couldn't hide her skepticism.

"From the case we worked with him in Pacific Palisades, my recollection of Brady is that he was lazy, slovenly and prone to inappropriate comments."

Ryan smiled at the thought of all that.

"Very true—he's inappropriate in general. But he's a solid cop. Plus, he owes me. And he's bored out of his mind. I could ask him to shadow Hannah, not even engage with her. She'll never know he's there. And if he understands that her safety is in jeopardy, he'll take it seriously."

"You're willing to entrust her welfare to him?" Jessie asked, unconvinced.

"Listen, he's not my first choice," Ryan admitted. "But you won't call Kat. And I can't think of anyone else who's qualified and has the day free to babysit a teenager from afar. What other option do we have?"

Jessie looked at him. There was something endearing about the enthusiastic puppy dog eyes he was giving her. He had that familiar impish, almost shy grin that had won her over, the one that seemed so at odds with the manly, muscled exterior the rest of the world saw before his injury. It was also a nice change of pace from the downtrodden demeanor that had defined him since Trembley's death and the Night Hunter's escape last night. Ever a flash of the old Ryan filled her with hope, and she wasn't about to dash this one.

"Give him a call," she relented.

*

Forty-five minutes later, Jessie drove north up Vermont Avenue, past The Dresden Room, made famous by the movie *Swingers*, past Skylight Books and House of Pies, and crossed over Los Feliz Boulevard into Vermont Canyon, just south of massive Griffith Park.

Even without Decker's directions, she would have been able to find Jax Coopersmith's house. It was the one with the nearly three dozen devastated fans out front, placing flowers and sitting vigil. Tabloid photographers walked up and down the narrow sidewalks just outside the property, like hungry vultures looking for anything they could pick at. One lone news helicopter continued to circle the area, hoping to zoom in on something new they could tease for the noon broadcast.

Jessie pulled into the driveway, flashed her LAPD consultant placard, and was waved through by a uniformed officer. As she drove up to the house, she wondered how hard it would be for the Night Hunter to find a spot on the sidewalk among the mourners. Could he be out there now, pretending to be just another senior citizen on his morning power walk?

Deciding these thoughts weren't constructive, she forced them from her head. There was a job to do, and she couldn't do it if she was distracted. She parked in the circular driveway next to the car she recognized as belonging to Detective Callum Reid and walked up the path to the house.

While it was clearly expensive, the mansion had a gaudy, Old South, plantation vibe that Jessie found off-putting. She was surprised that a supposedly edgy influencer would associate herself with such an anachronistic residence.

"I'm looking for Detective Reid," Jessie said to the officer guarding the front door.

"Yes ma'am, he's upstairs," the young man told her, pointing at the curved, flying staircase that wound its way elaborately to the second floor.

She nodded and headed that way, walking very deliberately in order to take in her surroundings. She noted that unlike the exterior of the house, the inside was much more befitting a modern young couple. There were abstract paintings and edgy photos on the walls, along with what looked like African and Native American art displayed in cases on several lighted pillars. As she passed through the foyer, she noticed a pair of high heels in the corner by the front door. Apparently the long, glitzy night had been taxing enough that Jax couldn't be bothered to take them upstairs.

Jessie knew that Coopersmith had been found in her bedroom. That meant that one of her last living actions was likely walking up the same stairs Jessie was now ascending. She looked for any sign that something was amiss as she made her way up but found nothing out of the ordinary.

Once she arrived on the second floor, she saw another officer guarding a room at the end of the hall and headed that way. As she approached the room, she felt the familiar mix of anxiety and anticipation that typically greeted her as she approached a crime scene.

She always felt a little guilty about the excitement but knew that it was that very eagerness that was a big part of what made her good at this job. Ultimately however, her fear that she liked it *too* much was what led her to step back and focus on teaching.

Admittedly, lecturing college students about the methods she'd used to solve cases wasn't as invigorating as actually solving those cases. But it was a steadier job, with normal hours, and it was a hell of a lot safer. No one had tried to choke or stab her because of the grade she'd given them last semester, at least not yet.

At the bedroom door, she again flashed her credentials and was let in. As she stepped into the room, she closed her eyes for a moment, allowing herself to prepare to absorb what was coming. She always liked to take a brief pause before assimilating a crime scene, finding that she saw things with a fresher eye if she came to them with an open, unassuming mindset.

When she opened them again, she found that there wasn't much to work with. The crime scene team was gone, along with Coopersmith's body, so the room was surprisingly devoid of people. There were two uniformed officers milling about. Callum Reid stood near the entrance to the bathroom with his back to her, talking to what appeared to be the assistant medical examiner.

The crime scene tape on the carpeted floor just outside the walk-in closet indicated where the body had been found. Without the tape, it would have been hard to discern where the dead woman had been discovered. There was minimal blood on the carpet and it looked to be muddied by some other substance. It was only as she got closer that Jessie realized that it was probably a combination of eye fluid and melted skin residue, almost certainly a result of the acid.

On the bed were Jax's handbag and a plaque of some kind, likely tossed there by Coopersmith as she entered the room. Jessie walked over to them. The purse looked undisturbed, reinforcing her doubt that that this killing was a robbery gone wrong. People didn't generally bring acid and syringes filled with drain cleaner for a typical smash and grab. This murder felt personal, vengeful, like the murderer didn't just want to kill the victim, but to punish her too.

The plaque lay face up on the bed and Jessie read it: *Annual Influencers Awards, Jax Coopersmith, Rising Star: Fashion.* It was so new that there were hardly any fingerprint smudges on it. Jessie felt a pang of sadness for this girl, so young, just on the cusp of achieving the success she so clearly sought. That was all over now, in one ugly, poisoned blink.

"Hunt," came a voice from behind her, snapping her out her reverie.

She turned around to find Detective Callum Reid staring at her. She smiled and walked over. Reid gave her a thin smile of his own.

He was an old school detective. Although Ryan had run HSS, Reid was the veteran of the group. In his mid-forties, with the hint of a belly, the start of a receding, brown hairline, and a pair of black-framed glasses, he looked just slightly past his expiration date. Jessie hadn't worked with him much, and never without Ryan along for the ride, but she'd always found him to be a competent, professional detective. He was little brusque and calloused, but with everything he'd seen, it was hard to blame him.

"Hi Reid," she said. "How's it going?"

"To be honest, I've been better," he said quietly. "I'm still trying to process what happened to Trembley. It's hard to believe that goofball is gone. How are you and Hernandez doing?"

"Same," she said. "It's tough. Ryan's trying to push through by catching the bastard. And taking this case will at least give me something else to think about." She made no mention of just how poorly Ryan was doing.

"Well, I'm glad to have you here," he said. "It'll be nice to have someone younger on this that gets this whole social media universe. From what I understand, this gal had over two million fans. That's a lot of potential stalkers."

"You mean followers?" Jessie asked. "Just because someone follows an influencer doesn't mean that they're a committed fan, much less a stalker. All it requires to be a follower is clicking a button."

"See, Hunt, you're already earning your keep around here. Other than reading the occasional Facebook post, I try to steer clear of this stuff, so it's nice to have a youngster around."

"Reid," Jessie said, trying not to laugh as she shook her head in amazement. "It's not like I'm an expert on this. And it's not like you grew up with the telegraph. What are you—forty-five? Don't you have kids who are into this stuff?"

"I'm divorced. No kids. Thanks for rubbing salt in the wound," he said, though it was clear that he wasn't actually offended.

"Glad to be of service," she said, giving as good as she got before returning to the situation at hand. "Speaking of wounds, what have we got?"

Reid nodded at the assistant M.E, a young woman named Gallagher with a tight blonde ponytail and an even tighter expression, who pulled up the photos on her phone. The images showed Jax Coopersmith dead, lying on her stomach, her body contorted painfully into a twisted variation of the fetal position.

"She was doused with the acid first," Gallagher said, "although it looks like it may have come from a spray bottle rather than just being tossed from an open container. The direction and force were pretty expertly concentrated right at the middle of the face. The injection probably came soon thereafter. She would have likely been blinded and in too much pain to even register the injection before it was too late."

"How long after she was injected with the drain cleaner before she died?" Jessie asked, half-afraid to hear the answer.

"No way to know for sure," Gallagher responded with impressive offhandedness. "Could have been seconds, maybe minutes, or even hours. I know of one case in Alabama where a woman injected a teenage girl with the stuff, but she didn't die at all, so the woman ended up shooting her. We know it didn't come to that here. But however long it took, it would have been excruciating."

Jessie tried to put the horrors she just heard described out of her head and turned to Reid.

"Do we know when she got home?" she asked him.

"The limo driver, a guy name Paul Wegman, registered the drop-off at 10:18 p.m.," he told her. "However long it took for this stuff to work its ugly magic, she was dead by the time the fiancé arrived home, assuming he can be believed."

"Have you talked to him yet?" she asked.

"Just briefly to let him know to sit tight. I only asked him the basics. I wanted to wait until you arrived to really go at him. He's downstairs in the living room now. You want to say hi?"

Jessie was about to say yes when her eye caught something in the bathroom. It looked like a snack on the counter.

"Give me a second," she said, walking over to get a better look.

When she got closer, she saw that it appeared to be a half-eaten rice cake with several slices of banana on top. The sight of such a pathetic snack made her heart sink. This was what Jax Coopersmith allowed herself as a cheat meal after winning a major award? It was almost too depressing to bear.

Jessie stepped back and glanced at herself in the mirror, wondering how many times Coopersmith had done exactly that and judged herself wanting. Jessie tried not to fall into the same trap but couldn't help noticing the dark circles under her green eyes.

Even after a decent night's sleep, the wear of spending nearly two full days awake gave her skin a dull pallor. Her shoulder-length brown hair was pulled back in ponytail, though not as tight as the M.E.'s. But even that couldn't hide how limp and tired it looked. Five foot ten, with a well-proportioned, athletic frame, she normally cut an imposing figure, but even that seemed to fail her today, as her shoulders slumped forward. She ordered herself to stand straight.

She glanced to her left. Pinned to the medicine cabinet mirror was a collage of off-the-shoulder wedding dresses, with one near the top asterisked. It was lovely— a warm cream color with a cinched waist that would have accentuated both Jax's beauty and her style.

In that moment, the M.E.'s horrific description of her death rang in Jessie's ears. Waiting one flight down from them was Jax's fiancé. The woman was supposed to be getting married soon. But that would never happen now. Jessie's heart sank even further. She turned back to Reid.

"Let's go downstairs," she said quietly.

CHAPTER SIX

He looked devastated.

When Jax Coopersmith's fiancé stood up to meet Jessie in the downstairs living room of the house, his eyes were red-rimmed and puffy. Despite that, he was a gorgeous man. Wearing an immaculate suit, he was tall, black, and ripped; his square-jawed handsomeness made Jessie wonder if he too was an influencer or some kind of model. He looked to be in his early thirties, which would have made him about half a dozen years older than Jax.

"Hello sir," she said, extending her hand, "I'm Jessie Hunt, a profiler consulting with the LAPD. I'll be working with Detective Reid, who I understand you already met. We're both very sorry for your loss."

"Thank you," he said, taking her hand and shaking it forlornly. "I'm Titus Poole. Jax and I were engaged. This is…a lot to handle."

"Of course," Reid said, stepping forward. "Why don't you sit back down? We need to ask you some questions, but can we get you water first?"

"No, I'm good," Poole said, slumping back down on the loveseat he'd just risen from. "Ask me whatever you need. I want to help however I can."

"We appreciate that," Jessie told him. She was sympathetic to his plight but had to keep open the possibility that this was all a ruse. So she decided to throw him a little off from the start as a means of gauging his sincerity. "I guess my first question might seem a little odd: why are you dressed in a suit? Were you planning to go into work this morning?"

Poole looked down at his attire, as if noticing it for the first time.

"No. This is what I was wearing last night. I just haven't changed yet."

"You wore a fancy suit on a Sunday night?" she asked, feigning ignorance as to what last evening's activities entailed.

"Yeah, Jax had a big awards thing. I went with her but had to cut out early to go to the office. I work for one of the studios and we were closing a deal, so I went straight from the party to the studio lot for the meeting, which had been going on all evening. I was there until late."

"I see," Jessie said, noting that his eyes were cast downward. She couldn't tell if that was a sign of exhaustion, guilt, or something else he hoped to hide.

"Forgive us," Reid said, "But we have to ask: is there anyone who can corroborate your whereabouts last night?"

Poole sank back into the loveseat, seemingly not upset so much as stunned that he was actually in this situation.

"Sure," he said. "There were five people in the meeting with me. And then I was on the phone in the car on the way home. I only hung up when I pulled in the driveway. I never should have gone back to work that night, not after what happened."

"What do you mean 'what happened?'" Jessie asked.

Titus Poole looked up at her, surprised.

"I thought you already knew about this. I figured that's why there were so many cops here."

"What are you talking about, Mr. Poole?" Reid pressed.

"It's just that the night before last, one of our friends was murdered. Her name was Claire Bender. She was actually going to be one of Jax's bridesmaids."

Jessie and Reid exchanged shocked glances. It was the first that either of them had heard of this.

"How did Claire die?" Jessie asked.

Poole's mouth dropped open. He was obviously stunned that they hadn't made the connection.

"I heard she was poisoned," he said.

Jessie's brain exploded at the words. Was it possible that they weren't just dealing with someone who had a vendetta against Jax Coopersmith, but a killer who was targeting people in her social circle? To his credit, Reid continued on, barely missing a beat.

"Where did Ms. Bender live?" he asked.

"In Beverly Hills," he said.

"Maybe that's why we haven't heard," Reid said to Jessie. "Sometimes BHPD gets a little proprietary with their cases. I have a friend in the department. I'll make a call when we're done here."

Jessie nodded. This was huge news, the sort that made her want to walk out and drive to Beverly Hills right now. But since there was nothing she could do until Reid made his call, she decided to keep the focus on what Poole could tell them.

33

"I know Jax was a big social media influencer," she said. "Did she have any enemies that you're aware of? Any followers who seemed a little too intense?"

Poole's face scrunched up as he tried to recall.

"Nothing jumps out at me," he eventually said. "I mean, she had her haters, of course. Jax's whole vibe was to be above it all, as if she was doing a favor by trying on whatever she was given. That way, when she actually got excited about something, her followers took it more seriously than a lot of the others, who will gush over anything. A lot of people didn't like the 'aloof' thing, so she'd get nasty comments here and there. Of course, that didn't stop those people from following her. And I never heard her express concern about any of them."

"What about people in her personal life or co-workers?" Reid asked.

Poole shook his head.

"She doesn't have traditional co-workers. She ran the business side herself, booked all her own brand shoots. For really high-profile stuff, she'd bring in a freelance photographer, maybe a makeup or hair person. But she was always great to them, paid really good rates. I can give you names, but I'd be stunned if any of them did this. She was a cash cow for all of them."

"And friends," Jessie pressed, noticing he hadn't volunteered anything on that front. "If this is connected to Claire's murder, we'll need to talk to folks in your social circle. Anyone among them jump out at you as a concern?"

"I can't think of anyone," he said with more finality than Jessie expected. Something about his suddenly clipped tone made her arm hair stand up.

"That's okay," she said carefully. "I understand that it might be a sensitive area. Why don't you write down a list of names and numbers and we'll take it from there."

He hesitated.

"I'm not super comfortable handing over the personal information of our friends," Poole replied. "I don't want them to have to suffer the trauma I'm going through now."

Jessie stared at the guy, whose eyes were locked on the coffee table in front of him. While there was no "normal" reaction to learning a loved one had been violently killed, this was well outside what she considered acceptable. She was about to say so when Reid jumped in.

34

"We appreciate your concerns, Mr. Poole," he said far more diplomatically than she would have. "But this is a murder investigation. Whatever discomfort your friends might feel is secondary to solving this. I'm sure they'll understand. We'd hate to have to formally request that kind of information. It could really slow the investigation down. I know you don't want that. So if you could just go through your contacts and give us what we need, we'll be on our way."

Titus Poole still seemed reluctant but ultimately pulled out his phone. As he wrote down the information, Jessie got up and walked out of the room. She wanted to both get away from Poole and clear her head.

As she walked around the house, she glanced at the doors and windows, wondering how the killer had gotten in. Did they sneak in and lie in wait or did Jax open the door to someone she knew? According to Reid, there was no security footage available to answer those questions independently.

If it was a stranger, how did the killer find her home? Did they follow her from the awards event? Had they been stalking her for some time? That last question sent her mind reeling in another direction.

She too was being stalked. How long had the Night Hunter been watching *her* home? How secure was it really? Despite her assurances to Ryan, doubts were creeping in. Her little sister was home right now. Ryan would be leaving for the office soon, entrusting Hannah's safety to a sloppy, undisciplined detective who might fall asleep while staking her out if the sun got too warm.

It was almost enough to make her rush home this second. But then Detective Reid was at her side again, and she had to set aside her personal concerns to focus on the murder she'd been tasked with solving.

"I think we've got all we can from this guy for now," Reid said. "I want to get back to the station and start diving into the evidence."

Jessie nodded. The sooner they solved this thing, the sooner she could focus her attention on the other killer on the loose.

*

Jessie met Reid back at Central Station. By the time she arrived, he was waiting at his desk in the bullpen in the section reserved for HSS. She noticed that Ryan's desk was unoccupied. Reid seemed to read her mind.

"He's back in the research department with Jamil Winslow," he said. "They're looking over surveillance footage from around the time of Trembley's murder in Santa Monica. Did you want to go say hi before we get started here?'

Jessie thought about it briefly but decided against it.

"No. I don't want to interrupt their concentration. Besides, I can tell from the way your feet are bouncing up and down that you have news to share."

"I do," he said with satisfaction. "My contact with BHPD got back to me on the drive over. Just like Jax Coopersmith, Claire Bender was sprayed with acid and then injected in the neck with drain cleaner. According to the time of death, she was killed soon after returning home from a trip to the drugstore. Her husband was allegedly away at a family event. The case detectives' preliminary theory is that it wasn't a random attack, that it was personal, either a stalker or someone she knew, maybe a spurned lover who was familiar with where Claire lived and knew the place well."

"Not a bad theory," Jessie conceded. "Even if neither individual killing was specifically about the victim, this whole deal feels personal to their group."

"Right," Reid agreed. "We've got two wealthy women, doing well in life. Maybe some guy who knew them became obsessed with them both or just resented them."

"How have the BHPD interviews been going?" Jessie asked.

Reid's expression told her the answer to that wasn't going to be very satisfying.

"What interviews?" he said disgustedly. "They've only had the most perfunctory chats with relevant parties. Plus, they've been keeping the method of murder quiet for fear of it turning into a circus."

"Why would that happen?" Jessie asked, confused.

"Because of the people involved."

"Should I have recognized her name?" Jessie wanted to know.

"Not Claire. She's a successful interior designer, but she didn't have a very high profile until she got married. It's her husband that you might know. Have you ever heard of Jack Bender?"

Jessie unsuccessfully searched her memory.

"I don't think so."

"He's the son of Vernon Bender, as in Bender Educational Publishing, the company responsible for a quarter of the college textbooks in the country. Jack is an heir to the fortune, which means

36

that, at least according to the internet, he's probably worth about four hundred million dollars. And like the rest of the family, he's known for spending it freely."

"Thus the circus?" Jessie said.

"Exactly," Reid confirmed, "which is why BHPD was more than willing to hand over the case to us. They acknowledge that we have more resources, but they also just don't want the heat. All their files are being transferred now."

"Great," Jessie said, settling in at what used to be her desk, right across from Ryan's. The fact that it was completely clean was a further sign that HSS was short-handed. No one had been sitting there. No one had replaced her. "While that comes in, I thought we could review Jax Coopersmith's background to see if there was anything new we could glean."

Reid was amenable so they each began poring over everything they could find on her. Jessie focused on Jax's social media feed and articles about her life and career while Reid sifted through her official file, including phone records, tax and property information, and business documents.

"I didn't find anything shocking," he said after a while, "other than that for a 25-year-old, she'd already amassed a small fortune. I may have to get one of our forensic accountants to determine her true worth."

"I didn't come across anything that made me pause either," Jessie admitted. "Obviously, her social media includes all the requisite stuff: tons of photos and video branding testimonials. There's endless footage of her at galas, premieres, parties, and hot, new restaurants. Titus Poole is on her arm for some of it, but he seems to generally keep to the background. I don't know if he's worried if it would undermine his credibility as a film executive, but he's rarely front and center with her. Then again, she's the star of the show."

"Is it really right to call her a star?" Reid asked borderline derisively.

"Depends on how you define it," Jessie acknowledged. "But by today's standards, I'd say yes. She had over two million followers on Instagram alone. If you add all her social up, it's probably double that number. That's a lot of influence. And I found multiple articles that mentioned that she was a real trendsetter. She was much more reticent to give a glowing review than a lot of other influencers and she tended to tout edgier, more avant-garde stuff. One independent handbag brand said their sales doubled after she shouted them out."

"But how many sales does that actually translate into?" Reid wondered. "Maybe she went from selling two bags to four."

"I don't know how many sales they had, but it took the company four months to fill all the back orders, so I'm guessing it was more than four. The same thing happened with a woman who makes artisanal scarves. After Jax mentioned her, she went from working solo out of her garage to employing fourteen people in a small warehouse in the arts district. Everything I read says Jax had taste and credibility and that she knew it, so she doled out the praise sparingly. It seems that she was well on her way."

Reid looked at her skeptically.

"Then why do I hear a 'but' in your voice?"

Jessie hadn't been aware that there was one. But now that Reid mentioned it, she realized that something was eating at her, if only slightly.

"It's probably nothing," she said after thinking about it for a moment. "But as I look at all Jax's photos, I get this weird feeling. It appears like she's living the perfect dream. But underneath it, I see this look in her eyes. I wouldn't call it desperation exactly. But there's an intensity behind them, like she's worried that everything she has could be ripped away at any second. Part of me wonders how much of her life, how much any of these influencers' lives, is a façade? If we scratch at it a little, I'm curious to see what we'd find underneath."

Reid nodded silently. He wasn't knowledgeable about this world, but he didn't have to be. Just like Jessie, he knew that young women came out to Hollywood every day seeking fame and fortune. Most didn't get a happy ending. And even those that did often had to make compromises that left them hollow-eyed and empty.

His phone rang, startling them both out of their trance. He answered it and listened silently for several seconds before thanking the caller and hanging up.

"You want the good news or the bad news first?" he asked.

CHAPTER SEVEN

He didn't wait for her to answer before launching into what was apparently the good news.

"That was the medical examiner. She says the acid and the drain cleaner were the same in both attacks. So we can be virtually certain that one person committed both murders on subsequent nights."

"I guess that's good, if not surprising," Jessie allowed. "We can focus on connections between Jax and Claire rather than doing deep dives into them individually."

"Right," Reid agreed. "And even though we already suspected it, the M.E. verified that neither woman was sexually assaulted. It appears that the killer came in, did their business and left right away, which is also the bad news."

"How so?" Jessie asked.

"Because it leaves us with little in the way of personally identifying physical evidence. There was no sign of struggle in either case. No fingerprints. No DNA as of yet. Plus, neither home was equipped with camera surveillance equipment. We're flying blind on all of that."

Jessie shrugged.

"I guess that means we're back to doing things the old school way," she said, "talking to people in order to establish connections between these two women."

"It sounds like you have someone specific in mind," Reid noted.

"I do," she replied. "I can think of one obvious person who might be able to help establish those connections, someone the Beverly Hills Police Department was apparently too scared to call: Claire's widower. I think it's time we pay Jack Bender a visit."

*

The Bender Mansion seemed designed to intimidate.

Reid had offered to drive. As a result, Jessie was able to get a full view of the place as they approached. It was in the Hollywood Hills, on Loma Vista Drive, just north of Sunset Boulevard. Like its more famous neighbors, the Waverly Mansion and the Greystone Mansion, it was apparently in the Tudor style, at least according to Wikipedia. But unlike those homes, this one had never been used for film shoots or walking tours.

"Remind me again why we're doing the interview here," Jessie requested.

"Because this is where Jack Bender is," Reid said as a massive white gate slowly opened to let them on the grounds. "His mother lives here and apparently he's been holed up with her since the murder."

"What about his father?" Jessie asked.

"It seems that Vernon lives most of the year in Monaco, where he spends his time with his longtime personal assistant. From what I read, she's younger than Jack. According to my BHPD contact, the Bender marriage is now mostly one of convenience. Vernon comes home for board meetings and black-tie events, then heads back to Monte Carlo as fast as he can."

"Sounds like a close-knit bunch," Jessie said sarcastically as they slowly rolled up the hill, surrounded on both sides by massive redwoods that must have cost a fortune to bring here.

She felt like she was at the start of a gradually escalating roller-coaster, approaching the top so that she could see the massive expanse below before the ride shot downward, leaving her stomach behind. Clearly that was the intent, as the actual home wasn't visible yet, hidden by the hill and huge trees.

When they finally reached the crest, she found that the wait had been worth it. Spread out in front of her wasn't so much a mansion as an estate. She'd been on large properties before, even solved a murder at the giant residence of a billionaire (and pedophile) mogul. But this was something different entirely.

It looked like the Benders had an entire hill that was all their own. A large, metal gate extended as far as the eye could see, encircling all the multiple structures on the grounds and suggesting the property might have no end. From where she sat, she could see a three-hole golf course, what appeared to be a polo field, stables, tennis courts, two pools, a garden the size of a football field, a fountain that rose at least twenty feet in the air, and a three-story manor complex that seemed to be comprised by as many as six different wings. That didn't include what appeared to be at least three guest houses and several small cottages she suspected were for on-site staff.

"Decent digs," she muttered under her breath as they descended down the hill toward the main entrance.

"Yeah," Reid agreed, "but I'd hate to see the utility bill."

They both chuckled as a young man in a red sports coat directed them to one of ten covered parking spots off to the side of the driveway.

"Detective Reid and Ms. Hunt?" he asked politely when they exited the vehicle.

"That's right," Reid replied.

"I'm Giles. May I escort you to the entrance where Mr. Miller will meet you?"

"You bet, Giles," Reid said, seeming to enjoy playing the philistine.

Mr. Miller, an older, wispy-haired gentleman in a tuxedo who Jessie assumed was some kind of butler, greeted them at the door.

"May I take your coats?" he offered.

It was unseasonably warm for early January, so Jessie handed hers over. Reid declined.

"Mr. Bender is waiting for you in the drawing room," he said. "May I take you there?"

Jessie and Reid nodded in unison and followed Mr. Miller as he walked briskly down a long marble-floored hallway. To Jessie's surprise (and if she was honest, her disappointment) he stopped after only walking about halfway down the hall and indicated for them to step to the left.

They reached the threshold and looked in to find a formal drawing room with multiple paintings, a large, ornate rug, and furniture that looked to be several hundred years old. Sitting on chairs at the far end of the room were Jack Bender and an older woman Jessie didn't recognize. Jack, in an expensive, black sweat suit, was looking down at the floor. But the older lady, dressed in a long skirt, a lavender blazer, and a white blouse with frills near the collar, was eyeing them with sharp, merciless eyes.

"Mrs. Bender, Mr. Bender," Miller said ostentatiously, "May I present criminal profiler Jessie Hunt and Detective Callum Reid? Ms. Hunt, Detective Reid, this is Lisanne Bender and her son, John."

"Please join us," Lisanne offered, waving at two high-backed, sculpted wooden chairs across from her. Everything about the woman was severe, from her gray hair pulled back into a tight, forehead-stretching bun, to the dress shoes that were so pointy they looked like they could double as ice picks.

As they approached, Jessie couldn't help but wonder why Jack Bender's mom was here at all. According to her information, he was a

41

twenty-nine-year-old executive at a gigantic publishing house. Did he really need his mommy around? She swallowed the urge to ask that very question, well aware that this interview could be cut short on a whim, leaving her and Reid to navigate a jungle of lawyers instead.

Once they sat down, there was an awkward pause. Mr. Miller tried to bridge the gap.

"May I offer anyone refreshments?" and when he got four heads shaking no, he concluded. "Then I will take my leave."

"Thank you for coming," Lisanne Bender said in her arched neck, patrician tone, as if she'd requested the presence of law enforcement in her home, rather than had it thrust upon her. "How can we help?"

"Well," Reid began. "We have a few questions for Mr. Bender that we think might help us quite a bit."

For the first time, Jack Bender looked up. Under normal circumstances he would have been an attractive man. His hazel eyes were deep set and his brown hair, even disheveled, had a casual waviness to it. But he clearly hadn't shaved in a few days. His skin looked blotchy. It was also immediately obvious to Jessie that he was on something. The eyes were glazed over, and his languorous movements suggested a man moving underwater.

"Jack has been distraught over the recent events," Lisanne replied before Jack even tried to speak, "first with the loss of his beloved Claire, and now upon learning of dear Jacqueline's passing."

Mrs. Bender's voice had the appropriate gravity, but her prim, officious manner hinted that neither death was hitting her all that hard.

"Did you know Jacqueline well, Jack?" Jessie asked, trying to engage him in some kind of communication but not wanting to dive right into the circumstances of his own wife's death just yet.

"Sure," he said, after getting a slight nod from his mother. "We were all friends. People even used to joke that they couldn't tell me and her apart. You know, Jax and Jack?"

"Right," Jessie said, pretending to be amused. "How did everyone first meet?"

Jack took a deep breath and managed sit up straight.

"Claire was doing interiors for a new house in West Hollywood," he said, speaking slowly and with great effort. "She was really proud of the design and wanted to generate interest and traffic to her website. She followed Jax on Instagram and had the idea that they could team up. So she reached out and offered the use of the house for some of Jax's shoots as long as her design work was prominently displayed.

They hit it off, the shoot did wonders for both of them, and they started collaborating regularly. Pretty soon they were fast friends. After a while we all started hanging out together. They were so close that Jax asked Claire to be a bridesmaid at her wedding later this year."

"I'm sorry," Jessie said sympathetically, watching closely for his response. "This must be so shocking, to lose both of them within a day of each other."

"It is," Jack whispered, sounding genuinely gutted. Despite his seeming sincerity, she wished there was some way she could throw him off without alienating his hovering mother.

"Is that why you're staying here rather than at your house?" Reid asked.

"I was actually already here," Jack answered. "I'd spent the night here on Saturday because of a family event. Claire was feeling under the weather, so she didn't come. I was just too exhausted to drive back down the hill at that hour, so I crashed in my old room. I found her when I went home yesterday morning."

"That must have been rough," Reid said softly. "Is that why you're still here?"

"Yeah," Bender said. "It was just too much for me. I couldn't stay in that house where...that happened to her. How could I sleep under the same roof where she suffered, where she breathed her last breath?"

"That's perfectly understandable," Jessie consoled. "I assume you spent last night here as well?"

"I did," he confirmed.

"And probably smart too," she said, suddenly thinking of a way to test what was really going on with him. "After all, you're much safer here."

The comment didn't seem to immediately register for Jack but it definitely did for Lisanne, whose head popped up immediately.

"What does that mean?" she demanded.

"It's just that we don't know the motive for these killings," Jessie said, her eyes still on Jack Bender. "I can't get into specifics, but it was as if the guilty party wanted the victims to not just die, but suffer. I'm sorry to be so blunt but it's important that you realize that until we know who is doing this and why, everybody in your circle could be in danger."

"But both victims were women," Lisanne protested. "What makes you think Jack could be at risk?"

"We just don't have enough to draw any conclusions yet, Mrs. Bender," she replied, providing a statement that was both true and designed to generate some kind of candid reaction.

"We'll have to double security," Lisanne said, shifting into immediate problem-solver mode. Jack didn't seem fazed. Jessie couldn't gauge whether it was due to a lack of fear or an abundance of drugs in his system.

"Unfortunately," Reid noted, "not everyone else in Jack's social circle has the same level of access to personal protection. That's why it would be extremely helpful if you could provide a list your friends, along with their contact information. We need to warn them."

Jessie noticed that he cleverly didn't mention that all of those people could also be potential suspects. She also saw that Lisanne seemed to have some reservations about the request and seemed about to voice them. She decided to beat her to the punch.

"And Jack," Jessie said, making sure that his eyes were fixed on her, "it would be especially helpful if you could include a list of all the bridesmaids and groomsmen from your wedding, and to the extent you know them, for Jax's too. Those folks are potentially the most vulnerable right now."

He pulled out his phone and immediately began scrolling.

"I have a list in my notes for our wedding. I could just send you the whole thing," he offered more eagerly than Jessie would have expected. "I'd have to double check, but I think there's some overlap with Jax's wedding party. I know they have the same maid of honor."

"We'll take whatever you have," Jessie said smiling broadly. She gave no indication that she found his offer mildly suspicious. Perhaps it wasn't as odd as Titus Poole's reluctance to share any information at all. But his sudden demeanor change, from drugged-up widower to eager-beaver information provider just felt off, even if she couldn't explain why.

Neither she nor Reid wanted to push the interview, especially since it was clear that Lisanne Bender's patience was fading. So they said their goodbyes and followed Mr. Miller back to the front. As they approached the front door, Jessie saw a thick-trunked man with an earpiece standing at the opposite end of the hall. He was clearly part of the family's security detail.

The sight of him sent her mind into overdrive. What she would give right about now to have a similar-looking man stationed in her own living room. Ryan was safe in the police station. But what about

44

Hannah? Was she still asleep? Had Ryan woken her to warn her to be especially careful today? How much had he revealed to her? Was Brady Bowen properly set up for a day of staking her out?

Jessie knew that Ryan was intently focused on finding the Night Hunter and she didn't want to mess with his concentration. But she also knew that until she got answers to some of these questions, she wouldn't be able to focus on her own responsibilities. Reid interrupted her thoughts.

"I'm thinking we should visit the maid of honor for both victims," he said as they walked from the mansion to his car. "She's got to have some extra insight."

"Sounds good," Jessie agreed, though she was only half-listening.

She was pretty proud that she made it all the way to Reid's car before dialing Ryan's number. As she waited for him to pick up, she made a silent promise to herself. She might not have armed security personnel at her disposal. But she would do whatever it took to keep her family safe.

CHAPTER EIGHT

Hannah was still amazed that she had the house to herself.

She had assumed that Jessie or Ryan, maybe even both, would hover over her all day, never letting her out of their sight. But Jessie was gone before she even woke up, off to investigate a case. She was about to get resentful when Ryan told her the name of the victim in the case: Jax Coopersmith.

Hannah wasn't sure why she took that news so hard. Her adoptive parents had been murdered in front of her; so had her foster parents. Garland Moses, the sweet old profiler who had gifted this very house to Jessie, had been murdered only six months ago. And yet the news of Jax's death seemed equally momentous.

Maybe it was because Jax felt, if not quite like a friend, at least like someone who *could* have been one. Her snarky, "prove it to me" attitude, combined with her edgy style and her warm, Louisiana twang made her seem both aspirational and approachable. Now all of that was gone.

Hannah wanted to begrudge Jessie going out to investigate a new case without a word of goodbye, but she couldn't. The truth was that she would have been pissed if Jessie had handed off the investigation to someone else in order to stick around for the day. Whatever her sister's flaws, and there were many, there was no one Hannah wanted on this case more than Jessie. If anyone could get justice for Jax, it would be her.

Nonetheless, as she puttered around the kitchen, looking for something interesting to make for breakfast, she remained surprised that she was alone. She cast her mind back to her conversation with Ryan before he too had left for the day, including his warning.

"I'm going to be spending the day hunting down the man who killed my partner last night," he said. "He's still at large and we have a real fear that he might go after the loved ones of the investigators. That means Jessie and you. Your sister can handle herself. She's armed and spending the day with another detective. You don't have those resources."

"So you want me to hole up in this fortress of a house all day?" she asked.

"Look," he replied, looking exhausted even though his day had barely begun," I can't make you do anything. Without getting into everything right now, you made that pretty clear to Jessie and me last night. All I can do is ask you to do is make smart choices. There is a threat out there. He's actually an elderly man, which is part of why your sister got so worried when she heard you got in a car with an older man. This guy apparently uses his seeming frailty as a tool to get close to potential victims. No one suspects what he's capable of."

To her surprise, he'd basically left it at that. He said a casual goodbye, wished her a good day, and walked out the door. As she listened to the metal bolt locking mechanism slide back into place, she wondered if this was intended as some sort of reverse psychology. A half hour later, she still wasn't sure.

Tired of thinking about it, she gave up on a fancy breakfast and grabbed some Raisin Bran. Though she prided herself on being a good cook and had even entertained the idea of going to culinary school after graduating, sometimes a bowl of cereal was all she had the energy for.

As she scooped a spoonful into her mouth, she tried to come to terms with her new normal. Despite her threats, Kat had spilled her secrets. Both Jessie and Ryan now knew, if not everything, enough.

They didn't know about the shoplifting or walking in front of cars to cause accidents. But they knew about her confronting a drug dealer last summer. They knew about her attempt to entrap a pedophile she thought had kidnapped a girl. They realized that her help in busting a sexual slavery ring was as much about the excitement of using herself as bait as catching the scumbags selling the girls.

In the cold light of day, that litany of poor choices didn't make her look great. In retrospect, neither did running away, even if she hadn't truly intended to go away for good. Sneaking out was something a petulant child might do. After pushing so hard for her independence, she felt ashamed that she'd resorted to behavior that seemed so beneath her.

It had worked out in the end, but it was one more example of the very behavior that had everyone so concerned. She'd done something reckless, even dangerous. This time it had been as much out of frustration as for the thrill of it. But usually the thrill was enough.

She hated that she did this. And yet, it seemed the only way she could really feel anything these days was when the situation was turned up to eleven. Contentment wasn't enough for her. She had to feel ecstatic. She rarely got irked but welcomed fury when it came. Anxiousness was an almost alien concept, but she understood fear. She couldn't continue to exist at those extremes and function much longer.

But what could she do? Kat certainly wasn't an option as a sounding board anymore. Besides, blackmailing her into being a confidante hadn't worked out that well. She doubted the woman would ever talk to her again.

There was too much emotion and history tied up in her relationship with Jessie for Hannah to really unburden herself to her. Her sister wanted to help. But she didn't seem capable of setting aside the guardian part of herself to just listen.

Ryan was an option. Hannah knew that while he cared about her well-being, he was less emotionally invested, which was generally a good thing when it came to these sorts of conversations. But it wouldn't fair to him to ask him keep any discussion in confidence. That would be hiding things from the woman he loved. Kat keeping secrets may have ruined her friendship with Jessie. Hannah didn't want to be responsible for blowing up her sister's relationship too.

If Edward Wexler was alive, even unconscious, maybe she could have talked to him. It might even have been easier that way, spilling her innermost fears to someone who couldn't judge or even hear her.

She punched up the man's name in Google to see if any plans had been made for his funeral. To her shock, a story popped up immediately in the "City" section of the Times. Edward Wexler wasn't just some old dude. He was a Holocaust survivor who had lost his entire family in a concentration camp.

She discovered that he had moved to the U.S. as a six-year-old, lived with relatives, and eventually settled in Los Angeles. He married, had three children, and at the time of his death, nine grandchildren. He became a lawyer, establishing a legal foundation with two goals: repatriating family heirlooms stolen by the Nazis and bringing the perpetrators to justice.

The article said that Wexler had realized that pursuing property crimes was often easier than proving war crimes. According to an old interview, he said he decided to make it his life's mission to bring some measure of justice to the people who had been violated, even if it could only be offered to their descendants.

The more she read, the more Hannah realized that last night, she'd unknowingly been in the presence of someone incredibly special. Edward Wexler was a good man who had done incredible things.

But something else spoke to Hannah more than his accomplishments. This was a person whose whole family was slaughtered when he was just a child, who had almost died himself, who was sent to another country to live with people he'd never met. His trauma was equal to hers by any measure.

And yet, rather than using the horrors he'd faced as justification for disconnecting from humanity, he'd used it as motivation to help people. He'd taken his pain and channeled it into something constructive that would long outlive him.

And in his last seconds on this earth, despite everything he'd been through, he asked about *her* life. He offered suggestions to make it better. He reached out to help a girl he didn't know that he could tell was in distress.

The memory of that moment filled her with an emotion she didn't even recognize at first: shame. She had no business stewing in her own sense of victimization when someone like Edward Wexler had refused to. She had to change. And in that moment, she thought of a way.

There was one other person she could talk to, someone she'd spoken to before but not in a long time. If she really wanted to change, this was the one person most qualified to help her. In fact, it occurred to Hannah that this might be the perfect—and scariest—choice, for the same reason: this person couldn't be played.

Maybe that's why Hannah had been reluctant to go back to see her. It felt like she might actually reveal something about herself with this woman. And for the longest time, making herself vulnerable had been more terrifying than dealing with how messed up she felt most of the time. But the scales seemed to have shifted slightly. Perhaps it was worth the risk.

Hannah put down her spoon and checked her phone. Sure enough, she still had Dr. Lemmon's address in her contacts.

*

An hour later, the rideshare driver dropped her off outside Dr. Janice Lemmon's downtown office building.

49

She stood outside, unmoving. Suddenly overwhelmed, she felt her breathing quicken and stepped off to the side of the building, next to a homeless man curled up and wrapped in a small tarp.

He glanced up at her and she thought he was about to say something. But something about her panicky expression must have changed his mind. He lowered his head and curled back into a ball, never saying a word.

She stared at herself in the office building window and noticed a marked difference from last night at the hospital. Her green eyes were bright. Her sandy blonde hair no longer drooped down like dying vines. Even though it was only twelve hours later, she looked stronger, even taller.

Reminding herself that her reservations about opening up weren't enough to justify bailing, she took one step and the another. Before she knew it, she was inside the building lobby walking toward the reception desk.

But when she picked up the pen to sign in, the self-doubt rose up in her chest again.

This is stupid. It's not going to work and I'm going to feel worse after I'm done. Time to leave.

She dropped the pen and spun on her heel but had only taken three steps when she heard a familiar voice.

"Hannah? Is that you?"

Hannah froze, realizing there was no way out now. Slowly she turned around and smiled at Dr. Lemmon. The woman was just as she remembered. The therapist was in her mid-sixties but didn't look it. She was in great shape and her eyes, behind a pair of thick glasses, were sharp and focused. Her curly blonde ringlets bounced when she walked, and she had a coiled intensity that was both impressive and borderline scary.

"Hi, Dr. Lemmon," she said, sounding plastic. "How are you doing?"

"I'm good," Dr. Lemmon replied. "How are *you*?"

"Oh, you know, I'm getting by."

"Are you here to see me?" she asked probingly, squinting at her like she was performing an X-ray with her eyes.

Hannah sighed heavily.

"Would you believe I was just in the area for a frozen yogurt?"

"Do you want me to believe that?" Dr. Lemmon asked with a gentle smile.

50

Hannah shrugged.

"You know," Dr. Lemmon said, not pushing for an answer, "I was going out for a hot tea because I have a free hour. But now that I think about it, I'd just as soon avoid all the foot traffic. Care to join me upstairs for a cup of chamomile and a chat?"

Despite the strong urge to say no, Hannah nodded. Dr. Lemmon smiled again and ushered her back to the elevators. As a sweaty, heavyset man with a mustache dashed to join them, failing to make it before the doors closed, she allowed herself a tiny giggle. It took that for her to realize she'd been holding her breath this whole time.

CHAPTER NINE

Rarely had such a simple text made Jessie so angry.

She and Reid were on their way to meet Allison Standish, the maid of honor to both Jax Coopersmith and Claire Bender, when it came in.

It was from Kat Gentry and it only had six words: *So sorry. Can we talk? Please?*

Jessie typed out a long, angry, accusatory response and was about to hit "send" when she stopped herself. After deleting the whole thing, she kept her reply short and to the point: *Can't now—working a case.*

She almost added "maybe later" but didn't. Frustrated with herself for even considering leaving the door open, she punched the "send" button hard and looked out the window. She still had more anger bubbling in her gut than she knew what to do with.

Yes, Kat had been trying to help Hannah. Yes, she had been trying to keep Jessie from carrying the burden of her sister's issues alone. And yes, Hannah had manipulated Kat into thinking that coming forward would end their friendship, which it may very well have done.

But still, her best friend had kept her in the dark for months, knowing full well that Hannah was teetering on the edge of a dangerous abyss. There was no getting around it: she should have said something. Suddenly, she realized that Reid was talking to her and snapped out of her angry daze.

"What was that again?" she asked.

"I was just saying that I think we're getting close to Standish's place."

Jessie sat up straighter and really looked at her surroundings for the first time. They were in the Franklin Village section of Hollywood, traveling east along Franklin Avenue past Beachwood Drive. This stretch of road was populated with improv comedy clubs, outdoor cafés, independent bookstores, at least one vegetarian-only corner grocery, and the ornate complex comprising the Scientology Celebrity Centre. Just a half block down was the equally infamous headquarters of the Eleventh Realm, a trendy but controversial spiritual sect.

"This isn't too far from Jax's house," she noted.

"Nope, we're only five minutes west," he agreed. "But from the area, it looks like Allison's place isn't going to be quite as hoity-toity."

He turned left onto Tamarind Avenue and drove up the suddenly steep hill, pulling over in front a charmingly Old Hollywood, but hardly ostentatious, apartment complex.

"What does she do again?" Jessie asked as she got out.

Reid glanced at his phone as they walked up the path to the entrance gate.

"According to the info I pulled, she's a makeup artist, though pretty junior from what I could tell. Her IMDB lists a lot of independent films and work on TV pilots that never went anywhere. I guess that until you hit it big, her line of work doesn't afford the same level of luxury as being an influencer."

"Or being married to a publishing heir," Jessie added acidly, immediately regretting her tone. Claire had been a success in her own right before meeting Jack Bender and didn't need her accomplishments diminished by the profiler investigating her murder, just because she was in a bad mood. "Forget I said that."

Reid looked over at her as they arrived at the gate, pulling up his slacks so that they better rested on his tummy.

"Don't be so hard on yourself, Hunt," he said. "With what you've had going on lately, you get a one-time pass from me, as long as you give me one when I inevitably say something out of bounds."

"That's a deal," she said, grateful for his consideration. "Let's see what's up with Ms. Standish."

She pushed the button to buzz the apartment. A few seconds later, a harried voice came over the intercom.

"Who is it?"

"This is the LAPD, Ms. Standish. We need to talk to you about the recent incidents involving your friends who passed away."

"You mean who were murdered?" the voice said bitterly, apparently not interested in his attempt at diplomacy.

"Yes, ma'am," he answered.

"Come on up," she said resignedly, buzzing them in without another word.

They opened the door and passed through the open-aired atrium, which was inundated by a plethora of overgrown plants. It was encircled by a mini faux creek that curled along the edge of the gate, ending at the foot of the stairs to the second floor. Reid led the way up to the exterior hallway leading to unit 216.

Reid was about to knock on the door when it opened, revealing a petite, attractive brunette with a black top and short, turquoise skirt. She had on thigh-high white socks and a pair of what looked like black tap shoes. Her blue eyes were slightly puffy, despite the obvious effort to hide what must have been a distressing last few days.

"Come in," she said, turning back inside and leaving them to close the door. Unlike Jax's plantation mansion filled with art, her place was much more modest. Her walls were adorned with framed posters that Jessie suspected she'd had since college and her furniture looked second-hand.

"I'm supposed to be at a commercial shoot in Culver City in an hour, so I hope this doesn't take too long," Allison said. She seemed to sense that the comment didn't come off well, which it didn't, and quickly turned back around to face them.

"I don't mean we have to rush or anything," she added, talking a mile a minute. "Obviously I want to help in any way I can. It's just that, despite what happened, I still have to pay the rent. And if I show up late for this shoot, it could affect future jobs. I work with this agency a lot. Besides, with everything that's happened, I could really use a distraction. Other than a few hours at a shoot last night, I've been going crazy sitting here in this place."

"What shoot was that?" Jessie asked, trying to sound casual and not like she was checking the woman's alibi.

"Just this crappy independent film," Allison said. "I'm not sure they're even going to have the money to finish the thing."

"But you were there last night," Jessie pressed. "For how long?"

Allison furrowed her brow.

"Maybe three hours? I know my call time was at 8 p.m. and I got back here after 11, so that sounds right."

"Were you shooting that film on Saturday night as well?" Jessie wondered.

Allison's face fell. At first Jessie thought it was because the woman had figured out that she was already being interrogated, but that turned out to be wrong.

"No," Allison admitted, looking ashamed. "On Saturday, I caught up on *The Bachelor* with my good friends—pizza and merlot."

Clearly trying to hide her embarrassment, she looked at her watch impatiently.

"I really do have to head out pretty soon," she muttered.

"That's all right, Ms. Standish," Reid said, showing a level of restraint Jessie doubted she could have mustered. "There's no reason this needs to take forever. We thought that, as the maid of honor for both Claire and Jax, you might have some special insight that could prove invaluable to our investigation."

Allison looked skeptical.

"I'll tell you whatever I know, but it's not like we bared our souls to each other. I think they both picked me because neither had sisters and I'm good at puncturing the tension in a room. That can be useful at a wedding."

"Sometimes keeping it light is more important than people think," Jessie acknowledged.

"Yeah," Allison said, adjusting one of her socks, which had slid down to her knee. "Plus they knew I'd do their makeup for free. I'll probably end up doing everyone's makeup before we're done. The wedding planner isn't psyched about that because she had her own go-to girl. But it can get really expensive. And even rich bitches like a bargain. Sorry, that was a term of affection among us."

"You really do know how to puncture the pomposity," Jessie marveled, making a mental note to find out more about the wedding planner she mentioned.

"It's a gift," Allison said. "I don't have many, but I've got that. So how can I help?"

Jessie looked over at Reid, happy to let him go first. He complied.

"We're trying to determine if Jax or Claire was being threatened," he told Allison. "Did either of them ever talk about stalkers? Did one of them have a falling out that you're aware of? Did either have a vengeful ex?"

Allison sat down at one of the barstools at her kitchen counter, her attention fixed on the question.

"Like I told you before, we didn't have the kind of friendships where they would necessarily reveal that kind of thing to me. But even so, I don't remember either of them ever mentioning anything like that. Jax never talked about her past and Claire lived a pretty cloistered existence, especially after she got married. I mean, Jack's family had personal security guards so if she ever felt unsafe, she had easy access to help."

"So neither ever expressed any concern about that stuff?" Jessie pressed.

Allison shook her head, but then seemed to reconsider.

"I guess you could say that Jax got hassled a little for some of her posts and stories. She'd sometimes read us comments that savaged her fashion taste. But nothing ever seemed scary. She thought they were funny."

"What about in your circle of friends?" Jessie wondered. "Was there any animosity?"

Allison gave her an "are you kidding?" look that spoke volumes.

"Sure," she said. "When you have a group of people who hang out and some are super successful and others aren't, there's going to be tension from time to time. I'll admit I was a little jealous. But it's not like people were scratching each other's eyes out; maybe a snide remark or a heated argument every now and then. That's about it."

Jessie had to admit that it was a fair point. A little jealousy among friends was natural and the fact that Allison voluntarily admitted that she'd felt it worked in her favor. To deny it, considering how disparate her world was from Jax's, would be suspicious. But admitting to jealously didn't mean she wasn't also capable of acting on it.

Of course, most fits of jealously didn't result in two horrific murders on consecutive nights. The thought resurfaced another concern, one that had been quietly bothering her for a while and was now doing so loudly: two nights of associated killings could be a coincidence or even a maniac on a drug-fueled spree. But three nights in a row constituted an unmistakable pattern. What would happen tonight?

"Allison," she wondered, "You said earlier that you'd probably end up doing the makeup for everyone's wedding. Are there a lot of them coming up?"

"For sure. Claire was the first in our group. Jax was going to be next but she and Titus pushed it back a few months. But I can think of at least two more in the next year. It's pretty incestuous. That's the word for it, right?"

Jessie ignored the fact that it most certainly was not and pressed ahead.

"Who's next on the wedding schedule?"

Allison checked her phone.

"That would be Caroline Ryan. Hers is in three months."

Jessie recognized the name. It had been on both Titus Poole's and Jack Bender's lists of friends.

"Where would she be now?" Reid asked. "Does she live with her fiancé?"

"They bought a place together recently. But if you're looking to talk to her now, she won't be at home. She's kind of a workaholic."

"What does she do?" he asked.

"She owns a little boutique on Melrose. It specializes in '80s era outfits. If someone wore it in a John Hughes movie, she probably has a version of it."

Reid turned to Jessie with a big grin on his face.

"I guess we're headed back in time," he said.

Jessie managed to stifle her groan at the cheesy comment, but Allison couldn't, so she got to experience it vicariously through her.

"Don't make that crack to Caroline," Allison warned. "She takes what she does seriously. If you get Dad jokey with her, she'll just shut down."

Jessie was happy for the advice on how to approach the interview. But when it came to solving murders, she wasn't interested in people's delicate sensibilities. Caroline would answer their questions, whether she wanted to or not.

CHAPTER TEN

Melrose Avenue was eerily quiet.

It was mid-morning on a Monday, so it wasn't that big a shock. But still, there was something a little creepy about a major shopping district looking like an abandoned old west town. Jessie half-expected a tumbleweed to blow past.

By the time they pulled up outside Caroline's shop, Abe Froman's, it was almost 11 a.m. The security gate was still pulled across the door, indicating it wasn't open yet.

"I don't get it," Reid said, looking at the storefront sign. "What's the name mean?"

"It's a reference to *Ferris Bueller's Day Off*," she said, shaking her head in disbelief. "He was the sausage king of Chicago. Didn't you grow up in the '80s?"

"Yes, but I was more into the Stallone and Schwarzenegger oeuvres," he replied drily.

Jessie thought of several snarky comebacks to that but chose not to share any of them.

"Since we have a few minutes, do you mind if I make a personal call?" she asked.

"Go for it," he said. "I was actually going to run across the street for a doughnut. You want one?"

"First of all, thank you but no. Second of all, you know you're a walking cliché, right?"

"And proud of it," he shot back, smiling.

Once he was gone, she called Ryan. He had updated her earlier when she texted, letting her know that Brady Bowen was sitting in his car, half a block down the street from their house, where he'd been ever since Ryan left for work earlier that morning. Hannah hadn't been outside at all at that point.

"How's it going?" she asked when he picked up. "Any leads on the Night Hunter?"

"Not much to speak of," he said, sounding incredibly agitated. "Jamil has meticulously gone through all the footage from near the Santa Monica hostel where Trembley was killed. We were able to track him to a block away from the place as he arrived and left. But then he just disappears. He knew exactly how to avoid cameras, dipping in and out of blind spots, entering parking garages. It's been a wild goose chase."

"I'm sorry," she said, frustrated for him but not wanting to feed into the guilt he already felt about what happened last night by asking questions that might make him defensive.

"Yeah, it sucks. Now we're starting to dive into connections through the initials. We know he killed Jared Hartung and Jenavieve Holt because they had had the same ones as you and he was trying to get your attention. But we're trying to determine if there might be another connection we're missing. So far, we've got nothing."

She heard an indecipherable mumbling in the background.

"What was that?" she asked.

"That's Jamil. He wanted you to know he ran a diagnostic on our home security systems and updated them with a few new patches. Otherwise, he says we're good."

Jessie was only slightly relieved.

"Please thank him for me. Still, I'm going to invest in some of the additional precautions we discussed."

"You mean the extra panic room?" he teased.

"That might take a while longer, as will the laser grid," she replied, refusing to give in to the taunting. "But there's no reason we can't have the heat sensors in place in the next 48 hours. Speaking of security precautions, have you heard from Brady lately?"

There was a moment of guilty silence on the line before he responded.

"I've actually been so focused on this stuff that I forgot to check in. But I haven't heard anything since I updated you last so I assume everything's fine."

She wasn't satisfied.

"That is, unless the Night Hunter has slit hit his throat and is inside our home right now," Jessie replied irritably before she could stop herself.

She considered apologizing for the harshness of her words but then decided not to. Ryan had told her that Brady could handle this. She needed to know he wasn't wrong.

"I'll check in with him now," Ryan said softly. "I'll update you with anything worthwhile."

"Thank you."

"Don't be pissed," he pleaded.

"Don't tell me how to feel, Ryan," she replied, not ready to forgive him yet. "This is my sister. I'm not going to feel bad about prioritizing her safety."

"I'm not suggesting you should."

A woman that Jessie assumed was Caroline Ryan walked up to the Froman's gate and began to unlock it. She looked to be about Jessie's age, maybe a couple of years younger. For a woman who ran an '80s-themed clothing store, she was dressed blandly, in blue jeans and a gray sweater.

Her red hair was pulled back in a ponytail and she had on a layer of white-tinted foundation that made her appear ghostly. There was an intensity to her manner that seemed at odds with everything around her. Jessie wondered what had her so uptight, though she could hazard a guess.

"I've got to go," she told him. "My interview subject just showed up. Please let me know what you learn."

"Of course," he said. "I love you."

"I love you too," she said, doing her best to set aside her irritation with him. She already had enough relationships in chaos. She didn't need one more.

After hanging up, she got out of the car and glanced across the street. Reid was paying for his doughnut. She decided not to wait and walked over to the store. She was a few paces from Caroline when the woman whipped around. Her eyes were wide with fear and she was pointing something at Jessie. It took a second to process that it was pepper spray.

"Easy, Caroline," Jessie said slowly, holding her hands out in front of her. "I don't think you want to start your day by assaulting a member of the law enforcement community."

"Who the hell are you?"

Jessie kept her hands up and took a small step back to stay out of spray range.

"My name's Jessie Hunt. I'm a criminal profiler working with the Los Angeles Police Department. I'm investigating the murders of Jax Coopersmith and Claire Bender. We're talking to all their friends and family. I just have a few questions for you."

Caroline still seemed dubious, and the spray can hadn't been lowered.

"Drop your arm!" a loud voice bellowed from somewhere behind Jessie.

Though she couldn't see him, she knew it was Callum Reid. The terrified look on Caroline's face told Jessie that he'd probably pulled his gun. Glancing behind her, she saw that she was right. He was aiming the weapon directly at the woman's chest.

"Caroline," she said calmly. "That's Detective Callum Reid. We're partners on this case. And cops don't like to see people pointing chemical sprays at their partners. So I think you'd be well advised to lower your arm as he instructed."

"How do I know that you're legit?" Caroline demanded, self-doubt creeping in even as her arm, which was now shaking, stayed up. "How do I know you're not planning to inject me with something and leave me to die?"

For the first time, Jessie got just how sacred this woman must be. Two friends of hers had been killed in the last thirty-six hours. She was paranoid that she was next.

"I understand your concerns," Jessie said in her most reassuring voice. "And you're right to be on edge. I don't blame you for having an itchy trigger finger. But we're on a public sidewalk in the middle of the day. I think you can rein it in a little bit. We're both happy to show you our IDs once you put that can down. You can call the department to check Detective Reid's badge number if you like. But you can't keep pointing that thing at me. Okay?"

She could see Caroline's resolve fading. After another few seconds, she lowered her arm. Once she did, Reid holstered his weapon and pulled out his badge and ID. Jessie did the same with her ID placard.

"I can read off my badge number if you want to call it in," the detective offered, doing his best to keep the gruffness out of his tone.

"No, that's okay," Caroline said, after peering at both their IDs and studying Jessie's face. "Now that I've had a second, I recognize you. You're the serial killer catcher."

"That's right," Jessie agreed, not in the mood to unpack that title. "May we come in?"

The woman nodded and unlocked the gate and the front door. Jessie and Reid waited just inside while Caroline turned on the lights. Jessie looked around the place. Allison Standish hadn't been kidding.

The boutique was small but not a foot of space was wasted. One clothing rack was packed with *Pretty in Pink*-style attire, complete with a dress that looked like the one Molly Ringwald wore to the prom.

Another had dozens of *Ferris Bueller*-style sweater vests. On top of the rack was a collection of berets. A third rack had surf shirts that looked like they had been taken straight out of Jeff Spicoli's closet in *Fast Times at Ridgemont High*.

A full third of the store was dedicated to New Wave fashion, including rows of leather pants and neon tops. It looked like someone had raided the wardrobe trailer for a Flock of Seagulls music video. An entire section of one wall was dedicated exclusively to scrunchies.

"Mind if I prep the store while we talk?" Caroline asked, walking over.

"Sure," Jessie replied, having trouble ripping her eyes away from the merchandise. "Let's start by discussing why you were so on edge outside. Had you been threatened or was it just because of what happened to your friends?"

"No, I wasn't threatened," Caroline said, as she set up spotlights to highlight particular items spread out on small tables throughout the store. "But when two friends are killed within a day of each other, it's pretty freaky. Can you blame me for being nervous?"

"Not at all," Jessie said. "Did you ever hear of either of them being threatened?"

Caroline shook her head.

"No. They both seemed fine. As far as I could tell, any stress they had came from their lives being so full of good stuff, not a fear of bad stuff."

Reid joined in for the first time.

"I understand that you weren't just friends. You were all in each other's weddings as well?"

"That's the other thing," Caroline said. "Claire was married recently. Jax was supposed to be soon. My wedding is coming up. We were all in each other's wedding parties. It was just weird that this happened to them. I wondered if there might be a connection."

"Might there be?" Jessie wondered.

"I don't know," Caroline said. "We're all getting married at different venues. But we have the same wedding planner, and she uses a bunch of the same vendors for her events. And like you said, there's a lot of overlap among the bridal parties. Jax and I were bridesmaids for Claire. Claire and I were both going to do the same for Jax and they were going to be in mine. Some of the groomsmen are in more than one too. Like, my fiancé, Brian, was going to be one of Titus's groomsmen."

Jessie wondered how much of these wedding party choices were made just out of obligation and how much was true friendship.

"So everyone mixed and matched?" she asked.

"Not totally," Caroline corrected as she broke open a box of what appeared to replicas of Lloyd Dobler's brown trench coat from *Say Anything...*"Like, Jack Bender wasn't going to be a groomsman for Titus."

"Why not?" Jessie asked.

"I'm not sure. I guess they just weren't that tight; more friendly because their significant others were close."

"You didn't mention Allison Standish," Reid pointed out. "She was the maid of honor for both women. Is she going to be for you too?"

Caroline looked aghast at the idea.

"No way," she insisted. "She's not in my wedding party at all. I know the other girls liked her because she's a walking *id*. They felt like she'd lighten the stress levels. But I mostly just tolerate her. Besides, I don't want to spend my wedding listening to her complain about how she can't find a man."

"Is that a recurring thing?" Jessie asked.

"Oh god, are you kidding? It never ends with her. If she's not complaining about her relationship status, she's upset that her career hasn't taken off. It's exhausting."

"She must have been jealous of how well things were going for Claire and Jax," Reid offered leadingly.

"That's the understatement of the year," Caroline replied, finding a hanger for one of the Dobler coats.

Jessie could tell that the comment made an impression on Reid, who scribbled a note on his pad. She agreed that it was suspicious but wasn't as excited. Allison had already admitted to being jealous. And her alibi for last night, if verified, sounded pretty airtight. Speaking of alibis, it was time to get Caroline's.

"Where were you on Saturday and last night?" she asked directly.

"Saturday I went to a dinner and movie with my fiancé," she answered without missing a beat. "Last night I was home going over store inventory. Exciting stuff, right?"

"Were you alone?" Jessie pressed.

"Most of the night, yeah. Brian was at a friend's place watching a football game. He's in the middle of a lawsuit so that's the only real down time he gets all week. I didn't want to take that away from him.

But I waited up for him because I was scared to go to bed after what happened to Claire the night before."

"What time did he get back?" Reid asked.

"I'm not sure," she said. "Maybe around ten something? I remember falling asleep before 11 for sure."

Reid looked over at Jessie to see if she had any more questions for now. She couldn't think of any.

"Okay, Ms. Ryan," Reid said. "We'll be in touch. In the meantime, I recommend that you be careful. Both these attacks took place in your friends' homes. For the next few days, I'd suggest no working late for you or your fiancé. Enter and leave the house together. Stay in regular touch with friends and family. Keeps your doors locked. Understood?"

Caroline nodded, now looking more scared than when she'd first pulled the pepper spray on Jessie.

"Don't worry," Jessie said. "We'll get to the bottom of this. My hope is that by the time of your wedding, the perpetrator will be long locked away."

"Thanks," Caroline said, fighting back tears. "I'm just sorry that Jax won't get to have hers. She was supposed to have already been married by now."

Something about the comment made Jessie's back straighten up.

"You know," she noted, "Allison mentioned something about that as well. She said that Jax and Titus pushed their wedding back a few months. Do you know why?"

Caroline looked hesitant to answer and seemed to be trying to form an appropriate response.

"I don't," she finally said. "They told everyone it was because they were so busy that they'd fallen behind in the planning and just needed more time."

"But you didn't believe that?" Jessie said more than asked.

"There was gossip. I don't know what made them push it, but the planning explanation never made a lot of sense to me. Jax and Titus are two of the most organized people I've ever met. With their jobs, they have to be to keep their heads above water. They would look months ahead on their calendar to book date nights. The idea that they couldn't square away their wedding, especially when they had a professional planner helping them, never sounded legit to me. But I'm not the type to butt into other people's personal business so I left it alone."

Jessie nodded, already lost in thought as Reid thanked Caroline for her time. Her mind was darting in multiple different directions. She didn't have any hard evidence, but her instincts were telling her to follow this lead. Earlier, something had made her wonder if Jax Coopersmith's life was as perfect as it seemed. The wedding delay only reinforced her doubt.

"So I'm guessing that after hearing that," Reid said as they returned to his car, "you want to talk to the significant other again. Shall we make a return visit to see Titus Poole?"

"You're half right," Jessie told him. "I absolutely want to talk to a significant other, but not that one just yet. We're going back to the Bender Mansion."

CHAPTER ELEVEN

Ryan didn't like being sneaky.

But he knew that if he said anything to Jamil about where he was going, the kid would pepper him with questions, maybe even demand to join him or send a uniformed officer along with him. So he lied.

"I just need a lunch break to clear my head," he'd told him before leaving the station.

It was partly true. He *did* need a break. For the last hour, they'd been looking for connections between the Night Hunter victims beyond their initials and come up dry. His brain was fried.

But it was more than that. He couldn't get away from the feeling that if the man killed again, the victim's blood would be on his hands. He flashed again to last night, to seeing the elderly murderer walk out of that hostel with blood on him, look over at Ryan, and smile. He couldn't forget how he'd frozen in that moment and let the killer get away. Nor could he escape the other fact eating at him: if he'd been healthy enough to go up to that hostel bedroom, Alan Trembley would likely be alive today. He *had* to atone for all of that.

Yeah, I definitely need a break. Otherwise I may lose it completely.

Besides, Brady hadn't returned any of his texts about Hannah and he was starting to worry. Jessie's sarcastic crack about him getting his throat slit was starting to seem more credible every second and he wanted to check in again.

But there was another reason he needed solitude: one he wasn't ready to share. He was so apprehensive about it that he couldn't stop himself from glancing back guiltily at the Central Station entrance as he waited for his rideshare to arrive. Once it did, he hobbled over as quickly as his cane would allow, hoping to be gone before anyone saw him and got curious about his destination.

Even as the vehicle pulled out, he was dialing Brady's number. His friend picked up after three interminable rings.

"Hey buddy," Brady said in a tone that immediately suggested he was hiding something, "how's it going?"

"Don't screw with me," Ryan told him, cutting straight to the chase. "What's wrong? Why haven't I heard from you?"

"Okay, man," Brady said, still trying to sound casual and failing. "I'll fill you in. I just don't want you to overreact."

"I won't overreact if you stop stalling. Update me now, Brady."

There was a brief pause during which Ryan suspected his friend was deciding how best to couch what was obviously bad news.

"So I kind of lost her," he finally said.

"You *what*?"

"Yeah, everything was cool for a while. She took a rideshare from your house about two hours ago. I followed her until she got dropped off outside an office building downtown just after ten. She stood outside for a few seconds, looked a little freaked out actually. But then she went in. So I went in too. She got in an elevator and I tried to catch it but the doors closed just as I got there."

"Was she alone?" Ryan pressed.

"There was an old lady in there with her," he said. "She looked pretty harmless."

"Are you sure it was an old lady and not an old man disguised as an old lady? Remember, the Night Hunter is elderly."

Brady's hesitation before answering was not reassuring.

"I only caught a glimpse of her, but it definitely looked like a female to me. Besides, you told me you warned the girl to be on the lookout for suspicious old guys, so I assume she had her guard up. She didn't look concerned. In fact, I thought maybe she even knew the lady. Anyway, I saw what floor they went to and I took the next elevator up."

"Did you find her?"

There was another long pause.

"No," he admitted. "The hall was empty by the time I got up there. But I checked the bathrooms to make sure no one suspicious was hiding in them. I also took photos of the names on every door. I've been researching them while I wait."

"Wait for what?" Ryan wanted to know.

"For her to come out of the building."

"She's still in some random office building after an hour and a half?"

"Actually, I'm not sure about that," Brady conceded. "After about an hour of waiting in my car, I went back inside and saw that there was an alternate exit to the street on the other side of the building. If she left that way, I would have missed her. I probably should have waited in the lobby."

"Ya think? Jeez, Brady. You are killing me here. What am I supposed to tell Jessie?"

"Why do you have to tell her anything yet? I found everyone from attorneys to therapists to accountants to importer/exporters with offices on that floor. Why assume that some elderly serial killer somehow forced her into one of them? The girl could just be talking to some lawyer about becoming emancipated. That takes time. Why jump to conclusions?"

"Brady," Ryan said slowly, trying to keep calm as he watched streets whiz by. "Hannah will be eighteen in a few months. She's not talking to a lawyer about emancipation. I'm in a car running an errand right now. Tell me where you are, and I'll come by."

"Don't be ridiculous," Brady retorted, sounding upset for the first time. "There's no reason for that. If she's gone, you showing up won't do any good. I'm returning to the lobby now. If she's still up there, I'll see her when she comes down and let you know. Continue with your day. You asked me to do this. Let me."

Ryan sighed, unsure how to respond.

"For how long? What if Jessie calls? She's not speaking to her best friend because she held out on her. What do you think she'll do to me?"

"Nothing," Brady insisted, "because you'll blame me. Give me another half hour. If I don't see her by then, we'll go to the next step. But I don't want you stressing out your already massively frazzled girlfriend if it can be avoided."

Ryan rubbed his temples as he thought.

"Thirty minutes," he finally said. "Good news, bad news, no news, you call me. Got it?"

"You can count on me, buddy."

Ryan waited until he had hung up to cuss his friend out. He'd barely had a minute to process everything before the car pulled over at the designated address.

"Thanks," he said, easing himself out the back door and shuffling over to the sidewalk. The car pulled away and Ryan allowed himself a moment to take in his surroundings.

Even though Central Station was located only a few miles from here, he was only slightly familiar with this district. He knew it was probably foolish to come to this place alone, without support, based only on a tip from one person. But he worried that if anyone else came along, word of his plan might get out and that couldn't happen.

He reconfirmed that he was at the correct address, which he'd hurriedly scrawled on a piece of paper earlier during his clandestine conversation about this place. It matched. As instructed, he limped down the adjoining alley along the building, past two dumpsters until he came to an unmarked door below a small, black awning. He rang the doorbell and waited.

After nearly a minute, a large, pale man with a shaved head wearing a too-tight sports jacket, a dress shirt, and slacks opened the door. Easily six-foot-five and 250 pounds, the guy looked like a retired professional wrestler who was just starting to let himself go. Ryan could see that the man had a handgun in a shoulder holster under his coat.

"You got appointment?" the man asked in a thick, Eastern European accent.

"Yes, for 11:30, with Johann."

"You early," the man said accusatorily, looking at his watch. It was 11:22.

"Light traffic," Ryan replied, not sure what else to say.

"Must search you," the man growled.

Ryan had been expecting that.

"I'm a cop," he warned, "so I'm carrying."

The former wrestler seemed unfazed by the admission.

"Have to take," he said, "will leave in lockbox."

Ryan nodded and handed over his service weapon.

"Ankle too?" the guy asked.

"Yeah," Ryan said, removing the small, extra pistol in his ankle holster and delicately placing it in the guard's massive hand.

The man handed the weapons to another, only slightly smaller man who appeared behind him with a metal box. That guard placed both guns in the box, locked it, and handed Ryan the key which was attached to a small bracelet. He put it on his wrist.

"Must still pat down," the larger guard said.

Ryan placed his cane against the wall and spread his arms out to his sides. The guard did a quick but thorough search that suggested he might actually have previously worked in a capacity other than professional wrestling. When he was done, he stood back and looked Ryan over.

"Must check stick too," he said, pointing at the cane.

Ryan gave it to him and waited while the guy tapped it in various places. He even pulled off the rubberized base to make sure there was

69

nothing hidden inside. When he was satisfied, he returned the cane and moved aside.

Ryan stepped through the door, as well as the metal detector that was just inside. The space was tight and dimly lit, with deep wood paneling. Once he'd passed through the detector and the door was locked behind him, he was directed to a small counter where a third man stood. This one was much older, well into his seventies, and looked like he'd spent way too many hours in the sun. When he squinted at Ryan, his face looked like it might actually crack.

"Mr. Hernandez?" the man confirmed.

"Yes."

"You were referred by Ray Vessey, correct?"

"That's right," Ryan said. He could feel both of the guards standing uncomfortably close behind him and did his best not to look unsettled.

"And you are consulting with Johann today, hoping to take advantage of his expertise?"

"That's what was discussed."

"Very well," the old man said and reached under the counter.

Ryan felt his muscles tense up even more than they already were, and tried to remind himself that, at least according to Ray, the likelihood of being assaulted in here was negligible. He heard a soft buzz and saw one of the wall panels to the right of the man slowly slide open.

Though it looked like wood, the hidden door was made of some kind of heavy metal. It took several, grindingly slow seconds for the thing to come to a stop. Behind it was another room. The old man gave a flourish of a wave, indicating for Ryan to pass through.

Once he did, everything changed. He was now in a much larger, brightly lit room, with three display cases, all of which held diamond rings. He imagined that the contents of this room alone were worth well over nine figures.

His anxiety level immediately ratcheted up a few notches. Was he actually doing this? Was he really considering buying an engagement ring? A shuffling sound to his right snapped him out of his thoughts.

"Hello, Detective Hernandez," said a man emerging from a small room behind the center display case. "So glad to meet you. I'm Johann Glitz."

Ryan made sure to keep a straight face despite the absurdity of a jeweler with the last name Glitz. The man was almost as ostentatious looking as his name. His black hair was slicked back and tied in a short ponytail. He had an immaculately groomed goatee. His face was unnaturally tan, and he wore a black turtleneck sweater that looked like it was about to choke him.

"Nice to meet you as well," he managed to say neutrally.

"I hear that we were recommended to you by Ray Vessey," Johann replied in a thick accent that Ryan guessed was South African. "What an interesting world we live in where a respected police detective can get a jeweler recommendation from a sports bookie."

"Well, before he was a bookie, he was a neighborhood friend. I'm not sure our professions played much of a role in me being here. How do you know him?"

"Would you believe we go to the same synagogue?" Johann asked.

"I actually would," Ryan said. "Ray mentioned that his temple attracted an eclectic mix of folks. Anyway, he tells me that you are a rare breed."

"How so?"

"He said that you have impeccable taste, ethically resourced merchandise, and that you rarely try to up-sell."

Johann smiled.

"The first two are unquestionably true," he said. "There might be some debate on that last claim. But seeing as how you are a dedicated civil servant rather than a twenty-something music producer, I'm less inclined to push on that front. My hope is if that you leave here satisfied, you'll mention me to some of your law enforcement friends. It never hurts to be well liked by the police."

Ryan didn't want the guy to get too far ahead of himself.

"I should warn you," he said. "For this visit, I'm really here just to look. I'm not sure I'm ready to pull the trigger just yet."

"Of course not," Johann replied. "I assume we're considering an engagement ring, yes?"

Ryan nodded. He couldn't bring himself to say "yes" out loud. He could still barely believe that he was actually in a place like this, considering looking for a ring. He knew he wanted to take the next step. But until today, he'd always told him himself that they should wait.

They should wait until he was healthier, until Jessie was more settled at the university, until Hannah had graduated and was on an independent path. That's what his head told him. But after last night, with Hannah running away and Trembley's murder, he'd come to a realization: there would always be something, some obstacle he could

71

use as an excuse for waiting, for delaying the life he dreamed of. But life was short, and he was tired of waiting. So he was here.

"Not sure about the young woman, is it?" Johann asked, pulling him out of his thoughts.

"Why do you say that?" he asked.

"You said you were just looking, that you're not ready to pull the trigger. Are you having doubts?"

Ryan knew he was being worked but didn't mind.

"About the girl? No. I'd give my life for her, so a proposal doesn't feel like a big leap. It's just that we've just had a rough year and I didn't want to add to the stress. Plus, I'm just not sure I'm quite ready to make the financial commitment that comes with a purchase like this."

He looked at the array of rings in the glass display case and tried not to choke on the prices marked in tiny print beside each one. Most went for at least five figures. A few cost more than he made in a year. At least one was more expensive than Jessie's house.

"I understand," Johann said soothingly. "The sticker shock can be daunting, especially for a trinket. Though you're not really paying for the trinket itself so much as what it represents, don't you agree?"

"I guess," Ryan said, shrugging.

"Detective Hernandez, may I try something unusual with you?"

Okay," Ryan said warily.

"Could you describe your beloved in one brief sentence for me? Take your time."

Ryan responded immediately.

"She's the toughest, bravest, smartest, most stubborn, beautiful, devoted person I've ever met."

Johann nodded, and then closed his eyes. He stood silently for twenty seconds. When he opened his eyes again, he moved over to the far end of the display case on the left and glanced down. He grinned slightly, and then motioned for Ryan to join him.

Ryan walked over and looked at the ring. The first thing he noticed was that he wouldn't have to sell a kidney to buy it. The diamond was a little smaller than some of the others, with an unfussy but still delicate, sparkly cut.

The ring itself, with a narrow, solid silver band, gleamed up at him. It was lovely in an understated way, the ring of a woman who was gorgeous but no frills, who appreciated romance and good sense in equal measure. It looked as if it had been designed specifically for Jessie's finger. It was perfect.

He looked up at Johann, who seemed to know what he was going to say.

"I'll take it."

CHAPTER TWELVE

There would be no return trip to the Bender Mansion.

Apparently, Jack had gone home to collect a few clothes before he returned to his mother's place. He'd agreed to meet Jessie and Reid there.

As they pulled up to his impressive house in the hills just south of the famed Greek Theater, just a three-minute drive up from where Jax and Titus had been living, Jessie was glad for the change of venue for this second interview. Without his mother lingering at his side, maybe the guy would be a little more forthcoming.

Jack came out to meet them, along with a short, muscular man that Jessie assumed was another member of Lisanne's security squad. As they walked up, Jessie took in the home. It was some kind of modernist cube concoction, with four levels that looked like large blocks stacked unevenly on top of each other. It was like a real-life version of a Jenga tower.

"Thanks for meeting me here," Jack said, shaking both their hands. "I was just packing up the last of my essentials."

"So you're planning to stay at your mom's for a while?" Reid asked.

"At least until I find a new place, yes."

"You're not moving back here?" Jessie asked, though she wasn't really surprised. She too had moved more than once because of the bad, violent memories associated with where she lived.

"I could never," he said. "Knowing what Claire went through in this house, I wouldn't get a single night's sleep. I'll sell it as soon as possible, probably at a loss, though you never know what the jackals in this town will find to be valuable."

Jessie wasn't going to argue the point.

"Shall we go in then and talk?" she asked.

He nodded and led them inside, seemingly oblivious to the expensive art on the walls or the elaborate sculptures on display tables throughout. They joined him in a decked out living room that, despite a large-screen TV, a pool table, and a wet bar, somehow seemed allergic to casual interaction.

He sat down in a plush leather easy chair that looked brand new and indicated for them to join him on the adjoining, equally unwelcoming couch. The security guard stood silently at the entrance to the room.

"Thanks for seeing us again, Mr. Bender," Reid said, not wasting any time. "We realize this is difficult for you but getting as much information as we can early on in an investigation can be invaluable. So do you mind if we dive right in?"

"Of course not," he said, staring back at them with clear eyes. It appeared that whatever he'd been on earlier had largely worn off.

Reid turned to Jessie. After all, she was the one who had wanted to talk to Jack Bender before revisiting Titus Poole, so it was on her to get things started.

"We've been speaking to a number of your friends," she began, "notably a few of the women who were part of the wedding parties, and some of what they told us had me curious."

"What about?" Bender asked, curious himself.

"Jax was a bridesmaid for Claire and your wife was going to return the favor. But it was clear that you weren't going to be a groomsman for Titus. Why is that?"

Jack considered the question for a second before answering.

"No real reason. We weren't super close. Claire and Jax were tight so we became friendly by association. But I'm not sure we would have hung out otherwise. We certainly weren't close enough to ask the other to be groomsmen."

His answer made perfect sense. But something about the way he shifted in his seat as he talked made Jessie dubious. It was as if he was dodging some invisible, incoming fire. She wondered what had him on edge and decided to tease it out.

"I totally get that," she said casually, hiding her suspicion. "I remember when I got married to my ex, only one of my bridesmaids was someone I actually liked. The rest were kind of foisted upon me. But I don't know that I would have outright rejected one of them being in the wedding party. There would have to have been some real animosity to risk rocking the boat. So I can't help but wonder if maybe there was a little more to you not being asked to suit up for him."

Jack Bender stared back at her and it was clear that he understood what she was getting at. It was equally clear that he had no intention of being forthcoming.

"I'm sorry you had that experience," he said, unable to keep the condescension out of his tone. "But our situation was much more boring. We just weren't besties, you know?"

They were at an impasse, one that might prove difficult to deftly navigate. Jessie was sure he was lying. But pushing him too hard might make him shut down completely or even bring up the idea of a lawyer. On the other hand, she might never get a chance like this again. It was highly unlikely that his mother would allow him to participate in any more unsupervised interviews. She decided to go for it.

"Well, if that's all you've got, then that's all you've got," she said nonchalantly. "Of course, if you're not able to help us, we may have to poke around a little more."

"What does that mean?" Bender asked, sitting up straighter in his chair.

"Well, it's just that I feel like you're holding back, which is your prerogative," she said without emotion. "But we've got a lot of unanswered questions. And we're not just going to simply leave them unanswered. So we may have to probe the history a little more with your social circle to see if they agree about why you might have been left off Titus's groomsmen list. We'll probably ask him directly as well. Sometimes that leads to embarrassing revelations which could have been kept quiet if the subject of those revelations was more forthcoming to begin with. Do you get what I'm saying, Mr. Bender?"

He obviously did, as his shifting in the chair was now accompanied a grimace he couldn't control. It took several seconds for him to find the words he was looking for.

"It would be nice if we could avoid dredging up embarrassing revelations, especially if they weren't relevant to your larger investigation," he finally said.

"Here's what I can offer you: if you have some unpleasant personal information you're willing to share, after we check it out and find that it isn't germane to our case, we could probably bury it deep within our case file. But if you hold back, once we start asking around, what happens next is kind out of our hands."

A long silence engulfed the room. Jessie saw the guard in the corner looking warily at them. He seemed to want to intervene but couldn't think of a credible reason to do so. Jack sighed deeply.

"Okay, I'll tell you," he said.

"Perhaps we should call Mrs. Bender," the guard blurted out, finally deciding to earn his keep.

"Zip it, sluggo!" Reid ordered, staring at the guy narrowly. "You're not part of this chat. Insert yourself again and you'll spend the afternoon securing bail on a charge of impeding an investigation. Got it?"

The guard nodded sullenly. Jessie and Reid returned their attention to Bender.

"Go ahead," Jessie prodded.

He closed his eyes, as if that would make what he said next less objectionable.

"Jax and I were sleeping together," he blurted out.

The pause between his admission and her question was brief.

"For how long?" Jessie asked quietly, not at all surprised.

"On and off for a few months now. It started as a drunken hookup at a Labor Day house party. We both agreed that it was a mistake. But then it happened again, and again. Pretty soon, it was a regular thing."

"So was it an affair," Reid wanted to know. "Were either of you planning to leave your significant others?"

"No," Bender insisted vehemently. "It was nothing like that. We were just having fun. Claire can—could—be controlling at times and Titus is so buttoned-down. Plus he's a lot older than Jax. The two of us were a little less intense, so we gravitated to each other. But we were both happy in our relationships."

Jessie wasn't convinced.

"But Jax and Titus postponed their wedding. Are you telling me that your hookups had nothing to do with that?"

Bender shook his head.

"I really don't think so. I know Claire had no idea it was going on."

Jessie didn't say anything, but she wasn't sure she bought that. After all, Jack Bender wasn't a pro at hiding his emotions. She'd gotten him to crack in just a few minutes. What if Claire had done the same? If she had found out the dalliance and threatened to reveal the truth, how far would Bender go to stop her?

And yet he seemed to have an iron-clad alibi. Upon a request earlier this morning, Lisanne Bender had agreed, without a subpoena, to turn over all the security footage from the mansion for the last two days. The tech team hadn't reviewed all of it yet. But just the offer suggested that the Benders weren't worried about Jack's alibi holding up.

"What about Titus?" Reid asked. "Any chance he found out?"

"No way," Bender said confidently. "He's a pretty jealous guy. If he suspected something, he's not the type to hold his tongue."

"Is he the type to get violent?" Reid pressed.

Jessie saw a flicker in Bender's eyes and knew he was thinking that saying "yes" might take the pressure off him. But ultimately he shook his head again.

"I've seen him get angry, but never violent. Usually when he gets mad, he starts speaking very slowly and deliberately. I remember he once said that a black man can't afford to get too angry in this world. It usually ends badly. I think he really took that to heart. Besides, if he did lose it, wouldn't it make more sense that he'd go after Jax and me? Why Claire? She was being cheated on too."

Jessie had to admit that it was a good point, although in her experience, when people reached the point of murder, logic often went out the window.

"Jax never told you why they postponed the wedding?" she asked. "Maybe a lovers' secret while you were in bed?"

"No," he insisted. "She said it was logistical, that they fell behind in the planning. I don't know, maybe she was lying to me. It's possible that she felt guilty about what we were doing and needed to sort things out in her head, decide what she really wanted. But she never said that."

Jessie wasn't sure where else they could go with this. Jack Bender was a cheating scumbag, potentially a drug addict, and a generally squirrelly guy. But his answers made sense and his alibi was likely to hold up. Going at him any more without something definitive felt like a mistake. There was no reason to make an enemy of Lisanne Bender if they didn't need to.

"I think that will be all for now," she said standing up. "We'll be in touch if we have additional questions."

"You're not going to say anything about what I told you, right?" he pleaded, standing up as well.

"I can't promise anything, Mr. Bender," she said as they began to leave. "Obviously if your infidelity turns out to be essential to the investigation, it will come out. But if we able to determine that it played no role in the crimes, we'll do our best to minimize your exposure. That's the best I can offer."

"I understand," he said as he opened the front door for them. "I appreciate any discretion you can provide."

Before Jessie could reply, she felt her phone, which was on silent, buzz. It was a voicemail from Ryan.

78

"We'll have to leave it there," she said abruptly and started down the steps.

"Let us know if you think of anything else," Reid said as he rushed to join her.

Jessie was about to listen to the message when Reid caught up.

"What's wrong?" he asked.

"I got a voicemail from Ryan," she said. "Usually he just texts during work. He only calls if it's something important."

"Go ahead then," Reid said as they got into the car.

"Thanks," Jessie said, reaching for her AirPods. But before she could put them in, Reid's phone rang. It was Captain Decker. She was tempted to tell him to send the call to voicemail so she could check Ryan's message. But she knew the captain was on edge and being put off would only exacerbate the situation. Reluctantly, she nodded and Reid answered and put him on speaker.

"What's up, Captain?" he asked.

"Is Hunt with you?" Decker asked, sounding even more irritable than usual.

"Yes, sir," Jessie volunteered.

"Good. Listen up, both of you. We've got a major problem."

CHAPTER THIRTEEN

Jessie steeled herself.

A major problem could mean anything from HSS having been shut down completely to another dead cop. She tried not to leap to conclusions and waited for Decker to explain.

"What is it, Captain?" Reid asked.

"This case is approaching DEFCON 1."

"What do you mean?" Jessie demanded.

"All those fans who were mourning outside Jax Coopersmith's house have moved. Now they're outside police headquarters. Only instead of dozens of them, now there are hundreds. And they're not just mourning, they're protesting. Some of them are lying in the middle of the street, making it impossible for vehicles to get by. We've had multiple arrests. News helicopters are everywhere. There's a march, complete with bullhorns and homemade signs. They're demanding to know if we have suspects. There's even a hashtag: #JusticeforJax. Please tell me you've got something because the Chief just called me, and my ears are still ringing."

Jessie and Reid exchanged frustrated looks. Decker wasn't going to be happy with the answer.

"Captain," Reid said, taking the bullet, "we're making progress, eliminating suspects. But no, we don't yet have anyone we like."

"No one?" Decker asked incredulously.

"We have a lot of credible suspects," Jessie said. "But that's the problem. Both victims had a large circle of friends and they overlapped. They were all in each other's wedding plans."

"Wait, did you say both victims?" Decker repeated, his voice rising. "What are you talking about?"

Jessie's heart dropped into her stomach. Only then did she realize that in all their driving around, neither of them had thought to update the captain on the connection between the victims: that they knew each other, were bridesmaids for each other, and most importantly, that they'd been killed on consecutive nights using the same method. If Decker was upset now, he was going to lose it completely when he found out the magnitude of the situation.

"Hold on one moment," Captain," Reid said, muting his phone.

"What is it?" she asked.

"This is about to get ugly," he said. "We should have kept him in the loop on this. But that's on me. I'm the LAPD detective. You're a consultant helping out the department. I should take the heat on this."

Jessie shook her head.

"We'll take the heat together," she insisted. "It'll be less painful if we tag-team him."

"No," Reid said firmly. "Call your boyfriend. I know you're worried about your sister. Find out what's going on. I'll smooth this over."

"Are you sure?"

"Don't worry about it," he said. "But maybe walk away from the car a bit. Decker doesn't yell much, but when he does, it really carries."

Before she could second-guess herself, Jessie leaned over and gave him a kiss on the cheek. Then she got out of the car. The door was just closing when she heard Reid saying "Sorry, Captain…"

She jogged over to the edge of the driveway and played Ryan's message. The second she heard the tone of the first word, she knew something was amiss: *Jessie, please call me back as soon as you get this. It's about Hannah. I'm not sure anything is wrong, but I need to talk to you.*

She called him back immediately, her mouth going dry as she waited for him to answer. He picked up on the first ring.

"Hey," he said, launching in without waiting for a response, "so Brady seems to have lost Hannah—."

"He what!" she interrupted, her chest tightening.

"He doesn't think she's in danger," Ryan added quickly. "He followed her into a downtown office building and saw her take an elevator up to the fifth floor. She went there on her own and didn't look under duress. But he hasn't seen her come out. He might have missed it or she could still be up there. I know you're trying not to be too much like Big Brother, or Big Sister, but I thought you might want to check that geo-location app you secretly installed on her phone."

She had already opened the app before he even finished talking. By the time he was done, she saw where Hannah was.

"She's at Tommy's Coffee, the coffeehouse near the house."

"Are you sure?" he asked.

"I'm sure her phone is there," she confirmed. "If you wait for a second, I'll find out for certain."

She put him on hold and called the place. The woman who picked up sounded like she didn't have a care in the world.

"Tommy's Coffee," she said sunnily. "How may I help you?"

"Yes, hi," Jessie said, trying to channel her best mom vibe. "My daughter is on break from school today and said she was going to be hanging out there for a while. I'm at work and don't want to call her to check up on her, but I worry that she may be feeding me a story so she can sneak off somewhere with her friends. Could you tell me if there's a girl in there, looks about early twenties even though she's a teenager; tall, skinny, beautiful, sandy blond hair just past her shoulders, green eyes, probably sitting curled up on the old, leather easy chair under the retro 'Here you go, a cup o' Joe' poster, staring at her phone?"

"She's right there," the woman replied, "Exactly where you expected."

"Thank you so much," Jessie said, the relief in her voice genuine. "It's a hard line to balance, giving freedom but being responsible."

"I understand," the woman said. "I've been through it with two boys. But if I can offer a suggestion, there are ways to mark her phone so you can see where she is. It's a little sneaky, but you might consider it."

"I may do that," Jessie said, feigning ignorance. "Thanks for the tip."

She switched back over to Ryan.

"I don't know what she was doing before but she's at the coffeehouse now," she said.

"Thank god," Ryan sighed.

"This doesn't say much for Brady," Jessie said, trying not to get too angry. Their last conversation had ended abruptly when she learned that Ryan hadn't checked in regularly with Brady. To get on him now, because he *had* checked in and come back with a disheartening status report didn't seem fair. Brady might be a mediocre tail but that wasn't Ryan's fault. He'd only been trying to help by suggesting him as an alternative when she rejected Kat as an option.

"No, it doesn't," Ryan admitted, not making any excuses for his friend.

Appreciating his admission, she decided to move past it.

"Can you let him know where she is please? And maybe remind him not to underestimate her. Part of the problem we have now is because I didn't consider what she was capable of."

82

"I'll reach out as soon as we hang up," he promised, sounding like he was about to end the call.

"Hold on," she said. "How is the Night Hunter investigation going?"

He took longer than expected to reply.

"I had to put it on pause briefly. Something came up. But we're getting back into it now. Unfortunately, there's nothing new to report so far."

She could tell he was holding something back but didn't press. There had been enough tension between them today and she didn't want to exacerbate it.

"Okay, well let me know if I can help. Otherwise, please be safe."

"I will," he assured her. "You do the same. I love you."

"I love you too," she said and this time there was no irritation to overcome.

She hung up and returned to the car, where Reid was waiting.

"How is everything?" he asked.

"Good," she said. "Sister's safe. Boyfriend's safe. Elderly serial killer is still at large but we can't have everything, I guess. What about you?"

"My call wasn't as great," he admitted. "Decker's really on edge. He seemed fixated on Jax Coopersmith's net worth. Apparently, all told, it's valued at north of five million. He kept saying he couldn't believe someone who reviewed clothes online for a living could be so wealthy. I told him to join the club. I don't get it either."

Jessie sat quietly for a moment. It occurred to her that one need not be a crusty old cop to be overwhelmed and possibly irked by a fact like that.

"You know, Jack Bender said Titus Poole was the jealous type," she said. "I wonder just how far that extended."

"What do you mean?"

"Titus may work as a studio executive. But I doubt he makes the money or has the influence of his younger, more famous fiancée. I think we should pay that visit to him now. Let's see what he really thought about Jax being the brightest light in the sky."

CHAPTER FOURTEEN

She hung up the phone. Her latest appointment was confirmed. That meant she'd have to take a pause in the planning of the next Rebalancing session. It was too bad. She was just getting into the nitty-gritty of the preparation.

But it was okay. This interruption would give her time to savor the anticipation. She was getting a real taste for it. Admittedly, she'd been nervous for the first one. But her loathing for that silver-spooned, high society wannabe Claire Bender had been strong enough to push her out of her comfort zone, to make her do the research on the chemicals she would need and how to safely employ them. Claire really shouldn't have been so smug.

Jax was a different story. She had never been mean. In fact, when she'd heard about the broken engagement, she'd been sympathetic. But it was clear that she didn't really get it. How could a beautiful, famous celebrity understand what it was like for someone else, someone without her gifts and her luck, to deal with a broken heart? She doubted that Jax had ever even been dumped, much less had an engagement ended just weeks before the wedding.

That's why she had been next on the list. The guilt almost stopped that one from coming to fruition. But when, from her hiding place beside the bed, she saw the gorgeous influencer toss her sexy gown on the comforter and wander into the bathroom to stare at her perfect body while munching on a late-night snack, the guilt disappeared, and the resolve hardened. When Jax's face started to melt to the point that even her moans were unintelligible, it provided an almost sexual thrill.

And it would all happen again this evening. But first she'd have to head out for another glamorous outing and pretend that she enjoyed all the doting and preening. After that, tonight would be her time. She could picture herself lying patiently in wait as the next target came closer, oblivious to the danger. She could almost smell the sizzling flesh.

As she imagined it all, she realized she was salivating and delicately wiped away the bit of drool that had formed on her lips.

CHAPTER FIFTEEN

As she waited outside Titus Poole's office, Jessie had just about reached the end of her patience.

First of all, it had taken well over an hour to get from Jack Bender's house to Dandelion Studios, where Poole worked. When they finally got to his office, Poole's assistant, Annaleigh, who looked like she'd just wrapped up her term as Miss Hawaiian Tropic, was less accommodating.

"Mr. Poole is in a meeting," she said, standing up to reveal that she was wearing a miniskirt and a cream blouse open about two buttons lower than Jessie would have been comfortable with. "He'll be with you as soon as possible."

Then she pushed a sign-in sheet across the desk and walked over to whisper something to another assistant outside the adjoining office of a nearby executive. As she passed, Jessie could feel Reid straining not to look at the woman's long, tan legs or her other attributes. Jessie reminded herself not to be too judge-y. Maybe the gal typed a hundred words a minute.

"Let's just pull rank," Jessie had suggested.

"I know you're anxious to get in there," Reid told her. "But Dandelion is the most successful studio in town. They hold an annual ball for LAPD every year. They've raised over four million dollars for the families of officers killed in the line of duty. Every boss I've ever had told me to use kid gloves as much as possible when we have to visit this lot."

"So you want roll over for them?" she objected, knowing that wasn't fair.

"No," he said, straining to keep calm. "We go wherever a case takes us. But it has been made clear that it's always better to maintain a smaller footprint here until we have to start stomping around. We're not in stomp mode yet. Let's give it a little more time."

Jessie relented, though she counted every second they sat there, imagining what she would do to Annaleigh if they ever met in a dark alley. It was already late afternoon and every second counted in a case like this.

Moments later Annaleigh told them Poole could see them and they stepped into his office, which was as large as her living room. She did a double take at the view out his massive window, which looked down on Dandelion Garden Plaza.

Along with the multiple benches and green spaces were ten large sculptures of different flowers, all painted in incredible detail, complete with human faces nestled among the petals. There was a red rose, a pink tulip, and an assortment of others, including a daisy, a carnation, a hibiscus, a bluebonnet and of course, smack dab in the middle of the plaza, a massive dandelion bursting forth like a yellow sun. Each flower represented a character in the studio's hugely popular collection of films about anthropomorphic flowers. As a kid, Jessie had always been partial to Bonnie the Bluebonnet, who had a little sass to her.

"I must admit I'm surprised to see you here," Poole said, snapping her out of her childhood memory before turning to his assistant. "Can you please close the door, Annie?"

"I was about to say the same about you," Jessie replied, regaining her focus. "After what happened, I'm surprised you're not in bed, sedated."

Poole, who was standing behind a giant desk, motioned for them to take seats opposite him, before doing the same.

"I thought about it," he admitted. "But it didn't seem like a great idea. There's no way I could sleep in that house right now. Besides, staying busy keeps me distracted. I'm actually glad that I'm in the middle of negotiating a big deal. It doesn't give me much time to fixate on…anything else."

"Well," Jessie said, sympathetic to his plight but not entirely convinced of his sincerity. "I'm sorry to tell you that we'll need you to fixate for a few minutes."

"On what?" he asked guardedly.

"How much do you make?" Reid asked bluntly.

This was part of the plan they'd come up with on the way over, to throw Poole off by asking frank, even impolite questions in quick succession. The hope was that maybe he'd inadvertently reveal something. Maybe he'd get pissed.

Based on the comment he allegedly made to Jack Bender about how black men couldn't afford to get too angry in this world, she knew it would be hard to get his goat. But if they were going to learn anything of value, they had to break through the wall he'd spent years building to protect himself.

86

"Do I have to answer that?" Poole asked, surprised but not upset.

"Of course not," Reid told him. "But it might help the investigation."

"How could that possibly be relevant?"

Reid pointed his thumb at Jessie.

"This one has a theory and I was hoping to test it," he said, intentionally attempting to sound like he was humoring the little woman he'd been assigned to work with.

"What's that?" Poole asked, curious despite his apprehension.

"Okay," Jessie said, leaning in. "I figure you make a pretty solid salary if you're high enough up the ladder to be closing deals late on a Sunday night. You probably rake in at least a couple of hundred thousand a year, right?"

Poole shrugged.

"You might be underestimating by a few hundred thousand," he couldn't stop himself from revealing. "But what does that have to do with anything?"

"I'm getting there," Jessie said, happily sensing the first hints of irritation in the executive's voice. "But even at that salary, I'm guessing you were still well below Jax's pay grade. Am I right? There was a news report that just came out saying she was worth over five million dollars when she died."

Titus Poole looked aghast that Jessie would broach such a thing, but when she remained silent, he realized she expected an answer.

"That sounds about right," he muttered quietly.

"Yeah," Jessie said, really getting into character now, needling him just a little more. "And I know it took her a while to break through. Her success started quite recently from what I read. So these last few years, she was probably pulling in well over one million a year, wouldn't you say?"

Titus nodded. Jessie studied his expression. He no longer looked irritated. He looked worried. She pressed on.

"That's a lot of money, Titus," she said, using his first name for the first time. "Like over double what you earn."

"So?" he asked challengingly.

"So," she countered, ready to pounce. "I can't help but wonder, did Jax ask you to sign a prenup?"

His pursed lips told her that she'd struck gold.

"What would make you say that?' he asked.

"Your fiancée makes twice what you do. She's famous, adored by her fans. When you go to red carpet events, paparazzi call out her name. You're already arm candy, one of thousands of interchangeable film executives in this town. You're already feeling self-conscious and then she asks you to sign a prenup? That must have been so emasculating, Titus."

Poole took a long, deep breath before answering. When he did, he used the slow, deliberate tone that Jack Bender had mentioned he employed when his temper was flaring.

"Yes, Jax asked me to sign a prenup. No, it wasn't emasculating."

Every word seemed to be a burden to him.

"Then why did she postpone the wedding?" she demanded. "It *was* her who postponed, wasn't it?"

It looked like she'd finally cracked through the façade. Poole's eyes were blazing, and his lower lip trembled slightly. He leaned forward in his chair as he clenched and unclenched his fists repeatedly. It looked like he might leap up at any moment.

But that wasn't what Jessie wanted. She needed him to explode verbally, not physically, and was about to say something else to redirect him when Reid jumped in.

"I wouldn't, Mr. Poole," he said, in a quiet but firm voice. "We both know that any rash decision you make won't end well for you. If you didn't kill Jax, your best bet is to simply answer our questions. Any other reaction will only make things worse."

Poole was still shaking slightly but seemed to have recaptured some control. He blinked twice, very slowly, then replied.

"Jax wanted me to sign a prenup. It hurt my pride a little, but I understood. I was just taking my time reviewing it with my lawyers. She thought I was dragging my feet because I had doubts about the marriage. That escalated and we decided to push pause on everything so we could get back to a good place."

"And did you?" Jessie asked.

"We went to therapy. I think it was working. I learned to admit that I was a little jealous. Here's the thing. When we first met, she was just an aspiring influencer. By the time we got engaged, she was huge. It was a lot. But we were getting there."

"I'm glad," Jessie said, aware that she was straddling the line between questioning and goading but knowing she might have to cross it to get the information she needed. It made her a little sick to her stomach, pushing a man to break who had spent his whole life forced to stay under control. But her job on this day was to get justice for Jax and Claire, not Titus Poole. "Then why did you lie about your alibi?"

"What?" he asked, genuinely stunned.

"You said that after the meeting you went home," she pressed, "that you were on the phone the whole time. But when our tech people checked the GPS in your phone and car, we found that wasn't true. You made a stop on the way home. Do you want to explain yourself?"

Poole's face hardened into a grimace, and then seemed to soften. It was as if he'd made some internal decision and was now at peace with it.

"You're right," he said, speaking barely above a whisper. "I wasn't forthright. I didn't go straight home. I made a stop."

"On North Curson Avenue in Hollywood, it seems," Jessie noted, looking at her phone. "What was so interesting at the Ocean Palms apartment complex?"

"That's where Annaleigh lives," he said, his throat choked with guilt.

"Ah yes, Annie," Jessie said, commenting on the nickname Poole had used for her when he'd asked her to close the door earlier. "What's that about?"

Poole, his eyes wet, took another deep breath and launched in.

"When Jax and I hit pause on the engagement, but before we started couples' therapy, I was feeling sorry for myself. I knew Annie had a crush on me. When she made a move, I didn't object. When Jax and I began therapy, I told Annie it had to stop. But she was insistent, and I didn't really fight her very hard. Pretty soon it became a regular thing—in the office, in my car in the parking garage, at her place. It was never more than physical. I still wanted to marry Jax. But it was nice to be with someone who didn't look at me with disappointment in her eyes. So I just…kept doing it."

Jessie looked over at Reid. His expression reflected how they both felt. Though it was satisfying to have answers, these didn't get them any closer to solving their case. If Titus was with Annaleigh, then he couldn't have killed Jax. And he had no reason to kill Claire.

Under normal circumstances, Jessie would consider Titus's devoted assistant/lover a suspect as well. But if she was with Titus last night, that ruled her out as well. They'd need to check her geo-data to be sure, but it didn't look promising.

She stood up to leave, giving one last glance at the Dandelion Garden Plaza. If nothing else, this trip had been worth it so she could see Bonnie the Bluebonnet in all her glory. But other than that, it had been a wash.

They were no closer to having a quality suspect than when Jessie first learned of the case this morning. That was bad enough, but what worried her even more was that the day was drawing to a close. The last two evenings had involved the brutal murders of young women. What did tonight have in store?

CHAPTER SIXTEEN

Ryan glanced around, trying not to appear suspicious and knowing full well that he was failing.

The rideshare pulled away and he hurried up the steps to the house as fast as he could. He kept his head on a swivel for two reasons. First, he was looking for anyone that might resemble the Night Hunter. Second, he wanted to make sure that Jessie didn't pull up. He needed time to stash the ring before she got home.

He had just reached the front door when he got a text. It was from Brady and read: *See that you're home now. Won't drive by in case Hannah's watching. She's been back since mid-afternoon. Heading out. Sorry for this morning. Talk soon.*

He lifted his hand high above his head as if he was stretching and gave an imperceptible wave. It bothered him that he didn't spy Brady when he'd looked around. But maybe that was a good thing, a sign that his former partner was more competent than he'd seemed most of the day.

He reached the door and looked around one more time to make sure no one was close by before opening up. The process was more involved than just turning a key in a lock. He punched a code into the keypad next to the doorbell. A metal cover pulled back to reveal a device that scanned his eyes. Then he placed his palm on a plate of glass below the scanner and waited for it to read his fingerprints. After that, he whispered a code phrase into a small speaker. Only then did the front door locks click open.

Once inside with the door locked, he stepped through the foyer into the living room and looked around. He could see the light on under Hannah's door. There was no noise, which suggested she had her headphones on. That was ideal.

Though he wanted to check in on her, this might be his only opportunity to hide the ring without prying eyes around. He had debated where to keep it on the ride home and eventually came up with what he considered an elegant solution: he'd put it in the panic room.

The three of them rarely had cause to go in there. In fact, Hannah never did, and he and Jessie only did so every few weeks to check that the battery for the security box was still charged. It was perfect.

As quietly as he could, he passed by Hannah's room. In the hallway between it and the bedroom he shared with Jessie was a bookcase that stretched from just above the floor to the ceiling. It was filled with actual books so that the hidden room behind it wouldn't be as easily discovered. But on the back of the third shelf, in the very upper right corner, was a small button that wouldn't be visible to anyone over five feet tall. Even then, it looked like a mild irregularity in the wood.

Ryan pushed the button and the shelf rolled quickly and quietly a mere two feet to the left, exposing a narrow entryway, leading to a small room, no larger than a constricted walk-in closet. He pushed the button on the left of the interior wall and, as fast as it had opened, the bookshelf rolled silently back into place.

Once the passage closed, a dim light flickered overhead. Ryan took a moment to let his eyes adjust before moving forward. Despite his teasing earlier, he understood why Jessie wanted a second panic room. This one was extremely basic. There was nowhere to sit. Other than one small cabinet in the back right corner, with some bottled water, granola bars, paper towels, and hand sanitizer on top, there was no furniture at all. That is, unless you counted the bucket in the back left corner for bathroom emergencies, which he did not.

The room wasn't designed to hunker down for an extended period, which is what Jessie hoped the second one might be. It was intended as a stopgap measure to hide from an intruder or hold one off long enough for backup to arrive. With some effort and tools, the bookshelf could be pried aside. The only thing separating the room from the adjoining bedrooms was drywall.

If someone was dedicated, prepared, and knew where to look, they could probably access the room in under five minutes. But the hope was that would be long enough. And it wasn't like the room was entirely without resources.

Between the cabinet and the bucket were three boxes affixed the back wall. The bottom one was a weapons locker, complete with two handguns and ammunition, a can of pepper spray, and a stun gun. The center box was comprised of a phone on the left, hard-wired to a different line than the rest of the house phones so that if the main line was cut, this was one would still work. On the right was a control pad that could operate several of the defensive systems throughout the house, including interior and exterior cameras, white smoke, and both a silent and extremely loud alarm. In the box at the very top was the battery they checked regularly, which could operate the security system, lighting, and phone, even if the power to the rest of the house was cut.

Ryan moved to the small cabinet, using the key on his chain to unlock it. He ignored the flashlights, gas masks, emergency thermal blankets, and notepads inside, going straight to the back. That's where he found extra hand sanitizer and a small, unopened box of tissues.

Taking out his pocketknife, he cut a hole in the bottom of the tissue box. It was just large enough to stuff the jewelry box with the engagement ring inside. He stared at the seemingly bland tissue box in his hand, still having trouble processing that it held an item that could change his world forever.

He knew that the next time he grabbed this hunk of cardboard and paper, it meant he was about to propose. Admittedly, he'd been married once before, but that always felt like the inevitable next step in a relationship that never had any real spark. This was different. Jessie was different.

He put the tissue box back, closed the cabinet drawer, and quickly left the panic room. Once the bookshelf slid back into place, he started for the bedroom when he heard a sound in the kitchen. He inched in that direction, undoing the holster clasp for his gun and he tottered toward the noise. When he emerged from the hallway, he was surprised to find Hannah with her back to him, leaning over the butcher block, intently studying a piece of paper.

"What's up?" he asked.

"Jesus!" Hannah shouted, jumping in the air. "You scared the hell out of me!"

"Sorry," he said.

"I didn't even know anyone was home," she said, her hand over her chest.

"I was about to check in on you after I got settled," he told her, which was mostly true. "What's going on?"

Hannah, still recovering, took a few deep breaths before replying.

"I was going to make dinner."

"That sounds awesome," Ryan said, happy that Hannah was engaging in anything that constituted normal behavior. She usually only cooked for all of them was she was in a good mood. "What are we having?"

93

"I was thinking something straightforward like herb-rubbed salmon with baby potatoes and lemon-garlic broccolini."

Ryan couldn't help but chuckle. The sound of it felt foreign to him. It was only then that he realized this might have been the first time he'd actually laughed all day. It was as if that small act served as some kind of release valve, allowing at least a bit the stress and guilt of the last twenty-four hours to escape his body. He felt as if the knot in his stomach has loosened slightly.

"See, when *I* say straightforward," he replied, "it means turkey sandwiches. But I'll take your version any day."

"Cool," she said, sounding almost pleasant. "You want to help?"

"Sure. Do you mind if I get cleaned up first?"

"Nope," she replied. "I'll start prepping."

"Great," he said, glad to finally be having some semblance of a positive interaction with her. Last night he wouldn't have thought it possible.

"Give me ten minutes and I'll be back, ready for apron mode."

He headed back down the hall, but not before he caught Hannah smiling involuntarily at his cheesy comment. The sight was so rare that it made him slightly giddy.

CHAPTER SEVENTEEN

Hannah moved quickly, not even thinking consciously about what she was doing.

She was almost done parboiling the potatoes. The salmon was herbed up and ready to go. She'd left the broccolini for Ryan, remembering that for some inexplicable reason, he found rubbing minced garlic into vegetable stalks relaxing.

As she worked, her thoughts drifted back to the events of the day, including the revelation about Edward Wexler's Holocaust foundation which had ultimately led her to visit Dr. Lemmon this morning. The memory of his hand squeezing hers tight, of him not wanting to let go, still burned bright in her mind.

Once the psychiatrist had coaxed her up to her office and brewed the tea, Hannah initially held back, refusing to tell Dr. Lemmon why she was there. But then the doctor stopped asking questions and just sipped her tea, happy to sit in silence.

Sometime during the stillness, Hannah had an epiphany. There was no point in holding out. Lemmon wasn't pressing her. She had come to the office of her own accord. It was incumbent on her to explain why. So she did, explaining everything she'd done since last summer. When she was done, Dr. Lemmon sat unmoving for a good thirty seconds.

"So what happens next?" she finally asked.

"What do you mean?" Jessie replied, perplexed.

"Well, you've just told me that for the last half year, if not longer, you've been putting yourself in dangerous situations, mostly so that you can feel something. I assume you're here because you've decided to either change that behavior or embrace it."

"Obviously, if I wanted to embrace it, I wouldn't be here," Hannah said crossly.

"Is it obvious?" Dr. Lemmon asked. "Are you sure this visit isn't just an excuse, so you can say you tried to stop one last time? So you can claim that not even the fancy therapist could help you, and you might as well continue with what you're doing?"

"You're just trying to push my buttons," Hannah replied.

"Not 'just,' Hannah. I'm pushing them for a reason. I need to know whether this is worth my time or if, when I say something you don't like, you'll shut down or storm out."

Hannah started to reply but the doctor held up her hand.

"We're at an inflection point here, my dear. You can't straddle this line any longer. From this moment forward you can either give into the urges that are putting your safety and emotional well-being at risk, or you can try to find a way out. The choice is yours. It always has been. Either way, I need to know what you want out of this get-together, because if you're here to get justification to continue on that darker path, nothing I can say or do will stop you."

"That's *not* why I'm here," Hannah retorted, trying to keep control.

There was another long pause before the doctor replied.

"Then I need a commitment from you," Lemmon said.

"What kind of commitment?"

Dr. Lemmon smiled. Her eyes twinkled.

"Most people pay me money. That usually works because it gives them incentive to keep coming. Otherwise they're just burning cash. But you don't have money, do you?"

"My adoptive parents left me some," Hannah told her. "But I can't access any of it until I'm eighteen, and even then only a portion."

"So that option is out," Dr. Lemmon said.

"Jessie paid for my previous sessions."

"Ah, yes she did," Lemmon agreed. "But that won't work this time. That would be a commitment from her, not you."

"So what then?" Hannah asked, "Should I start getting paid for providing my plasma or something?"

"I have an idea that might be a little less drastic. How about getting a job?"

Hannah was embarrassed to admit she'd never even considered the idea.

"Doing what?"

"I don't know. What are you passionate about? If you find something that you feel strongly about, it might serve two purposes. One, it wouldn't feel so much like work. But perhaps more importantly for our purposes here, it would allow you to channel that restlessness you feel into something constructive. I'm not saying it would solve all your problems. But maybe the numbness that's deadening your spirit would subside a bit if you trained yourself to find joy, or even just satisfaction, in accomplishing something of value. What do you think?"

Hannah sat with that for a bit.

"I like to cook," she said. "I'm pretty good at it. And it doesn't suck when people go on about how much they like what I've made."

"Excellent," Dr. Lemmon said, sounding positively giddy. "Cooking it is then."

"But I've never had a real job," Hannah said. "It might take me a while to find something; that is if Jessie even lets me do it. Apparently, there's another serial killer out there. They're worried the guy might go after investigators' families."

"I'll tell you what," Lemmon said. "Until you get the job, we'll put our sessions on your tab. You can start paying once it's safe to look and you've secured something. I'll even lower my rate a little, sort of a student discount."

"How much would it be?"

"My normal rate is $300 for a 50-minute session, but for you I'll do it for $50. Does that sound fair?"

Hannah nodded. Lemmon continued before she could muster the nerve to say 'thank you.'

"But remember, you can't expect to just walk in somewhere and become a line cook. You might need to start as a dishwasher or a hostess and work your way up. Beggars can't be choosers. Even if you don't love what you're offered, if you get an offer, you take it. Are we clear?"

Hannah nodded again and said what she couldn't before.

"Thank you."

"You're welcome," Lemmon had said, "Now let's begin."

The sound of Ryan's cane squeaking on the kitchen floor yanked Hannah out of the memory.

"What have you got for me to do?" he asked, now wearing sweats.

She blinked a few times, trying to get back into a social headspace.

"You get to knead the garlic into the broccolini," she said, handing him a plastic glove.

"My favorite," he exclaimed, "So satisfying after a long day."

"Speaking of," Hannah asked, as she sprinkled salt and pepper on the baby potatoes and tossed them in the oven, "any luck catching the geriatric killer?"

"I'm afraid not," he said. "We have leads but nothing solid. So please, really stay alert when you go out. This guy could be anywhere."

Hannah smiled to herself, debating whether to say what had popped into her head. Ultimately, she couldn't stop herself

97

"Is that why you and Jessie sicced that chunky guy on me?" she teased.

"What?" he asked, so startled that he dropped the stalk in his hand.

"You know," she continued, "the heavyset set dude with the barrel chest and the mustache, not to mention the sweat pouring off his brow and shirttails poking out of his slacks. Is he an actual law enforcement professional or just some golfing buddy you pressed into service? Because he was not great at the whole surveillance routine."

"You saw him?" Ryan asked, not even trying to pretend it wasn't true.

"Sure," Hannah answered. "I first noticed him when he looked like he was about to have a heart attack while trying to catch the elevator I was in. Then I saw him parked out front when I came downstairs. I left through the back entrance while he was munching on what looked like a pop tart. He showed up outside Tommy's Coffee later that afternoon. I saw him run into the convenience store next door to use the bathroom. He appeared a little distressed. I think he'd been holding it in for a while. Then he followed me back here. I told the rideshare driver to go slow so he didn't lose us. When I got dropped off, he set up shop down the block. I'm assuming he left when you got home."

"You're not pissed?" Ryan asked.

"I chose not to be. I get that you guys were worried about me, even before the concern about this killer you're looking for. I wish you would have been straight with me, but I've decided to give you a pass."

"Thank you," Ryan said, looking truly stunned.

"All the same," she replied, done with the heart-to-heart stuff, "I think you could do better. That guy was junior varsity material at best."

"He's actually a pretty solid detective," Ryan told her. "We used to be partners when I worked on the Westside. He's let himself go a little. But in a pinch, he's someone I know I can count on."

"Unless the job requires running," Hannah countered.

"Touché."

She was giving the salmon a final once over when she heard the garage door open. Jessie was home.

"You better finish up that broccolini," she told him, as she opened the oven door. "Your girlfriend's going to be ravenous, I bet."

He resumed kneading in the garlic while Hannah added the salmon to the oven. She was just debating whether she had time to whip up a dessert when Jessie walked in. She hadn't even put down her purse before the tirade began.

"Where the hell were you this morning?"

CHAPTER EIGHTEEN

Jessie hadn't meant to sound so accusatory, but upon seeing Hannah casually moving about the kitchen, seemingly untroubled by the anxiety she'd caused, the words came out with more venom than intended. She tried to reframe them.

"Didn't we tell you how dangerous it is out there right now?" she pleaded. "I just don't understand how, after everything we said, you could just saunter out of here like it's no big deal."

"Jessie—," Ryan started to say but she didn't want to hear it.

"No, Ryan. I can't take any more of this. I feel like my heart is going to explode out of my chest. Hannah, please tell me you've got a good explanation for today."

Her sister looked at her without speaking. That alone was surprising. Normally by now, she'd be yelling or barreling to her room. Instead, she pulled a sheet of paper out her back jeans pocket and handed it over. Jessie opened it. It was on letterhead from the office of Dr. Janice Lemmon, her therapist.

Hannah Dorsey has voluntary consented to twice-weekly sessions to address areas of behavioral concern. She will pay for these sessions (at a reduced rate) with funds secured through gainful employment, when it safe to pursue such employment. In the interim, her counseling bills will be put on hold. If Dorsey's guardian consents to this treatment plan, please sign below and return this document at the next session.

Even after she'd finished reading, Jessie kept her eyes locked on the paper, pretending she wasn't done. She needed a few seconds to acknowledge the significance this moment. But before that, she waited for the wave of heat at the back of her neck to dissipate.

She had jumped the gun and now felt like an idiot. She thought back to what Ryan had said about Hannah going to the fifth floor of a downtown office building. Dr. Lemmon's office was on the fifth floor. That's where Hannah had been this morning. She'd gone for help on her own.

Jessie finally looked up at her sister, who was staring back at her with a mix of stubbornness and apprehension. There was no way Jessie could convey the mix of emotions that were swirling within in her at that moment. She was so happy—and relieved—that Hannah had taken the initiative to deal with all this. From personal experience, Jessie knew that any progress her sister made was much more likely to stick if she was the one leading the charge.

But she also felt deep sadness, mostly because Hannah hadn't felt she could come to her. She realized that was in large part due to the reaction she'd just displayed: making accusations, lashing out, and demanding compliance.

After everything that had happened, she certainly had the right to act that way. But it hadn't helped Hannah. Instead, it pushed her away. But now there was a chance to rectify that. And doing so started with one statement.

"I'm sorry," she said quietly.

Hannah didn't respond for a few seconds.

"That's okay," her sister finally replied. "I know you were worried."

"I was," Jessie admitted. "I really was. But this is great to hear. I'm so proud of you for taking this step."

Hannah nodded but didn't say anything. It looked like she was trying to keep her emotions in check. Jessie couldn't.

"Would it be okay if I hugged you?" she asked.

Hannah nodded again. Jessie reached over and wrapped her little sister in her arms. They squeezed each other tight. Jessie glanced over at Ryan, who was smiling broadly as he rubbed broccolini stalks with a plastic glove.

"You know," Jessie said, her voice catching as she fought through her tears, "I haven't talked to Dr. Lemmon in months. Maybe it's time for me to go back to see her too."

"I think maybe you should," Hannah said, her voice muffled by Jessie's chest. The she lifted her head up and looked in her big sister's eyes. "But that can wait. Right now, you need to get washed up. Dinner will be ready soon."

*

That night, Jessie snuggled up close to Ryan in bed.

They were about to turn out the lights, but she wasn't quite ready to sleep, still jazzed by Hannah's decision to get help.

"This could be the first step on the road to culinary school," she said hopefully. "I wonder how long she'll have to do grunt work before any restaurant actually lets her start cooking."

"Let's not get ahead of ourselves," Ryan reminded her. "She can't even start looking until we have the Night Hunter in custody."

"I know. Plus she starts up school again tomorrow. How are we supposed to make that work safely?"

"I've already got it covered," Ryan said. "Before I left work today I got a commitment from Decker. I said that if I was going to keep working this case, he needed to assure the safety of my loved ones. He guaranteed me that a patrol unit will stay within one block of her school at all times until this is resolved."

"That's great, but what about coming home?" she asked.

"If one of us can't pick her up and she gets a rideshare, she'll have multiple escorts," he assured her.

"What does that mean?"

"It means the patrol car will follow her home. Plus, Brady has agreed to continue watching her. He's on paid leave the whole week and he wants to make up for today. Besides, now that Hannah fingered him, he won't have to try to stay hidden. He just has to watch her."

Jessie shook her head.

"I still can't believe a teenage girl identified him within hours of him staking her out," she said, recalling Hannah's story during dinner about spotting Brady.

"She's no average teenage girl," he countered, kissing her. "Just like her sister isn't. Speaking of impressive women, how's your case going? We didn't get to discuss it earlier. I was surprised to see you come home at a decent hour."

Jessie sighed.

"There wasn't much more we could do today," she said, deflated at the thought of it. "We have lots of suspects, but none we feel great about. Reid called to set up an interview with the wedding planner for both victims, but she was out of town at some fancy event and won't be back until late. So we had to push that until tomorrow. My bigger concern is that we've had two murders on consecutive nights. I'm worried that whoever's doing this might not be finished."

"Well, if they strike again, I'm sure Decker will let you know right away," Ryan said.

"The same goes for you, I guess," she replied. "Are you confident that the Night Hunter won't be active tonight too?"

102

"Not at all," he replied. "Obviously killing Trembley wasn't part of his meticulous plan and that may have him back on his heels. Decker thinks he's going to lie low for a while, but I'm worried that almost getting caught might make him more brazen. He knows we're getting closer. That's why I want to get him fast. This guy is always dangerous, but even more so when cornered."

"I have real concerns that he might try to get in here," she said, voicing the fear she knew he shared.

"Me too," he said. "That's why I think we should add the measures you mentioned— the heat sensors, the external laser grid—let's do it all. I'm even game for the second panic room."

"Really?" she said, borderline shocked, "Because if you're serious, I have just the place."

"Where?"

"There's an unfinished room below the laundry room. It's accessible through the linen closet."

He looked over at her, stunned.

"How did I not know about this?" he demanded.

"I only discovered it myself back when I was looking at the architectural plans for the house in Garland's office," she explained. "I was trying to determine where we could situate a new room when I found it marked but not labeled. So I spent twenty minutes in the laundry room searching for an entry point. Eventually I found a false wall in the linen closet next to the pull-down ironing board."

"Why didn't you tell me?"

"Because I knew you'd tease me when I said what I wanted to do."

He laughed at the absurdity of the situation.

"So we already have a second panic room?"

"We have space for it, but right now that's all it is. I'll show you tomorrow. There's nothing but a cement stairwell leading to a cement-encased room. I think Garland had big plans to turn it into something state-of-the-art. It has outlets and all the proper wiring. But I guess he never got around to it. I can see why. It's a major project. If I could, I'd get started on it tomorrow. But doing it right will require a lot of research and time."

"Time is something we don't have right now," Ryan noted darkly.

"Believe me, I know," Jessie said. "No matter what I'm doing or where I am, somewhere in my gut, I always feel the Night Hunter's eyes on me. I'm tired of being in a permanent defensive crouch. I want to take it to this guy."

103

"That mission resumes tomorrow," Ryan promised her.

But as he turned off the lights, they both knew it wasn't as simple as that.

CHAPTER NINETEEN

Brian Clark was tired.

As he unlocked the front door and walked into the dark house, he finally allowed himself to exhale.

He'd spent all day in depositions. When those were done, the team had a marathon three-hour meeting in the conference room to discuss the case. The take-out pasta dinner they'd ordered was sitting like a stone in his stomach.

But now he could let all that go. Sure, it was after eleven at night, but if he was going to keep up this pace, he had to allow himself some down time to decompress. That's why he went straight to the kitchen and poured himself two fingers of scotch.

But before taking a sip, he had to get things in order. As he walked down the hall to the bedroom, he could already hear the sound of the shower. That typically meant that his fiancée, Caroline, was less than fifteen minutes from sleep. He wanted to make sure to catch her before that happened. Besides, he felt bad about coming home so late after she'd specifically told him that the detectives she'd talked to today had warned against it.

"I'm home," he said, poking his head into the bathroom.

He heard her startled yip at his voice. He loved giving her a little scare every now and then.

"You know I hate it when you do that, especially with everything that's been going on lately," she complained. "Now it's going to take me an extra fifteen minutes to fall asleep after that adrenaline rush."

"Sorry," he said, forgetting how on edge she was. "I made myself a scotch. I could brew you a late-night tea to calm your nerves, if you like."

"I think it's the least you can do," she replied, quickly getting over her agitation.

"I'll see you out there," he said, closing the door.

He took off his suit and put on sweatpants and a t-shirt. Glancing at himself in the dresser mirror, he thought he didn't look too bad, even after such a long day. His thick brown hair still had a bit of the waviness from this morning. His hazel eyes were sharp. He could stand to lose a little weight, especially if he planned to look good in his wedding tux. But all in all, he was holding up okay.

Satisfied, he returned to the kitchen. After he put a chamomile teabag in a mug and started to boil the water for Caroline, he grabbed his scotch and stepped out onto the back patio. He allowed himself one small sip, which he swirled around his mouth, letting the kaleidoscope of flavors envelope his tongue before slowly swallowing.

He needed moments like this. With the stress of the case and the upcoming wedding, he never seemed to have time to unwind. Add to that two of their friends being murdered in the last few days and it was getting harder to keep a healthy perspective on things.

Brian turned to face the backyard and had just let a second sip pass his lips when he heard what sounded like someone spraying water on a nearby plant. It was a fraction of a second later when he felt the stinging on his face and realized the spray had hit him. He opened his mouth to scream but only seemed able to grunt as the scotch dribbled out of his sizzling lips and down the dissolving skin on his chin.

He dropped the glass and reached up to his face just as the syringe plunged into his neck. As his body burned from the inside out, he slumped to his knees and then collapsed to the wooden deck. He could barely hear the kettle in the kitchen begin to whistle.

CHAPTER TWENTY

Jessie heard Caroline Ryan crying even before she reached the front door of the house.

Girding for what was to come, she allowed herself a moment of stillness. After having been ripped from sleep by Reid barely two hours after drifting off, she still felt a little disoriented. She reminded herself what she was about to walk into. The fiancé of the woman she'd interviewed today was dead on the back deck, the killer's third victim in as many nights.

Blinking slowly, she took in the house that Caroline shared with Brian Clark. It was a Craftsman style home, refreshingly understated compared to the residences of their more showy friends.

She took a deep breath and opened the door. Callum Reid was already there, sitting on a living room couch with Caroline, talking quietly. Jessie moved past the room silently, walking through the more formal sitting room so as not to get pulled into the painful exchange.

She walked slowly, in part to avoid detection, but also so that she could take in her surroundings. The room was meticulously designed, with art on the walls and on multiple tables. On top of the piano was a collection of photos, some of the couple alone, others with family and friends. Other than one slightly discolored spot where some item had clearly once sat but had yet to be replaced, the space was immaculate.

Jessie made her way back to the kitchen and the adjoining back patio. That's where Reid had said the murder occurred when he called just after midnight. Jessie looked at the time. It was 12:38. The crime scene crew was out on the patio where the body of Brian Clark still lied, covered in a white sheet.

She blinked several more times, still trying to shake off the effects of her disrupted sleep as she glanced around the kitchen. She did her best to focus on the details of the room. A mug rested on the kitchen counter with an unused teabag sitting in it. There was a kettle on the stove. Outside, she could see a tumbler on the deck next to Clark's limp, right hand.

"We've got nothing," a familiar voice said from behind her.

107

She turned around to find Callum Reid standing in the kitchen doorway. He looked as bad as she felt, maybe worse. His face was almost gray.

"You look terrible," she said. "Are you okay?"

He shook his head.

"I think I may be close to clocking out for good, Hunt," he said, with alarming matter-of-factness.

"What does that mean?' she asked, perturbed.

"My body just can't handle these 'middle of the night' calls the way it used to. And arriving to find a young guy contorted and unrecognizable doesn't help. I'm seriously thinking of putting in for early retirement. To be honest, I probably would have done it already if Decker wasn't in such a bind with HSS."

The thought of the unit losing the only really experienced detective it still had left filled her with concern. It was already teetering on the edge. His departure would almost certainly send it off the cliff.

"Maybe you just need a vacation," she suggested meekly.

"My doctor thinks I need a lot more than that. Decker doesn't know this, but my ticker isn't tip top. The phrase 'early-stage congestive heart failure' was used, along with the term 'pre-diabetic.' Apparently my stress level and lifestyle choices haven't been the greatest for the last…quarter century or so."

"But are you okay right *now*?" she asked, refusing to deal with the big picture at this moment. "You look a little ashen."

"It's always the worst on an overnight call. Bad sleep exacerbates things. I'm feeling a little short of breath and even more tired than usual. It'll pass but the doctor says that stuff's only going to get worse over time unless I do something drastic."

"I'm sorry, Callum," she said, using his first name for perhaps the first time ever.

"A concern for another time," he said, waving his hand. "Let's focus on the guy on the deck. He's got it way worse."

"Right," she said, sensing that he'd reached the limits of his comfort zone when it came to discussing his personal life. "You said we've got nothing."

"As far as we can tell, so far," he told her. "Like I told you on the phone, it's the same M.O. as with the others, but this time the killer didn't even have to get into the house to commit the crime. The team is still dusting for prints, but they're not optimistic."

Jessie hoped that would change over time but didn't attach her hopes to the possibility.

"Did Caroline have anything useful to offer?" she asked.

"She helped with the timeline a bit; said he got home while she was showering a little after eleven. He offered to make her tea. When she got out of the shower, she could hear the kettle whistling. She got into her robe and rushed out to find the sliding kitchen door open and him lying face down on the deck. She freaked out, locked the door, and called 911. She's beating herself up because she didn't go to check on him first."

"If the other victims are any indication, he was likely dead before she even got there," Jessie said.

"That's what I told her, but it didn't help much. She couldn't remember the exact time she found him but the call to 911 came in at 11:19. She says she got in the shower at about 11:05 and had been in there for about five minutes when he poked his head in. So if she's to be believed, our window for the crime is from about 11:10 to 11:18."

"That's tight," Jessie noted. "It means the killer was either already waiting here or followed him home, then injected him and left, all in less than ten minutes."

"Pretty bold, too," Reid added, "What with the fiancée just down the hall."

"I assume there's no security video," Jessie guessed.

"You assume right. How did you know that?"

"It seems to be part of the pattern. Neither of the other victims had it either. It makes me think the killer had been to the house before and knew it well enough to be confident they wouldn't be discovered that way."

"That fits with the theory that this was someone in their social circle," Reid pointed out.

"Very true," Jessie agreed, "although now that we have a male victim, I think we can eliminate the hypothesis that this was the work of a guy who had a vendetta against woman."

"Or that this was a woman who was jealous of other women exclusively," he added.

Jessie wasn't as comfortable with that conclusion.

"I'm not sure I'd go that far," she countered. "Jealousy could still play a role, even if a victim was male. If this was a woman whose envy had reached lethal proportions, she might consider killing a fiancé to be just a different kind of punishment. Claire and Jax paid the ultimate price. But Caroline will suffer too. That might be what the killer is after, causing all different kinds of pain."

"Those are a lot of theories, Hunt," Reid said, sounding beaten down by the multitude of unpleasant options.

"Agreed. That's why we need to talk to that wedding planner in the morning. I'm hoping that her perspective will help us narrow things down a little. In the meantime, I think we should go back to the station and dig into Brian Clark's life a little more. Maybe the legal case he was working on played some part in this. Or maybe he's got a dark side we don't know about."

"You don't really believe either of those, do you?" he asked skeptically.

"No," she conceded. "But I find that making assumptions usually ends badly for me. Besides, we've got to do something to stay awake until the sun comes up in five hours."

She felt guilty the second she said that, as Reid seemed to turn an even more sickly shade of gray at the prospect of spending all night poring through the personal and professional life of Brian Clark.

Still, they didn't have much choice. Somewhere out there was a murderer who seemed to enjoy making people suffer as much as killing them. And Jessie had a feeling this murderer wasn't done yet.

CHAPTER TWENTY ONE

It was almost dawn when Walter Nightengale left the house.

As he walked to the old clunker halfway down the block, he switched the small, brown, beaten-up travel bag from his right hand to his left. With all the supplies he kept inside, it tended to get heavy after a while and he wasn't as strong as he used to be.

He had intentionally left the front door open, knowing that the homeowners would notice it when they checked their security system. The Morgans, a family of four, were on vacation in Mexico and had left their palatial Brentwood mansion in the care of a house sitter.

They'd used Hallie Douglas for this before and trusted her. She'd babysat for their kids for years. House sitting was comparatively easy, merely requiring keeping an eye on the place, watering the plants, and turning on the security system when she was out. It was that last task that the Morgans would find incomplete when they checked the system status on their phones later this morning. And that's what would make them call the security company to check.

Walter knew all of this. In fact, he was counting on it. How else could he get Jessie Hunt's attention on such short notice? He needed her, almost certainly via her boyfriend, to learn that a young woman had been murdered in his particular style. He needed her to discover that the woman, a twenty-one-year-old college student at Pepperdine University, was skinny, about five foot nine, with sandy blonde hair just past her shoulders and bright green eyes. He needed her to notice that, at least on the surface, Hallie was the spitting image of someone Jessie knew quite well. He needed her to pick up on the fact that Hallie Douglas had the same initials as someone Ms. Hunt cared about deeply. He needed her to grasp all these things so that she knew that he was taking the game to the next level.

As he got into the old car and pulled out onto the quiet suburban street, he was confident that she would figure it all out. Like her mentor, Garland Moses, Jessie Hunt was very smart. But the Night Hunter was smarter.

111

CHAPTER TWENTY TWO

Jessie thought she might throw up.

No matter how much mouthwash she swigged or how many times she brushed her teeth, she couldn't get the lingering taste of bad police station coffee out of her mouth.

I guess that's what happens when I consume eight cups over the course of the night in a desperate attempt to stave off the exhaustion invading the edges of my brain.

It didn't help that, overnight, the media had figured out the friendship connection between Jax Coopersmith and Claire Bender. The local news was already in a frenzy over Jax's death and the subsequent, collective and anguish and anger of her fans. Now that they had a whiff of an interconnected murder spree, all restraint was gone. Jessie could only imagine how bad it would get when they realized that Brian Clark's death could be tied to the others too.

The worst part that all her efforts to stay alert—the caffeine, the sugar rush from the doughnuts she broke down and inhaled, the jumping jacks she did on the sly in the restroom—didn't do any good. They were hitting a dead end with Brian Clark.

It was approaching 8 a.m. and they still hadn't discovered anything incriminating or unusual about Clark's life. The more Jessie saw, the less she expected that they ever would. He was a straight arrow—a corporate attorney for a blue-chip firm, no criminal record, no debts to speak of, no known enemies.

The case he was currently working involved two financial outfits haggling over a minor dispute in profit percentages on the sale of a farming equipment company. It was soul-deadening stuff, apparently even to the competing parties, and didn't appear to be murder-worthy. So once again, suspicion returned to his friends, in particular the bridesmaid connection among the women in the group.

Or, she thought as she rinsed her mouth out yet again, maybe the connection was weddings more generally. Was it possible that she and Reid were coming at this backwards? Could the weddings be the essential link and the specific social circle just happenstance? It seemed like a reach but one they had to explore. The urge to call the wedding planner overcame her.

"Hey Reid," she said to the detective sitting one desk over from her in the Central Police Station bullpen, "it's eight. How about we reach out to that wedding planner? What's her name again?"

"Her name is Jeanie Court," he said, sounding as wiped out as she felt. "And it's not eight, it's 7:47 a.m., which is still early for a lot of people. I know we want to interview the woman but let's wait until nine. That's a reasonable hour. No one can complain about a call by then. I don't want there to be any excuse for pushback."

"Fine," she grumbled, turning her attention back to a list of Brian Clark's previous, equally uninspiring cases. She could feel the need for another cup of coffee coming on when her phone rang. It was Ryan.

"What's wrong?" she asked almost before answering the call.

"Everybody's safe," he assured her immediately. "I shared a ride with Hannah to school, and just dropped her off a few minutes ago. I'm actually on my way into the office right now. I don't want you to stress, but there's been an incident."

"What does that mean?" she asked, struggling to keep her tone even.

"The Night Hunter struck again last night," he said, his voice heavy. She could almost hear him beating himself up through the phone, struggling to stay on top of things even though he surely felt like he was collapsing under the weight of this new revelation. "Details are still coming in but here's what we know for sure. The victim's name is Hallie Douglas."

"Oh god," Jessie said, immediately making the connection between her initials and Hannah's. He had changed targets.

"Unfortunately, there's more," Ryan said. "She's a college student, twenty-one. She has shoulder-length blonde hair and green eyes, just like Hannah. Her height and weight are also solid matches. From the photos I've seen of this girl, the two of them could be sisters, even twins, unless you look really close."

Jessie gave herself a few seconds to process what he'd told her and what it meant.

"He's speaking to me, Ryan," she finally said. "He's playing some kind of sick game. He's telling me that if we go after him, like you and Trembley tried to do, he'll come at what's precious to me."

"I know," Ryan said quietly.

"Think about it," Jessie continued. "He must have had this girl picked out for a while, waiting to use her as a message when the time was right. He scouted her. An innocent kid is dead just because she shares Hannah's initials and looks like her."

"I know, Jessie!" Ryan shouted through the phone. "You don't think I know that? You don't think I know that if I hadn't frozen last night, she'd be alive right now, just like Trembley would be alive? Believe me, I know."

"I'm sorry, Ryan," I didn't mean to suggest—."

"Jamil's down the hall from you right now," Ryan said, cutting her off. "He's gathering security footage, tracking nearby traffic cameras. We're on his trail."

Jessie was dubious about how much success they'd have, even someone as brilliant as Jamil. The Night Hunter knew what he was doing. He'd only be seen if he wanted to be seen. But she didn't dare say that to Ryan, not in his fragile state. Then another, more pressing thought leapt into her head.

"You said you were coming into the office?" she confirmed. "Why aren't you turning around to get Hannah right now?"

"Because Brady is already doing it," he told her. "He was there when I dropped her off—had already spoken to a vice-principal about getting on-campus access. He texted me a minute ago to say that he's collected her from her classroom. They're in the office, just waiting for the assigned patrol car to pull up. It's going to escort them back to the house. He'll stay inside with her once they get home. One unit will remain parked on the street nearby with another one circling the area. She's safe, Jessie."

"Still, I should probably go home."

Out of the corner of her eye she saw Reid, who had pretended not to be listening, stiffen at hearing those words. But frankly, she didn't care.

"There's no need for that," Ryan insisted. "She'll be in a virtual fortress with five law enforcement officers with or near her. You going back won't make her any safer. Besides, you're on a case. Three people have died in the last three nights. They deserve justice. And what if the person who killed them is planning a fourth attack tonight? Are you just going to play checkers at home with Hannah while that goes down? While HSS crumbles? No—you've got to stop these murders. Just like I need to be there so I can track down the Night Hunter. We both need to work our cases and trust that the people entrusted with Hannah's safety will do their jobs. Besides, I'm more worried about you."

"Why?" she asked.

Even though he knew he wasn't on speaker, Jessie noticed him lower his voice.

"Because this guy is after *you*," he whispered urgently. "So far he's only been messing with your head, but I doubt he intends to end it there. We don't know what his ultimate plan is. And while you can handle yourself, that alone may not be enough. You may need backup and, no offense to Reid, but he's a little long in the tooth."

Jessie thought about recent Reid's admission about his heart. He had basically conceded Ryan's point, which didn't fill her with confidence.

"What do you suggest?' she asked.

She heard an almost imperceptible sigh of relief from him and knew he'd been waiting for the chance to make his case.

"You're a consultant for the LAPD. Your contract, which I know well, states that you can bring in 'preferred personnel assistance' that you deem necessary, as long the cost doesn't exceed the rate for a comparable department employee. Basically, you can select a personal wingman on the department's dime."

"What, as my bodyguard?" she asked skeptically.

"Yes, he said bluntly, "but not exclusively. Sure, I'd be more comfortable if someone we could count on had your back. But what if there was a person who could assist in both a security and investigative capacity? I'm thinking you could get a twofer, someone who has sleuthing experience but is also a badass, an expert at taking people down in dangerous situations. Can you think of anyone who meets that description and would love to get back in your good graces?"

Despite the stress of the situation, Jessie almost laughed. Ryan was being intentionally, almost insultingly transparent. But he wasn't wrong. There was exactly one person who had all the skills she needed right now, along with the deep desire to redeem herself, if only Jessie was willing to let her.

"Are you still there?" Ryan asked.

She realized she hadn't actually responded.

"Yes," she finally said. "I get it. I'll call Kat."

CHAPTER TWENTY THREE

Jessie wasn't hungry but she ordered oatmeal anyway.

Her text to Kat, asking her to meet at the Nickel Diner at 8:15, got an immediate response: *I'll be there.*

While she waited in the red-cushioned diner booth, she texted Hannah.

Sorry for this morning's craziness. I know this is scary. Will call later to explain.

Hannah's response was short, and though Jessie tried not to read too much into it, seemingly curt: *Okay.*

Finally, she texted Reid to let him know she'd be back soon. He had offered to join her so they could work the case while getting a bite. She appreciated his desire to keep his nose to the grindstone but didn't want him around for what was sure to be a very awkward personal conversation.

In an effort not to obsess, she put her phone away and looked around the diner. This was the same place, only blocks from Central Station, where she used to meet with Garland Moses all the time, where he was such a regular that all the servers knew his order without asking. And though she hadn't yet established that kind of rapport with the staff, she liked being here, amid the morning bustle.

Sometimes she thought she could feel his presence, as if her mentor might sit down across from her and offer some sage advice. She missed him terribly. Somehow being here left more of an ache than living in the house he'd left her, maybe because this was where they'd forged the closest thing she'd had to a paternal relationship since her adoptive father was murdered by her real one.

Her ache at his loss was compounded when she thought of the others she'd lost recently. First her adoptive parents were murdered by her serial killer birth father. Then her mentor was killed by her ex-husband. And most recently, sweet, goofy Alan Trembley had died on the dirty floor of a youth hostel at the hands of an old man. What must he have thought as the life leaked out of him? And who else would suffer because of the Night Hunter's obsession with her? Would Kat be next?

The front door opened to reveal the person that she'd been waiting for with both hope and dread. Kat looked around, searching the diner, not sure if she had arrived first. Jessie used that moment to size up the woman who, until two days ago, she'd considered her closest friend.

Kat was in her standard private detective uniform these days: blue jeans, a professional but utilitarian shirt that was rolled up near the elbows, and a leather jacket, currently swung over her shoulder. She wore work boots, always useful in a dustup. At about five foot seven and 140 pounds, she was both solidly built and sneakily attractive.

The average person might not realize what she was capable of at first glance. But upon closer inspection, there were clues. Her gray eyes were focused. Her dark blonde hair was pulled back into a no-fuss ponytail. Her visible forearms were well-muscled. And then there were the pock marks on her face, along with the thick vertical scar beneath her left eye, permanent reminders of her run-in with an IED in Afghanistan.

Kat caught sight of her and walked over, sliding into the booth without a word.

"Thanks for coming," Jessie said.

"Of course."

Before she could say anything else the waitress walked over, put Jessie's oatmeal on the table, and asked to take her order. Kat looked at Jessie.

"How much time do we have?' she asked.

"Not a lot."

"Then just toast and coffee please," Kat told the waitress before looking at Jessie's food and beverage choice.

"No coffee?" she asked, noting the glass of water beside the bowl.

"I try not to consume more than nine cups in any six-hour period," Jessie answered.

Kat nodded, unsure how to proceed. Jessie felt just as awkward but did her best to push it aside.

"Listen," she began, "I know we've got a lot to work through but that's not why I asked you here. We'll have to deal with that some other time. Right now, I need a favor—a huge one—and it's been brought to my attention that there's no one better suited to the job than you."

"I'm in," Kat asked without hesitation. "What do you need me to do?"

117

Despite her best efforts, Jessie couldn't help but be moved at the immediate willingness to help without even knowing the task. She did her best to hide the emotion as she replied.

"I can give you more details later, but here are the essentials. I'm consulting on a case for the department—three murders in three nights, all mutual friends. I've been paired with Callum Reid. He's a sharp, solid professional. Normally that would be the end of it. But you know the elderly serial killer I mentioned to you a while back, the Night Hunter?"

"Yeah," Kat recalled, "You said he went dark for a couple of decades after Garland nearly nabbed him, but has been active recently in L.A."

"Correct. But in the last thirty-six hours, we learned some new information. His first two Los Angeles victims both had the initials 'J.H.' It was pretty clearly a message to me. But last night he killed a third person, a dead ringer for Hannah named Hallie Douglas."

"H.D.," Kat muttered, almost to herself.

"That's right," Jessie said. "We're worried that he's escalating things, killing more often and obviously taunting me. Ryan's working the case. He thinks the Night Hunter may be on the verge of moving past taunting. Hannah is safe at the house with a phalanx of officers protecting her. But here I am, out in the world trying to solve a series of murders and prevent another. Unfortunately, my partner on the case just confided to me that he has a heart condition and is thinking of retiring any day. So he's probably not in the best position to provide quality backup if things go south."

"Jeez," Kat said softly before going quiet when the waitress brought over her coffee and toast. When she left, Jessie continued.

"But apparently I can hire assistance at the same rate the LAPD would pay for comparable services. So I was hoping that, if you aren't too busy, you'd consider signing on for a day or two?"

Kat seemed troubled and for a second, even though she'd already said yes, Jessie thought she might change her mind.

"Of course I'll do it. No case I have is as pressing as this. But what about Reid? I don't want to step on his toes."

Jessie shook her head.

"I can massage that when I tell him. I'll focus on the investigative angle. Frankly, we're both exhausted and I'd bet he'll be happy for the hand. Besides, he's already working with one contractor so what's one more? We'll keep the 'cover my ass' element of the job just between us."

"That sounds like a smart move," Kat agreed. "Either way, like I said, I'm in."

"Good," Jessie said, relieved. "Then finish up your toast. We've got to get to the station to fill Reid in and then make our first stop."

"Where's that?" Kat asked.

"We're talking to someone I thought I'd never deal with again: a wedding planner."

*

Jessie was getting pissed.

She knew that fatigue was making her prickly but that wasn't the only reason. The assistant to wedding planner extraordinaire Jeanie Court was trying to give her the run-around.

"I'm afraid Ms. Court is with clients and can't be disturbed," an assistant named Yasmine told her over Jessie's speakerphone as they drove to the planner's office. Reid was at the wheel, with Jessie in the passenger seat and Kat in the back.

"That's not acceptable," Reid replied, speaking up before Jessie started yelling. "I reached out last night to let Ms. Court know we needed to speak to her this morning. We're conducting a murder investigation. She needs to make herself available on our timetable, not hers."

"I think she'll be back in the office by eleven," Yasmine said, seemingly unimpressed with the gravity of the situation. "I can pencil you in for her 11:15 slot. Just know that she has a lunch client at noon."

Reid looked over at Jessie and gave her his best "I tried to help her, do your worst," shrug. She was happy to oblige.

"Hi Yasmine," she said in a saccharine sweet voice. "This is Jessie Hunt. I work with Detective Reid. How are you?"

"Okay," Yasmine said guardedly.

"That's great. I wanted to give you my name so you know who to blame when you're arrested and charged with impeding a criminal investigation. That's what's in your immediate future unless you start giving us the answers we need. Do you understand, Yasmine?"

There was a long pause before the assistant finally spoke.

"I'm just doing my job," she said, not conceding but definitely sounding shaky.

"I respect that," Jessie told her, still using an over-cheerful, sing-song-y voice. "And you can be proud of that work ethic while you sit in a downtown jail cell, swapping stories with women in there for things like public defecation and assault with a sharpened plastic hanger. Alternatively, you can help us out. Because when it comes to murder, we don't play. So are we going to meet your boss where she is right now or are we coming to her office to cuff you?"

This time the pause was briefer.

"She's at a cake tasting with clients at the Hillhurst Bakery," she said sullenly.

Reid immediately moved into the left lane.

"Thank you, Yasmine," Jessie replied, still maintaining her faux chipper tone. "Assuming your information is accurate, you won't have to be strip searched today."

She had barely hung up when Reid spoke.

"That's only about five minutes from here," he said as he made a U-turn.

"You really lit a fire under her," Kat marveled from the backseat. "But aren't you worried that she'll tip Jeanie Court off?"

Jessie shrugged.

"I'd be surprised," she said. "But so what if she does? If the wedding planner decides to make a run for it, it will reflect pretty poorly on her."

"Still," Reid added. "I think we'll go without sirens, just in case."

"That's fine," Jessie agreed. "I need a little quiet. I was hoping to call Hannah. I don't know when I'll get another chance anytime soon. You mind?"

Reid shook his head. Kat didn't say anything, but simply sat back in her seat uncomfortably. Jessie knew this might be awkward for her, but right now she didn't care. She needed to talk to her sister. Hannah was trying to turn over a new leaf; now it was her big sister's turn to come clean.

CHAPTER TWENTY FOUR

Hannah almost didn't take the call.

Getting dragged out of class (again) was embarrassing enough. But having to spend the day with a portly, sweaty detective was even worse. Now Jessie was calling, almost certainly to make sure she wasn't causing the guy trouble.

No. This is a fresh start. Give her the benefit of the doubt.

She repeated the mantra in her head as she picked up.

"Hi," she said.

"Hey," Jessie replied. "You home safe now?"

"I am," she answered, unable to totally eliminate the sarcasm. "I'm just hanging here with my best bud Brady Bowen. We're getting set to play tiddlywinks."

In truth she was in her room with the door closed. Brady was in the kitchen, rifling through their cupboards in the hopes of finding an unhealthy snack.

"Sounds fun," Jessie said, not taking the bait. "So you're probably wondering what's going on."

"I think I get it,' Hannah assured her. "Elderly serial killer, may go after investigators' families, must take precautions."

She heard a little hesitation in her sister's voice and knew something bigger was coming.

"That's true but it's more than that," Jessie said. "He's not just going after investigators' families. He's going after our family."

Hannah sat, numbly holding the phone as Jessie gave her a primer on the Night Hunter's history.

"He used to cut people up with machetes," she concluded. "But Garland found him; this was twenty years ago. They fought. Both men almost died. Then the Night Hunter disappeared for decades."

Her sister described how he-remerged with a new method of murder, immobilizing victims with an injected drug, then cutting their flesh into ribbons with an exacto knife. But only when Jessie got to the kicker did her numbness begin to make way for a creeping sense of horror.

121

"Both victims had the initials J.H.," she explained. "It was clear that these were messages intended for me. Then Jamil Winslow, our police researcher, discovered that he's been staking out our house. And finally, last night, he killed someone else. Only this time the victim had the initials H.D., and she looked like you."

"Are you sure?" Hannah muttered, more to make certain her voice was working than because she doubted what she was being told.

"I saw pictures of her," Jessie said. "She's a little older than you, blonde hair just past her shoulders, green eyes, same height and weight. I wouldn't have been able to tell you apart from a distance. Ryan learned all that just after he dropped you off at school. That's why he had Brady pick you up. That's why there's a patrol car parked down the block and a second one circling the neighborhood. This man is playing games with us. But we're worried that he's decided games aren't enough anymore."

Now it all made sense. Jessie wasn't just furious that she had been lying about her whereabouts and what she was doing. She was terrified that her little sister was about to be abducted and skinned alive. That's why learning that Hannah had gotten into the car of an old man the other night had freaked her out so much. She wasn't angry as much as worried. Still, she'd kept this from her.

"How long have you known all this?" Hannah demanded. "How long have you been keeping me in the dark?"

The delay in getting a response told her that her sister was trying to stay calm before answering.

"We've suspected for a while that it wasn't a coincidence that he showed up here in L.A., where his long-time nemesis lived and recently died. But it was only in the last couple of days that we began to suspect that he might be starting up a new cat and mouse game with me, Garland's protégé."

"But you knew something unusual was up," Hannah challenged.

"Yes," Jessie conceded. "But the idea that all this was personally directed at me, and apparently at you, is new. Until we realized that, we thought that standard safety precautions would be enough. We didn't want to upend your world again. We really wanted you to finally have something like a normal life. But now that we understand the magnitude of this, we had to take action. That's why we have to lock everything down. No running off, no going anywhere unsupervised, and no attending school in person until we nail him. I know that sounds Draconian, but we don't have much choice."

122

Hannah ignored the bitterness bubbling in her gut and did her best to focus on the bigger picture.

"I understand," she said, trying to put herself in her sister's shoes. "I don't like it, but I understand."

"Thank you."

Another thought popped into Hannah's head.

"What about you and Ryan? This guy killed his partner the other night. Are you safe?"

"We are," Jessie said reassuringly. "Ryan is operating out of the station. He's hunting everywhere for this guy, but he's still confined to desk work. I'm working the Jax case with Detective Reid and we've brought on an additional team member to help us out and serve as an extra set of eyes."

"Who?" Hannah asked, noting that her sister had pointedly avoided mentioning a name.

"Kat."

The name sent a cascade of emotions coursing through her system. She'd been so intent on resenting Jessie that she'd barely made time for her sister's best friend. But it was too hard to wade through her feelings about Kat—a jumble of animosity, affection, and guilt— right now. She decided not to address it.

"How's the investigation going?" she asked.

"Not sure yet," Jessie confessed. "But we're following up on a lead right now. I know you really want us to solve this one."

"Not just me," Hannah reminded her. "She meant a lot to a bunch of people. I always told myself that if some girl from Podunk, Louisiana, could go from barely scraping by to influencing fashion around the country in half a dozen years, I could make my dreams real too. There are hundreds of thousands of girls who feel the same way."

"I know," Jessie said quietly. "I promise that I'm doing everything I can. In fact, we're pulling up to talk to someone of interest now. I've got to go."

"Good luck," Hannah said, "and be safe."

"I will," Jessie said before hanging up.

She sat quietly in her room, thinking. Her sister was trying to catch the person who killed one of her heroes. Meanwhile she was stuck in this house, at risk from an old man who still somehow managed to murder three people much younger than him.

She knew better than to underestimate the guy, especially after learning what people in their later years were capable of. Edward

Wexler had taught her that. He'd spent his final years selflessly dedicating himself to helping people. If the Night Hunter was half as driven, he could do as much harm as Wexler had done good.

As much as that frightened her, it also unearthed another feeling, one she was all too familiar with: excitement. Despite everything she'd told Dr. Lemmon and all her pledges to herself to rise above her urges, she couldn't help but acknowledge the truth: she felt a little thrill at the possibility of coming face to face with the Night Hunter. How would he try to ensnare her? How would she react? Yes, the prospect was scary, but at least it wasn't something else: boring.

CHAPTER TWENTY FIVE

The car screeched to a stop.

Despite the lack of sirens, Reid had pulled up to the bakery hard and fast and his under-pumped tires let everyone around know. That wasn't a big deal to the average person. But if someone in that bakery heard it and was already on edge, it would almost certainly set off their internal alarm.

With that concern in mind, Jessie leapt out of the car the second it came to a stop and dashed to the front door. Hillhurst Bakery was an unassuming storefront situated along a stretch of funky, eclectic businesses. To the left of the bakery was an Ethiopian café. To the right was a hookah shop called The Suck.

Under other circumstances, Jessie would have loved to window shop, but right now her focus was on what was happening behind the window directly in front of her. There was a sizable group of people inside, hard to tell apart because of the sun's glare.

She stepped inside, sensing that Kat was right behind her. It took a second to orient herself. At least a dozen cakes, some as much as five tiers high, sat on tall tables scattered through the room. Many more decorated the counters closer to the walls. She thought she might get a sugar high just from the scent of the place.

Everyone in the group looked up when she entered. Four of them were standing around a smaller table, where they appeared to be partaking of a much more modest cake. Three other people—two women and a man—stood slightly off to the side, observing. One woman was holding a camera. Another held a pen and notepad.

One of the people eating the cake, a woman in her forties wearing a gray pantsuit, appeared to be slowly separating herself from the others. With her elaborate updo, fully made-up face and panicky eyes, Jessie knew it was Jeanie Court. Everyone else in the store looked confused by the two harried women who'd just burst in, now joined by an older man, breathing heavily.

"I'm afraid the bakery is appointment only," the woman who was clearly the cake baker said in a polite but firm tone. "I'm busy right now but you can call and I'm happy to schedule something with you for later in the week."

"That won't be necessary," Jessie said, watching Court inch toward the short hallway that led to the back of the establishment. We're here on other business. We just need to steal Jeanie Court for a few moments."

That seemed to set the pant-suited planner over the edge. Without a word, she turned and scurried toward the back, kicking off her heels as she ran. She inadvertently bumped into a three-tiered cake with a figurine couple on top. It teetered for a few seconds, and then toppled over, splattering the floor with icing. Jessie and Kat shared a disbelieving look. Was this woman really trying to make a run for it?

"You follow her," Kat said quickly. "I'll go back outside and cut her off in the alley."

She was gone before Jessie could reply. Reid looked slightly taken aback but got over it quickly.

"Go ahead," he said. "I'll catch up."

Jessie nodded and darted after Court, still astonished that the woman thought this was her best course of action. The wedding planner had just exited the back door and, despite her desire to barrel after her, Jessie moved with caution, dodging the sweet mess on the carpet. Her heart was pounding harder than she thought the situation deserved. She unholstered her gun and peeked out into the alley.

Court was running down the alley as fast as she could in her confining business slacks. Jessie gave chase but lost sight of her as she rounded the corner from the back alley to the driveway that connected to the main street. She slowed when she reached the driveway, preparing to take another cautious look.

But before she could peer around the building, she heard a grunt, followed by heavy thud. She carefully stepped out to find Jeanie Court sprawled out on her stomach, with Kat straddling her, pinning her wrists behind her with zip ties.

Jessie walked toward them, holstering her gun as her breathing returned to normal and the tingling in her fingers started to subside.

"Jeanie Court?" she asked, after stopping and staring down at the woman, who still looked winded from Kat's takedown.

"Lawyer," she managed to grunt before resting her cheek on the asphalt.

"Really?" Jessie asked, hoping to get her to reconsider. "All we wanted to do was talk. But first you decide to go on the lam and now you're clamming up? This feels a little extra for a wedding planner, no?"

"Lawyer," Court said more forcefully.

"Hunt, shut it down," Reid said from behind her. He'd finally managed to join them in the driveway. He looked pale and winded but mumbled his objection anyway. "I know you're not LAPD. But the rules still apply to me. We've got a suspect who ran away at the sight of us rather than be questioned. That's pretty damning. Let's not screw this up by fudging procedure."

Jessie was frustrated but knew he had a point. There was no point in forcing an interrogation when it might jeopardize a conviction, especially when it appeared not to be necessary.

"Okay, okay," she relented, raising her hands in surrender.

"Why don't you two go back inside, see what you can glean from the others?" Reid said. "I'll call for a patrol car to take her down to the station."

Jessie was happy to let him handle the bureaucratic work and walked back around to the front. Kat fell into step beside her.

"I wish I could have seen that tackle," Jessie said. "It sounded like you really laid her out."

Kat smiled.

"Most people don't know this, but I was drafted as a strong safety in the second round by the Bears."

"I don't doubt it," Jessie said, enjoying the moment despite the chasm that still remained between them. Kat knew not to push and said nothing more. When they returned to the bakery, everyone was still inside. Most looked as confused as they had before. No one was eating cake anymore.

"What the hell just happened?" the woman with the camera asked.

"That's what we're trying to find out," Jessie said non-responsively. "We're hoping you can help with that. My name is Jessie Hunt. I'm a consultant for the LAPD and this is my associate, Katherine Gentry. The man outside with Ms. Court is Detective Callum Reid. Can everyone please identify themselves and explain your connection to her?"

Everyone was briefly silent before the camera lady, an unassuming thirty-something in a long, modest skirt, finally spoke up.

"I'm Sloane Baker," she said. "I'm a wedding photographer. I work with Jeanie a lot. I was here to take photos of the cake tasting for the Wyatts."

127

"I assume you're the Wyatts?" Jessie said, looking at the couple wiping their faces with linen napkins.

"Yes," the guy said. "I'm Gary and this is Hilly."

"Congratulations," Jessie said before her turning attention to the woman in the apron. "And you're the baker?"

"Uh-huh," she muttered, apparently still shell-shocked. She looked over at the remnants of the cake that Court had knocked over and shook her head. "I'm Stacy Barrett. I work with Jeanie all the time."

"We all do," said the woman with the notepad next to the photographer. She was older, likely in her forties, and gave off a mom vibe. "I'm the caterer, Deb Carl."

"And I'm Chet Hamilton, the deejay," said the tall skinny guy next to her. He looked like he was barely out of college.

"Why is the deejay at the cake tasting?" Kat asked, voicing the very question Jessie had.

"Jeanie's big on that," he answered. "She likes the whole team working as one collective unit, so everyone is on the same page. She doesn't like when a wedding seems disjointed."

"When a couple wants live music, I've seen her bring in the bandleaders to tastings," Sloane the photographer offered. "She once had the lead singer of a heavy metal band come to a wedding shower so he could get a sense of the energy of the bride's friends."

"So you work with her on all her weddings?" Jessie asked.

"Not all," Deb the caterer volunteered. "It depends on what the couple is after. Jeanie has a small stable of vendors she works with regularly, including us. We all know each other pretty well."

"Can you please tell us what this is about now?" Hilly Wyatt asked, understandably disconcerted. "We're supposed to be getting married in six weeks and you just chased our wedding planner out the back door. What did she do?"

"I'm afraid we can't get into the details of that at this time," Jessie said. "But we'd appreciate it if you could all give us your contact information. We'll be in touch if we have additional questions."

As the others wrote down their details, Chet the deejay shimmied up to Jessie.

"If I give you my contact information," he whispered to her, "do you promise to get in touch even if you don't have questions?"

"What?"

"I love older women," he said by way of explanation.

Jessie turned to Kat, not sure whether to laugh or ask for help. Without even blinking, Kat stepped over and wrapped her arm around Jessie's waist.

"Sorry," she said with utter seriousness. "She's taken."

Jessie barely managed to keep a straight face as the guy skulked off. She didn't say it, but Kat was making it increasingly difficult to hold a grudge. Then she reminded herself why she was upset in the first place.

The memory of her sister using herself as bait with a pedophile popped into her head, along with her friend saying nothing about it. The smile sneaking to the edge of her lips was immediately erased.

"Let's get to the station to question Jeanie Court," she said coldly. "We've got a lot of work to do.

CHAPTER TWENTY SIX

Jessie couldn't decide if Court was incredibly devious or just plain stubborn.

She'd been read her Miranda rights and left to stew in an interrogation room while they tried to reach her lawyer. Apparently, the guy was tied up in court all day. One of his associates was available but Court wouldn't speak to anyone but him, which meant they couldn't proceed until he got here.

Jessie wasn't satisfied with that. If they had their killer in custody, it wasn't a big deal that they were sitting on their hands. But if Court was innocent, that meant there was a murderer still out there, possibly plotting another attack for tonight. She had to know.

Jamil was tied up helping Ryan out on the Night Hunter case, so they had a junior tech ready to backfill Court's GPS data from her car and phone for the last few days. Unfortunately that required a court order, which they didn't have yet. They'd already been waiting around for two hours. It was mid-afternoon and time was fast ticking away. Jessie decided she had to take drastic action.

"I promise I won't ask her any questions," she assured Reid, who looked as agitated as she'd ever seen him. "I'm just going to offer some theories to her. If she says silent, fine. But if she happens to get chatty, then at least we've got something to work with."

"That's super risky," he said. "It's the sort of thing that could be used at trial to toss the case. Juries don't like it when cops skirt around the edge of the law."

"Yeah, well they also don't like people getting away with murder," Jessie snapped. "And remember, I'm not a cop."

"You've been leaning on that point a lot for your last few cases," Reid retorted, coming back just as hard. "Eventually a judge is going to lose patience with you walking that tightrope of a technicality."

Jessie knew he had a point, but it wasn't one she had the time to address right now.

"It hasn't happened yet," she replied acidly.

"Easy guys," Kat said. She'd been quietly standing by observing the argument until now. "Callum, I understand your concerns. But if

130

Jessie goes in there without you, clearly states that she's not an LAPD officer, and refrains from actually asking questions of the suspect, that seems like it would fall within the letter of the law. Am I wrong?"

Reid's furrowed brow suggested that he didn't have a good response. Kat seemed to view that as a positive sign and kept going.

"If Court isn't our killer, we need to know," she pleaded, reading Jessie's mind. "We could be less than eight hours from another murder. Isn't it worth giving Jessie a shot? If Court doesn't talk, we're no worse off than we are now. Come on, Callum."

That last earnest line seemed to break him. He looked over at Jessie.

"No questions," he insisted, "only statements."

"Understood," she said, leaning over and giving him a second kiss on the cheek in as many days. Then she darted out of the room before he could change his mind.

She allowed herself one long, slow deep breath, then opened the door and stepped into the interrogation room. Jeanie Court looked up. She was sitting in a metal chair bolted to the ground with her right wrist cuffed to a metal loop on top of the table, also bolted down. When she saw who it was, her eyes went from worried to ferocious. It wasn't a great start to the interview.

"Hi, Jeanie," Jessie said, pretending as if their past interactions hadn't all been hostile. "I just wanted to update you on the situation with your attorney. He's still in court and could be for another couple of hours. Are you sure you don't want to consider speaking to his associate?"

She knew what the answer would be but hoped that the question might get Court talking, even monosyllabically. The woman shook her head.

"I'm afraid I need a formal, spoken "no" for the record," she said, not certain if that was even true.

"No," Court spat.

"Understood; so, we'll wait," she said, sitting casually on the edge of the table as if she didn't have a care in the world. "In the meantime, I thought I'd tell you a few things that were on my mind. No need to respond. In fact, you *shouldn't* now that you've invoked your right to counsel. I'm just a consultant for the department, not a cop, so I don't think that stuff applies to me. But all the same, you should just listen."

She glanced at the two-way mirror knowingly, giving the unseen Detective Reid her best "are you satisfied?" look. Then she turned back to Jeanie Court, who was eyeing her warily but silently.

"Anyway," she continued, adopting the tone of a girlfriend who wanted to share a secret over coffee, "like I said, I've been brainstorming while I was out there. And I figured that as long as we're stuck here, I'd run some of my crazy ideas by you, just to keep us entertained while we wait. Okay with you?"

Jeanie looked like she was about to object but Jessie cut her off.

"Remember, don't talk. You still have that right to remain silent," she reminded her. "But here's what I'm thinking. It just seems weird to me that a respected wedding planner, who hasn't committed any crimes, would up and run out of a bakery in the middle of a cake tasting just because some random people walked in. It's almost like you were on tenterhooks, waiting for a shoe to drop. I mean, we hadn't even identified ourselves yet."

Jeanie Court stared back at her like she would have enjoyed ripping out her throat if she could, or maybe spraying acid in her face. Jessie acted as if she didn't notice.

"It really was odd, considering that we fully went to that bakery just hoping to chat," she said. She went silent, musing wordlessly to herself for a few seconds to increase the pressure on Court. "So here I am, sitting out there, wondering what could cause such a desperate reaction. And then it hits me—I don't have to guess. There are ways to find out. First among them would be to get a search warrant for your office, which we've since requested and should be approved soon. I expect a knock on the door telling me so any minute."

She paused and stared at the door, as if that act alone might cause it to open. When it didn't, she shrugged and turned back to Court.

"What I think we'll do for starters is get a full list of all your clients, past and present, so we can talk to them. I got the sense from chatting with Yasmine that she'll be pretty accommodating."

That was not at all the sense that she'd gotten from their conversation, but Jeanie Court didn't know that. It was clear that the woman was getting increasingly worked up. The mention of reaching out to clients seemed have particularly hit home so Jessie pressed on that. She looked at her watch.

"Yeah, I think I have just enough time to get to your office, confiscate all your records, and start making calls before I have to be back here to meet your lawyer. Truthfully, before I even ask all these couples my questions, I'd want to warn them. I think it's only fair to give them a heads up about the situation so they can make alternate plans to find a new wedding planner if need be."

"What situation?" Court demanded, too curious to realize that she'd violated her no-talking policy. Jessie briefly debated answering but decided that since the woman was asking a question rather than answering one, it was probably safe to reply.

"Jeanie, I think you know the situation quite well: their well-regarded wedding planner is being held on suspicion of murdering three people she worked with. I hope sharing that with everyone doesn't hurt business too much."

"Wait," Court said, her eyes a mix of fury and distress. "This is about *that*?"

Jessie studied the woman closely before she answered. The woman's panicky energy was making it difficult to determine the sincerity of her response.

"Of course it is, Jeanie. Three of your clients are dead."

"What? Three? I saw the stories on the news about two of them and I assumed it had something to do with Jax and Claire being friends. And I don't even know about a third death."

"There was a third last night— Brian Clark. Now maybe all these murders are about some animosity among friends. Or maybe it has something to do with the wedding planner they all shared who ran away when she saw us. All I can tell you is that no one else we wanted to speak with took off at the sight of us."

Court sat there with her jaw open. Jessie tried to gauge whether she was genuinely stunned at the allegation or at the realization that her reign of terror had come to an end. In the end, she just couldn't tell. If she wanted to be more certain, it was time to amp things up. She stood up and straightened out her top.

"Anyway, I'll be back in a few hours," she said, starting to leave the room. "You hang tight. When I return, I'll let you know how many clients you have left."

She was almost to the door, afraid her bluff was about to be called, when Court called out.

"Wait!"

Jessie made sure to wipe the smile off her face before she turned around.

CHAPTER TWENTY SEVEN

"Yes?" she asked innocently.

"That's not why I ran—," she started to say.

"Hold on," Jessie interrupted holding up her hand. "You've invoked your right to remain silent. You've asked for a lawyer. I can't have you telling me whatever it is you want to tell me unless you waive that right. It wouldn't be proper. So why don't we just wait until he gets here, and you can talk it over with him first. In the meantime, I'll go reach out to those clients."

Court, despite her desperation, was no dummy.

"I get it," she said. "You don't have to twist my arm anymore. I waive my rights. Just hear me out before you start calling my clients."

Jessie didn't know what the woman was trying to hide, but she was increasingly getting the sense that it wasn't murder. Whatever it was, she decided that laying out everything clearly on the table was to her advantage.

"Are you sure you want to do that?" Jessie asked. "You heard what Detective Reid told you earlier. If you waive your rights, anything you say could be used against you in court. And considering that we're talking murder here, what you say next could be what gets you a lifetime in prison."

Court spoke slowly and emphatically.

"Considering that I didn't kill anyone, I waive my rights. Just let me explain before you call anyone."

Jessie wished she could see through the mirror to tell if Reid considered Court's words emphatic enough for her to continue. But at this point she was committed. She returned to the table and sat down, this time in the chair across from Court.

"Go ahead," she said.

"The reason I ran was because I saw the detective's badge on his belt when you all were walking in. I knew he was a cop."

"Why should that matter if you didn't do anything wrong?" Jessie demanded.

Court breathed a frustrated, defeated sigh.

"I didn't say that I didn't do *anything* wrong. I said that I didn't kill anyone. A few weeks ago, a client named Amanda Nelson accused me of skimming money at her wedding reception. She threatened to sue me and to have me arrested. I've been on edge ever since. When I saw the detective, I jumped to conclusions and panicked."

Jessie waited for her to continue but when she didn't, prompted her.

"There'd be no reason to panic if her allegation was meritless," she noted.

Jeanie Court didn't respond. Jessie didn't have patience for this woman's wounded pride and let her know it.

"Jeanie," she said sternly. "You are under investigation for murder. Do you get that? Whatever other crimes you may have committed are inevitably going to come out. The client who accused you—this Amanda Nelson— is going to do interviews. There is no way you can keep this quiet. Right now, your best bet is to cooperate with us. If committing some other, lesser crime absolves you of murder, admit to it. Lots of thieves have eventually rebuilt their lives after getting caught: multiple murderers not so much. Tell me exactly what you did and why it clears you of these killings."

Jeanie's whole face scrunched up like a raisin for several seconds. Her eyes were closed tight. When she finally opened them, she started talking fast and without a breath.

"I'm not admitting to anything," she said. "But Amanda accused me of swiping cash gifts from her at their reception. I often suggest that my clients mention to guests that they would be happy with cash as opposed to wedding registry items. That allows them to choose what they want and when they need it, rather than be boxed into to getting some china set they don't really care about. Plus there are potential advantages to having a pile of undeclared cash at their disposal, especially early in a marriage. It also makes it a lot easier on guests. There's less thought involved. They can just hand over and envelope and be done with it."

"This all sounds relatively reasonable so far," Jessie said. "Maybe get to the accusation part."

"I am," Court said snappishly, before regaining control. "At weddings, I set out a lockbox for cash gifts attached to a rolling table for traditional ones. Guests just slide their envelopes in the lockbox slot, knowing they'll be secure. At a certain point, me and my team move all the gifts, along with the lockbox, to a secure room at the wedding venue. Amanda accused me of unlocking the box, going through the envelopes, and removing some of the money."

"How would she know what had been taken?" Jessie asked.

"She said a friend accidentally mentioned how much they gave a few months after the wedding. The amount differed from what she remembered so she started asking other guests who'd gifted cash how much they gave." There was a pregnant pause before she added, "there were a number of discrepancies."

"I see," Jessie said slowly. "How much did she accuse you of taking?"

"$3700," Court said flatly.

Jessie nodded.

"How many weddings do you plan a year, Jeanie?"

"Usually between eighty and ninety," she said.

Jessie pulled out her phone did a little calculation.

"Wow—that really adds up. If her allegation was accurate and that haul was typical for a wedding, we're talking well over quarter of a million in a year. And as you noted, there are potential advantages to having a pile of undeclared cash at one's disposal."

Jeanie remained silent. That was okay. Jessie wasn't done.

"And she threatened to sue you, as well as go to the police with her suspicions?" she reconfirmed.

"Yes, and to tell everyone she knew who hired me."

"Did Amanda know Claire Bender, Jax Coopersmith or Brian Clark?" Jessie asked.

"Not that I'm aware of," Court said. "I think they travel in different circles."

"But you're not sure. It's possible that she mentioned it to one of them?"

"Anything's possible," Court said.

"Is it possible that she talked to one of them and *they* reached out to you? Is it possible that you decided to eliminate everyone who knew what you were being accused of?"

Court got so upset at the question that she slammed her cuffed fist down on the metal table, making a clanging sound.

"I didn't eliminate anyone. I have no idea who she told so how could I go after anyone? Besides, if I was going to kill anybody, wouldn't it be Amanda? To the best of my knowledge, she's alive and well."

136

"We'll check on that," Jessie assured her, not saying that Court had made a strong point—why *wouldn't* she go after Amanda Nelson first if she was trying to keep her financial misdeeds quiet? "Where was this wedding you handled last night?"

"On the beach in Santa Barbara."

"That's almost two hours north of here," Jessie noted. "When did you get back to the city?"

"It was an early afternoon wedding, but the reception lasted well into the evening. Traffic was rough coming back. I think I finally got home around midnight."

"Did anyone drive back with you?"

"No. I released all my staff about a half hour before I left myself."

"What about Sunday?" Jessie pressed, not allowing the woman time to ponder her answers for too long.

"I had a light day: church wedding in the morning downtown at St. Vincent De Paul Catholic Church. They had their reception at the Hotel Figueroa. It was over by 1 p.m. I spent the rest of the afternoon and evening at home prepping final details for the Santa Barbara wedding the next day."

"Was anyone with you?"

"No," Court said resentfully. "I live alone."

"And Saturday," Jessie demanded, keeping the heat on. "What was your schedule like?"

Court thought for a moment.

"I had a noon wedding at The Peninsula Hotel in Beverly Hills. It ended at 4 p.m."

"What did you do after that?"

"I caught a movie, picked up takeout, and went home."

"Again, by yourself?" Jessie asked, feeling slightly cruel but setting the guilt aside. Court's feelings were secondary to getting answers.

The woman nodded with downcast eyes.

"So to be clear, you have no alibi witnesses for any of the nights on which the victims were killed?"

Court's face flushed.

"Had I known I would need an alibi witness, I would have called someone up," she said bitterly. "Too bad I dumped my Tinder account recently, I guess."

"There is a way you could help yourself out," Jessie said, refusing to be pulled into a testy back and forth.

"How?"

137

"Give us permission to look at your GPS data without a court order," Jessie said. "If the location information on your phone and car reinforces what you're saying, it would go a long way to helping clear you."

Court didn't hesitate.

"How do I do that?"

"Just sign a release," Jessie told her.

"Bring it to me now," the woman insisted, "the sooner the better."

Jessie walked out without another word. By the time she got into the observation room, Reid was holding the release in his hand.

"What do you think?" Jessie asked both him and Kat.

"Hard to say," Reid replied. "There's no telling if this cash skimming operation played out the way she describes. How do we know Claire or Jax wasn't the first one to notice and told Amanda Nelson? Court could be fuzzying up the timeline to protect herself."

"All the more reason to get this GPS data," Kat said. "At least then we can get a sense of her movements."

"True," Reid said, "but she could always manipulate that too— leave her phone at home, take a cab to these people's homes."

"Agreed," Jessie said, feeling the post-interrogation exhaustion settle in on her. "But we have to start somewhere."

"We'll start with the release," Reid said. "Why don't you take a breather, have a seat? I'll get her to sign it."

Jessie nodded and plopped down in one of the chairs facing the observation mirror. Kat sat next to her. They both stared at the wedding planner, who seemed to be studying her nails.

"What are you thinking?" Kat asked. "You like her for this?"

Jessie closed her eyes, trying to clear out the mental clutter.

"I wish I could say," she muttered. "The GPS data will help. But Reid is right. If this *is* her and she conceived it well in advance, she'd have anticipated us pursuing this stuff. And she'd have crafted a diversionary explanation like this money skimming thing. She could be playing games with us. And the fact that she has zero witnesses for her whereabouts on three consecutive nights bothers me."

"But..." Kat said leadingly.

Jessie opened her eyes and studied the woman on the other side of the mirror.

"On paper, she's a solid suspect. She's smart, meticulous and clearly resents planning perfect days for these people when she hasn't gotten one of her own. *But* in my gut, I think we may have the wrong person. I'm worried that while we're spinning our wheels with her, someone is out there, planning to do evil tonight."

CHAPTER TWENTY EIGHT

This would be her big night, so she checked her makeup one last time in the mirror.

It was a delicate balance, looking nice for a wedding but not wanting to show up the bride. In recent years, she'd become a master of it. She liked to think it was because she had developed a sense of these things, but she knew there was another reason: no matter how much she did herself up, people didn't really notice her.

She'd come to that realization quite recently and accepting it had brought another epiphany: because she was a blandly pleasant looking person—a little plump, a little short, and a little mousy—she was almost invisible. That could be a curse, but it also meant that she had total freedom.

She could walk among the glamorous people without drawing attention to herself. Often their gaze seemed to skip over her completely. Sometimes she felt like a wraith, passing among the living but not really of them.

Maybe that's why Hardy had left her weeks before their wedding. Maybe that's why he'd taken up with her closest friend. Maybe that's why she'd been oblivious as the two of them engaged in the perfect deceit right under her nose for six months before suddenly moving back to Philadelphia a month ago. She just wasn't a very interesting person. Or at least, she hadn't been until three days ago. That's when everything changed.

She'd admittedly been nervous before the first Rebalancing. But she told herself to be brave and found an unexpected reserve of strength. She went to Claire's home, where she'd been previously, and did the deed. The pressure wasn't as intense as she'd feared once she determined that Claire's husband, Jack, wasn't home. Once it was done, as she listened to the woman's anguished moans, she knew she'd made the right choice. Every pained grunt gave her an erotic tingle.

Doing Jax had been even more satisfying. She wasn't sure if she got greater pleasure from listening to the woman's agony or knowing that her death would be all over the news the following day. Ultimately, the buzz she got from immersing herself in the subsequent media frenzy and public grieving was almost, but not quite as delicious as the murder itself.

She'd changed things up a little last night. Caroline Ryan had always been nice to her, in a distant, mildly condescending way. Had it not been for the fact that she couldn't remember her name—she kept calling her Joan—she might have escaped judgment.

But after getting it wrong multiple times, the indignity became too much to ignore. She decided not to punish Caroline directly. Instead that Rebalancing would be achieved via her perfectly charming fiancé, Brian, who had always treated her well and *did* get her name right. But that wasn't the point. Caroline needed to be taught a lesson.

Now the woman would live in grief and fear, knowing an unseen threat was out there, always ready to strike at her more directly. And if the cops ever caught her, she felt confident that Caroline would remember her name from then on. Whatever remorse she felt at making Brian suffer was more than mitigated by the suffering his beloved would experience going forward.

That was the reason she had to keep going. The Brian Clark Rebalancing had left a bit of a bad taste in her mouth. She needed a palate cleanser and tonight offered the perfect opportunity.

Nicholas and Janet Goodsen were celebrating their tenth anniversary at a gorgeous venue in Palos Verdes, on a cliff overlooking the Pacific Ocean. It was a converted Spanish mission, now a historic landmark, with a restored bell tower and the mission's original walls, which were over two hundred years old. In addition to being beautiful, it had many dark, narrow halls. That would make a surprise, sneak attack easier to carry out. It would also allow for the perpetrator to escape unseen.

The Goodsens had been selected partly because they were next in line on her schedule. She didn't have another worthwhile event to attend until next weekend. But the choice was made easier by the couple's arrogance. They had insisted that all their friends journey out to a hard-to-access area on a chilly weekday evening rather than delaying it until the weekend because "Tuesday was their anniversary, dammit," as Nicholas Goodsen had bellowed.

They were also a good choice because of Janet Goodsen's demand that the party have a ball theme and that everyone dress as if they were attending some celebration at a 18th century French palace. The pretention and narcissism were unmatched. She couldn't wait to watch as Janet's flesh melted onto her fancy ball gown. Maybe she'd finally

141

learn a little humility, however briefly. The thought of it made her heart beat a little faster.

Satisfied that she looked presentable but not noticeable, she started to turn away from the mirror when something caught her eye and she glanced back. Some aspect in her manner was more vibrant that unusual. She would never delude herself into thinking she was actually pretty, but there was a healthy glow to her cheeks and a sparkle in her eyes. She just seemed more vital than usual. It was exhilarating.

She turned off the bathroom light, walked over to her bed, and sat down. She knew she had to leave but she couldn't help taking one more glimpse at the framed photos on the bedside table. There were three of them. All were of happy couples, smiling warmly for the camera. Or at least they had been smiling before she had scratched out the faces of the victims, mutilating them just as she had with their real faces. She planned to add another photo to her collection tonight.

With a kick of anticipation and a sense of purpose, Sloane Baker grabbed her camera equipment and headed out. The happy couple expected their photographer to be at the venue early. But it was what they *didn't* expect that had her grinning from ear to ear.

CHAPTER TWENTY NINE

Jessie could barely keep her eyes open.

Unlike Jamil Winslow, her usual go-to guy for all things technological, the tech who was gathering Jeanie Court's GPS data wasn't especially gifted at making the search compelling to observers. At a certain point, she decided there was no point in her, Reid, and Kat hovering over his shoulder.

"Joel, "she said to the clearly anxious tech, "We're going to let you do your thing. Please let us know the second you have something worth sharing."

Both Kat and Reid seemed relieved that she'd made the call and followed her out into the hall. Standing up in a bustling corridor seemed to give her a small jolt of energy.

"I'm not optimistic," she said, immediately voicing the same thought the other two had. "It's almost 5 p.m. and it's starting to get dark out. We're only about five hours from the time window for the other murders. And there's no guarantee that timing will continue. We need to be pursuing other leads in case Jeanie Court falls through."

She heard the anxiety in her own voice as she spoke. The way Callum Reid looked at her, she knew he'd noticed it too.

"We've got Court in custody until at least tomorrow, no matter what her lawyer does," he said, doing his clumsy best to sound comforting. "The forensic accountant is going through her financials. I'll go back in and work with Joel on the GPS data. Two sets of eyes are better than one. After that it gets a little crowded. Why don't you too take a little mental break and then you can dive into whatever other leads we have."

"We have other leads?" Kat asked sarcastically.

"I don't know," he said, sounding defeated. "Maybe there's some connection among the victims we haven't noticed yet. Maybe reviewing the crime scene photos again will spark something. It can't hurt."

He went to rejoin the tech, leaving Jessie and Kat alone. Feeling a sudden awkwardness between them, Jessie spoke quickly.

"I'm going to check in on Ryan," she said. "I'll catch up with you in a few."

"Okay," Kat said, not pushing, "I'm going on a bathroom break. Reconvene in five?"

Jessie nodded and walked down the hall to the research room. She could hear furious tapping on a keyboard and was not surprised to find Jamil sitting before a bank of three monitors, his eyes darting around almost as fast as his fingers.

Jamil Winslow didn't look like much. The twenty-four-year-old was short and appeared so frail that Jessie often worried what a strong gust of wind might do to him. But she'd learned from her first interaction with him that the young researcher was brilliant. If Jamil told her something, she knew she it was accurate, vetted several times over. He was also relentless and seemingly impervious to fatigue.

Ryan, however, apparently was not. He was lying on the couch along the back wall, snoring softly. Jessie tiptoed over to Jamil and waved to get his attention.

"Hey Jamil," she whispered. "How's it going?"

"Hi, Ms. Hunt," he said, looking up at her ever so briefly, still typing. "Not great to be honest. We still don't have any more leads than this morning. The Night Hunter parked much further down the street from the victim's location this time, away from any surveillance cameras. We don't have any idea what kind of car he used."

"There's nothing useful from the crime scene?"

"Not really. He seemed to be wearing prosthetics and a wig during the murder. Ryan said he looked much different than when he saw him outside the hostel on Sunday night. In addition, he wore gloves the whole time; there were no fingerprints. He even sprayed the room down with some kind of industrial antiseptic. CSU thinks it was to degrade any possible DNA that might have been left behind. If so, it worked. They found none. But that's not the worst part."

Jessie tensed up at those words.

"Tell me," she said though she didn't really want to know.

"We saw the whole killing on the family's interior security cameras. He appeared to be…performing for us, knowing we'd see it later. He moved her into a room with a camera and turned on all the lights. Detective Hernandez thought that was so everything would look clear and bright. He wanted us to see him at work. And he took his time, like hours. The girl was immobilized but her eyes were moving, and she would twitch slightly when he used the exacto knife to remove a fresh layer of flesh. Eventually her movements stopped so he gave her an injection of something to wake her up. After a while, even that didn't work. But he kept going. He got there around nine at night, but the coroner's estimated time of death was between 3 a.m. and 5 a.m. That means he was skinning this girl alive for at least six hours."

Neither of them spoke for several seconds, processing the horror of what the girl had suffered. When Jessie finally replied, it was to change subjects.

"How's *he* doing?" she asked, nodding at Ryan.

"He's pushing himself pretty hard," Jamil said. "I told him to take a break since all I'm doing right now is searching through city cameras for old clunkers spotted in the area of the crime. It's a long shot and he couldn't help. I told him I'd wake him if I found anything."

Jessie looked at her boyfriend, his right arm splayed out, nearly grazing the floor, his body bent at an unnatural angle.

"Change of plans," she said. "When he wakes up, tell him I came by and insisted that he go home. There's no reason for him to be here unless you find something useful."

"I don't know if he'll go for that," Jamil warned.

"Then please remind him that my sister is at home with a detective who deserves to be relieved of duty after watching her all day. Until this guy is caught, Hannah isn't safe, and I'd feel better with Ryan protecting her, even at half strength, than just about anyone else. If he has a problem with that, he should call me or find me. Tell him I sounded...unyielding. That should get his imagination going."

"I'll tell him," Jamil said. "How's your case going? I know Decker's on the warpath about it."

"Not much better than yours," she said, avoiding details. "But I'm about to dive back in. Wish me luck."

"Good luck," he said sincerely. Jamil was almost always sincere.

She returned to the hall just in time to see Kat push open the door to the station's interior courtyard. With a sense of trepidation, she followed. Once outside, it took a second for her eyes to adjust from the fluorescent indoor lighting to the last, fading rays of the evening sun. Kat was sitting alone on a bench in the middle of the courtyard, under a large tree. It was the same spot where Jessie had engaged in so many conversations with Garland. She walked over and sat down beside her.

"How's it going?" she asked.

Kat looked over at her apprehensively, clearly unsure exactly which topic she was being asked about. Jessie saw her decide to play it safe.

"I think I agree with what you said back in the observation room. My gut tells me Jeanie Court didn't do this. I think our killer is still out there."

Jessie closed her eyes and exhaled slowly. She knew that there would never be a more opportune moment to address the episode that had them so at odds. Kat had apologized and wouldn't bring it up again on her own for fear of making things worse. It was up to Jessie to open the door to any reconciliation.

"Me too," she said quietly. "But that's not what I meant. How's it going with *you*?"

Kat looked straight ahead, afraid to make eye contact. When she responded, her voice was almost too quiet to hear.

"I know I failed you, Jessie. I kept secrets from you and secrets leave stains on relationships, ones that often can't be undone. And I *so* want to undo what I did; to make things right. But I don't know how. I don't know what I can do to earn your trust back. And I'm terrified that I've lost the best friend I've ever had. I feel helpless."

Jessie sat there stiffly, unsure how to respond. All of Kat's fears were well-founded. She wasn't certain there was any way her friend *could* fully win back her confidence. And without that, how could their friendship ever truly be repaired?

Jessie didn't know. But in this moment, she did recognize one thing: despite the fracture between them, she longed to have Kat back. Selfishly, she missed her as a sounding board, as her emotional backstop. But mostly, she just missed her sister-in-arms.

"Listen," she finally said. "I can't tell you that I didn't feel betrayed by what you did. You allowed my sister to continue engaging in behavior that put her at grave risk and you kept me in the dark. I can't excuse it. But I understand it."

Kat looked over at her, surprise on her face. Jessie went on.

"I know you thought you were helping Hannah, trying to get her to work through her thrill-seeking. I know you didn't want to create any more tension between the two of us when there was already so much. And I get that once you made the decision to keep the truth from me, you were trapped: tell me the truth and lose Hannah's trust. Don't tell me and risk her putting herself in danger. You made the wrong choice, and it was a long, slippery slope from there."

Kat nodded, not daring to speak. Jessie continued.

"And I'm not blameless in this," she said. "My sister, who I am ultimately responsible for, was doing these things while she lived in my

146

house and I never had a clue. I get that she's an incredibly smart, extremely convincing girl. But I'm a frickin' criminal profiler and I was oblivious. Maybe it was because I was focused on Ryan's recovery or my new job or the parade of killers I was hunting, but I missed what was going on. So I can't be too high and mighty."

"You couldn't have know—," Kat started to say but Jessie interrupted her.

"Don't do that," she said more harshly than she intended. "Don't try to comfort me. We're not there yet. Just because I understand you, that doesn't mean that I absolve you. It just means that I want to... find a way to get there."

"I'll take what I can get," Kat whispered.

Jessie looked over at her and a wave of unexpected goodwill washed over her.

"What you can get, if you want one, is a hug."

Kat allowed herself the briefest flicker of a smile.

"I do want one," she said.

Jessie stood. Kat rose as well and allowed herself to be wrapped in her friend's extended arms. Neither said anything for a while.

"What do we do now?" Kat finally asked quietly.

"We try our best to clean up the stain of the secrets," Jessie said. "It might take a while, but I think we can get there."

"I know we can," Kat replied before finally pulling away. "Should we work on that some more *after* we catch this sick killer?"

But Jessie wasn't really listening. Her own words, a callback to something Kat had said moments earlier, had caused a jumble of disconnected thoughts and images in her head to collide all at once. Her brain was filled with flashes of stained carpets and faded paintings hanging in lonely houses. Slightly dizzy, she reached for the back of the bench to steady herself.

"Are you okay?" Kat asked, concerned.

Jessie wasn't sure. The cascade of thoughts was almost physically overwhelming.

"Something you said just made me think about the case," she eventually managed to mutter. "I think I have an idea. We should get back inside."

She started for the door.

"Do you want to tell me what I said that caused this epiphany?" Kat asked, jogging to catch up."

Jessie didn't even look back as she responded.

147

"Stains."

CHAPTER THIRTY

It didn't take long to find what she was looking for.

Reid and Kat stood over her desk in the bullpen as she flipped through the crime scene photos taken at the home of Caroline Ryan and Brian Clark.

"Here it is," she said, pulling one out and slamming it down on the desk. It was photo of the top of the piano from the couple's sitting room, with multiple photos strategically lined up.

"What are we looking at?" Reid asked. "Kat said there was a stain. I don't see any stain."

Jessie shook her head.

"Not a stain so much as a discoloration," she said, talking as fast as her brain would allow. "I noticed it when you were talking to Caroline last night. I went through the sitting room to avoid being seen. That's when I noticed it."

She pointed to a spot on the piano top between two photos where the wood looked darker than elsewhere.

"Okay," Kat said. "I see it, but I don't get the significance."

"From everything I know," Jessie said, "both Caroline and Brian Clark were very meticulous, even anal people. I don't think they would have missed something like this. The color in this spot is different than everywhere else. I think that's because when the sun streamed into the sitting room, over time it affected the color of the wood. In places where the piano was exposed directly to sunlight, the wood was lighter. Where the wood was covered for an extended time, by say a piece of art or a photo, it would be darker. This portion of the wood is darker than everything around it."

"Okay, so they had something there and they moved it," Reid said, unimpressed.

"Doubtful," Jessie replied dismissively. "Those two would never have moved an item without replacing it with something to hide the spot. Everything else nearby is a framed photo. How hard would it be to just put a new one in the empty space? But they didn't do that. And look at the gap between the two photos on either side of the spot. It's much wider than the separation between any of the other photos on the piano top. No way Caroline Ryan would have let that stand."

"So what are you saying?" Kat asked.

"I'm saying that I think there was a photo on top of that piano and that it was taken very recently," she said, pausing before making the leap she hoped they would take with her. "I think it was taken by the killer."

Reid and Kat were silent. Reid managed to regroup first.

"But why?" he asked.

"I don't know," Jessie said, pulling out her phone and dialing a number. "And I won't until we know what was taken. That's why I'm calling Caroline Ryan right now. I need you both to do the same thing. Reid, call Jack Bender. Have him look around his house to see if anything is missing or out of place. Tell him to look specifically for framed photos that might have been taken from a mantle or wall, somewhere where it might not be immediately missed. Kat, you call Titus Poole and do the same thing."

Before either could respond, Caroline Ryan picked up.

"Caroline," she launched in, dispensing with any initial words of sympathy. "It's Jessie Hunt. Are you at home?"

"Yes," the woman responded groggily. "I had a few sleeping pills. I was taking a nap."

"I need you to go down to your sitting room right now," she instructed.

"Why?"

"I'll explain when you get down there, but please hurry. This is important."

"Okay," Caroline said, sounding more alert already. "Give me a minute."

While Jessie waited, she looked over the other two.

"Bender's walking a real estate agent though the house for a potential sale," Reid said. "I'm having him look right now."

"I keep getting Titus Poole's voicemail," Kat said. "Maybe he's not picking up because he doesn't know my number. Should I use a station hard line?"

"Sure," Jessie said.

"Okay," Kat said, her eyes suddenly lighting up.

"What?" Jessie asked.

"I have an idea that may work even if he doesn't answer," she said. "I'm going to look at the—."

Jessie held up her hand. Caroline was back on the line.

"I'm down here," she said. "What now?"

"Look at the top of your piano," Jessie told her. "Do you see a discolored spot in a gap between two photos?"

There was a long pause.

"Yes!" came the piercing reply. "It's missing."

"What is?"

"One of our engagement photos," she said, her voice wounded. "We took them at the pier in Hermosa Beach."

"Did Jeanie Court organize that?"

"Yes, she was there supervising the whole thing along with Joan Baker, the photographer. She even brought in a hair and makeup stylist to touch me up."

"I thought the photographer's name was Sloane," Jessie prompted.

"Oh yeah, that's right. I always get that wrong."

"Who was the stylist?" she asked.

"I think her name was Steph; something like that."

Reid was waving at her excitedly with his phone.

"Thanks, Caroline," she said hurriedly. "I'll get back to you if I have any more questions."

"Does this help?" she asked.

"I hope so," Jessie told her, then hung up. The second she did, Reid dived in.

"I have Jack Bender on mute. He didn't have a clue. He said he doesn't notice stuff like that. But apparently the real estate agent with him did. She pointed out an unusually large gap on the mantle. Once he saw it, he remembered that they kept one of their wedding photos there."

Jessie felt a flush of excitement. This couldn't possibly be a coincidence.

"Ask who was at the photo session. Jeanie? The same photographer, Sloane? Was there a stylist named Steph or something similar?"

Reid unmuted Bender and asked the questions. Jessie waited impatiently, glancing over at Kat, whose eyes were fixed on the computer monitor in front of her. Before she could ask what that was about, Reid spoke up.

"Jeanie was there. He doesn't remember the photographer's name; said it was some chunky gal who didn't talk much. He doesn't remember the stylist either, but it wasn't anyone named Steph. In fact, he said it was a guy. Any other questions for him?"

Lost in thought, Jessie absently shook her head without speaking. She tried to put the pieces together without making assumptions. Just because someone was at these photo shoots didn't automatically mean that they were the one who stole the pictures, who committed these murders.

But whoever did this obviously had animosity toward these couples, though not necessarily because of anything specific to them. Could it just be the very fact that they were couples at all? It was clear that Jeanie Court resented that her entire life was about creating perfect romantic moments for people when her own life seemed so devoid of them. Could the same be true of Sloane Baker?

She was about to pull up whatever info they had on the woman when Kat looked up. Her eyes were sparkling with excitement.

"I found something," she said giddily.

"What?"

I've been comparing crime scene photos from Jax's place with photos from her Instagram account. She took a *lot* of them. I matched up her most recent personal photos with the ones taken by CSU and found a discrepancy. Look here."

Jessie and Reid crowded over her monitor as she laid two photos on the screen side by side. Even before Kat started explaining, Jessie saw what she was referencing, but she held her tongue.

"Here, on her Instagram," Kat noted, "there's what looks like a framed engagement picture on the dresser in her bedroom. But that picture isn't in the crime scene photos. The space is empty. I searched further back in Jax's account and found the original photo that she ended up framing. She posted a bunch of them all on the same day."

Kat scrolled to the day and clicked on the image. It was of Jax and Titus sitting on a bench with the famed Griffith Observatory in the background. In the lower left corner of the image was a watermark that read "courtesy of Sloane Baker Photography."

"It could just be a coincidence," Reid said, clearly also trying not to jump to conclusions. "Just like Jeanie Court planned all the victims' weddings, Sloane Baker was the photographer for them too. That doesn't mean she's our killer."

"You're right," Jessie said. "But it's the best lead we've had in hours. Even if it's not her, she's bound to have some useful information. Either way, I think we should go see her now."

"I just pulled up her address," Kat said, reading Jessie's mind. "She lives in the Fairfax District. I bet we can be there in twenty minutes if you use your sirens."

Jessie grabbed her jacket as Reid did the same.

"I'll try to make it fifteen," he said.

Jessie hoped it wasn't too late.

CHAPTER THIRTY ONE

Jessie shut the siren out of her head.

As Reid tore through the city streets, she focused on the limited information she'd been able to collect on Sloane Baker. Other than a driver's license indicating that she was thirty-two, some LLC paperwork for her photography business, and two traffic citations, there was almost nothing.

Baker had moved here from Philadelphia seven years ago, established her photography business, resided in three different apartments over the years, and lived what appeared to be a generally drama-free life. Of course, paperwork couldn't reveal what might be lurking underneath, but on the surface, everything seemed normal.

Her phone buzzed and she saw a text from Jamil, along with an attachment. It read: *Sent Detective Hernandez home. He didn't put up a fight. Had a little lull in my vehicle search and heard about your new suspect. Did some web sleuthing. Found this. Hope it helps.*

She clicked on the attachment and saw that it was Baker's school record from her time attending Temple University in Philadelphia. Jamil had specifically highlighted two notations from her junior year. The first said: *Health services incident report (redacted); 12/8/2007; 2007 fall semester.* The second was equally succinct: *Sabbatical approved; 2008 spring semester, personal/medical reasons.*

It was hard to draw too many conclusions. Maybe Sloane Baker had gotten sick. Maybe she'd been the victim of some kind of assault. Maybe she'd harmed someone else. But whatever happened, it occurred late on a Saturday night in the waning weeks of the fall semester. Then she didn't return for the spring semester. It was reasonable to assume the two were connected. And it was the first sign that Baker's life wasn't always as milquetoast as it first seemed.

Reid shut off the siren and Jessie looked up to see why. She saw that they had turned left off North Fairfax Avenue onto Oakwood Avenue, a residential street near Canter's Deli. Baker's apartment complex was just a few blocks west.

When they arrived, a patrol car, also without sirens, was parked at the curb with two uniformed officers waiting for them. They hopped out and while Reid filled the two men in on the situation, Jessie looked over at Kat.

"You okay with this?" she asked.

"This is why I'm here," her friend said with cool confidence. "I've got your back."

With everyone on the same page, Reid led the way. He pushed open the front gate, which had a broken latch, and jogged toward Baker's first floor, back corner unit.

"Remember," he said, sounding slightly winded. "If this is our girl, she has access to sprayable acid and injectable drain cleaner. Keep your distance. Don't take any chances."

Everyone nodded. Reid knocked loudly on the door.

"Sloane Baker. This is the Los Angeles Police Department. We have a warrant to search your home. Open the door now."

There was no response. Reid waited about ten seconds before trying again.

"Open the door now, Ms. Baker. This is your final warning. LAPD has a warrant to search the premises."

After another ten seconds of silence, he nodded to the uniformed officer holding the battering ram and stepped aside. Everyone unholstered their weapons. The officer wasted no time slamming the door, which gave easily, shooting wide open. The second officer moved in first, followed by Reid, and then the other officer, who dropped the battering ram on the ground and took out his gun. Jessie and Kat followed close behind.

The unit was cleared in under a minute. There was no one home. Jessie walked around, finally stopping at the entrance to Sloane's bedroom. A second pair of officers arrived. One took up a position at the front door of the apartment. The second walked up to Reid.

"Are you Detective Reid?" he asked.

"I am."

"I'm supposed to give you a message from Captain Decker at Central Station. He says he got emergency authorization for a search of Baker's GPS phone and vehicle location data. Nothing has come back yet on the car. There seems to some confusion as to what vehicle is actually registered to her. He said her phone isn't pinging at all and that the researcher doing the search thinks she took out her battery completely."

"Thanks, officer," he said, turning to Jessie and Kat. "So this means we have no way of knowing where she is now."

Kat said something in response, but Jessie was no longer listening. Her eye had drifted to a series of pictures on Baker's bedside table. She walked over. They were the missing photos from the victim's houses. As she leaned in closer, she saw that the faces of Claire Bender, Jax Coopersmith and Brian Clark had all been scratched out.

She felt a surge of vindication mixed with horror. They knew who the killer was but had no idea where to find her.

"She did it," Jessie said quietly, ending whatever conversation Reid and Kat had been having. They joined her.

"Oh god," Reid said, speaking for them all when he saw the photos, "We have to find her. She could be out wreaking havoc right now."

"Her laptop is on the dresser," Kat pointed out. "Maybe I can search her calendar and see where she's supposed to be right now. The murders don't usually take place until later at night. She could be working an event."

As Kat searched, Jessie noticed that the bedside table drawer was open slightly. She pulled the drawer all the way out to find one more framed photo lying face-up. It was of Sloane with a schlubby-looking guy, his armed wrapped around her shoulder. She couldn't tell much about the man's facial appearance because, like the recent poisoning victims, it was scratched out. A grunt from Kat made her look up. Based on her friend's body language, she knew the laptop was a bust.

"It's password protected," Kat said. "I'm sure it won't be hard to crack but that's beyond my skill set. By the time we get it to someone who can access the thing, it might be too late."

Jessie looked at the photos again, absorbing the pain of all the couples who had looked so happy in them. And then it hit her. Feeling like an idiot, she pulled out her phone.

"Who are you calling?" Reid asked.

"We don't need her laptop," Jessie said. "We have someone in custody right now who probably knows exactly where Sloane Baker is at this moment: Jeanie Court."

She reached the shift officer managing the cells.

"I need you to get Jeanie Court on the phone right away," she said.

She listened as the officer barked instructions to someone else, then waited helplessly, flinching slightly at the sound of each shouted voice and clanging metal door. The three minutes it took to get her on the line felt interminable.

"Hello?" Jeanie Court said tentatively.

"Jeanie," Jessie said, cutting to the chase, "It's Jessie Hunt. I may have a way for you to help yourself, assuming you can help me. If your information pans out, I'll put in a good word with the prosecutor on your case. How does that sound to you?"

"Good," Jeanie said without hesitation.

"Okay. Did you have Sloane Baker contracted to work an event tonight?"

There was a long pause that Jessie assumed was Court searching her memory. But when she replied, it was clear that wasn't the problem. Court just didn't want to give her bad news.

"I don't have any events scheduled for tonight," she said slowly.

Jessie felt her whole body sink in on itself. She was out of ideas. Maybe they could still track Baker's car. But there was no guarantee that she'd even used it. They'd find her eventually. But that would be of little solace to the family of whomever she was targeting tonight.

"But," Court said, sending a jolt of adrenaline through Jessie's body, "I might know where she is."

"Where?" Jessie asked, trying to keep her voice even.

"When we were wrapping up after the wedding in Santa Barbara, I remember her complaining about an anniversary party she had booked for this week. I don't remember the exact day. I just know it didn't conflict with any of my events, which would have made it tonight, tomorrow or Thursday."

"What was the event, Jeanie?" Jessie asked calmly despite her desire to scream at the woman to get to the point.

"I'm trying to recall. She said it was this ridiculous thing where the couple insisted that everyone attending wear 18th century ball gowns," she said, before suddenly adding excitedly, "Oh wait, now I remember. It's at the Ángel Montaña Misión in Palos Verdes Estates. And I think that it *is* tonight. I feel like I remember her complaining that it would take forever to get out there on a Tuesday night."

Jessie looked over at Reid.

"How long will it take us to get there?" she asked.

"From here at this time of night," he said, "Probably an hour at least."

"Then we better get moving."

*

They made it in forty-eight minutes.

157

Reid used his siren until they got to the border of Torrance and Palos Verdes, about three miles from the venue. Then he switched to flashing lights only and ordered all other vehicles to do the same. By the time they reached the bottom of the large hill where Ángel Montaña Misión was situated, even the lights were shut off.

Worried that she might not have a cell connection when they got higher in the hills, Jessie shot a quick text to Ryan: *Found likely suspect location. Could be out of coverage range for a while. Will reach out when able. Keep Hannah and yourself safe. I love you.*

She got a return text seconds later that was simple and straightforward. *Be careful. I love you too.* Feeling unburdened, she shoved the phone in her pocket and focused on the task ahead.

After getting up the winding road as fast as they safely could, they pulled up on the edge of the road just before the entrance of the venue. There were two vehicles already waiting there. With the additional two that had accompanied Reid's car from the Fairfax district, that made five in total.

"What's the situation?" he asked the assembled officers once they'd hopped out. Jessie remained silent, taking everything in.

"We did as you asked," said Sergeant Hughes, the Palos Verdes Estates Police Department officer in charge of the scene. "The area is secured so that she can't get out of the place by car. Escape by foot is another matter. There are several hiking trails that pass along the edge of the property. If she's aware of them, she could slip by in the dark."

"Hopefully it won't come to that," Reid said. "Nobody has approached the venue, correct?"

"No, Detective," Hughes assured him, "though I had trouble convincing my people that someone shouldn't go in wearing plainclothes just to keep an eye on things. Why can't they?"

"All the murders have occurred later at night," Reid explained. "If there's no imminent threat to guests, we don't want to do anything that will tip her off to our presence."

"But if they're in plainclothes, that shouldn't be an issue," Sergeant Hughes countered.

"Everyone at this party is supposed to be wearing outfits from an 18th century ball," Jessie said, speaking for the first time. "Anyone not dressed like someone from that era is going to look out of place."

"But *you're* going in?" Hughes challenged.

"We spoke to the facility manager on the drive over," she said. "He's set aside some server uniforms for us. Hopefully that will help us

158

blend in. If you want to select a couple of officers you think can stay low-profile, we'll bring them along as backup."

Hughes pointed at two officers. One was a woman, a petite brunette named Chavez with an impressive scowl. The other was a lanky guy named Coyle with sun-bleached hair. Jessie thought they were solid choices. Both looked young, like they could pass as twenty-something actors working as catering servers to make ends meet.

"Chavez and Coyle, you're with these folks," he ordered. "Take off your uniforms out here."

As they undressed, Jessie gave them the rundown.

"Our suspect is Sloane Baker," she said, showing them the woman's ID photo on her phone. "She's the photographer for the event. We believe she's killed three people on each of the last three nights. She sprays them in the face with some kind of acid to disable them, and then injects them in the neck with drain cleaner. Do not approach her if it can be avoided and if you must, do so with extreme caution. I'm not kidding. This acid alone is incapacitating—it melts the skin off faces. Got it?"

Both officers nodded, though Coyle's eyes were wide with astonishment. Chavez looked more taciturn.

"Our goal here is to get her in custody quietly and without incident," Jessie continued. "The last thing we need is her seeing us, panicking, and running around a crowded party, spraying acid in people's faces. So make yourselves scarce until told otherwise. Detective Reid will be monitoring events from the security office while the rest of us look for Baker. He'll have access to multiple camera angles and can direct us as needed. Any questions?"

Neither officer had any.

"All right then," Reid said, taking over, "let's move out."

CHAPTER THIRTY TWO

Sloane could barely control her excitement.

For the last three nights, she'd simply waited at the victims' homes and completed the Rebalancing there. But this evening would be different.

This time, she would eliminate the offending individual at her *own* event. That way, all of Janet Goodsen's guests would get to watch her face melt in real time, as if she was the Wicked Witch of the West. They would be able to observe her death spasms, horrified by the sight of her but too scared to help; not that there was anything they could do anyway.

The trick was to complete her task without being seen, but still keep close enough to other people so that she could shove the dying woman into their sightline. Then she would sneak around and join the crowd, gasping in shock and disgust along with them. She might even take a few photos to share with the police when they conducted their investigation.

Carrying this secret knowledge around with her, aware that within mere minutes, she would be changing the course of multiple lives, was almost too much too bear. She felt like a bottle of soda that had been shaken violently. If she didn't keep the top on tight, she feared she might explode.

As she wandered among the guests, snapping photos, she tried to maintain her persona. She was the bland woman that no one paid attention to, who blended into the background, almost invisible. She listened to nearby guests gossiping, oblivious to her presence, saying nasty things they'd never speak out loud if they thought someone who mattered might hear.

But she never lost sight of Janet Goodsen. She kept looking for the perfect moment to make her move. And then, an hour into the party, it finally came. Goodsen walked off alone, away from any other guests. Sloane, on the other side of the venue, snapped one last photo for an elderly couple who looked like they might collapse under the weight of their costumes, and then darted off after Goodsen, trying desperately to both catch up to the woman and stifle the giggle gurgling up in her throat.

*

Jessie buttoned up the red jacket on her server uniform and looked at the others as they stood in the crowded security office. They all looked like they could credibly pass for wait staff, though she and Kat would have to be cautious as Sloane had seen them at the bakery earlier that day. They couldn't afford to be recognized, so both altered their look slightly. Jessie put her hair back in a bun and Kat brushed her hair so that it covered much of her face.

Reid stood at the bank of monitors. Jessie had convinced him to run point, teasing him that none of the uniforms would fit him and even if they did, no one would buy him as a struggling waiter. She didn't mention the other reason she didn't want him out there. After what he'd told her about his heart condition and his seemingly repeated shortness of breath, she worried what would happen if things got ugly out there.

"Let's split up," she said. "Everyone take a food tray. Try to avoid eye contact with guests. Don't get noticed. Don't be obvious when you talk on the radio. If you see Sloane Baker, alert the rest of us. Don't take any action alone. Keep a safe distance at all times. Everyone clear?"

Kat, Chavez, and Coyle nodded.

Then she pointed at a poster she'd pulled off the wall as they walked into the place. It was an elaborate one-sheet, designed to look like something one might see in a movie theater, with the Goodsens standing back-to-back, posing like they were the stars of a James Bond film.

"If you see either of these people, alert the rest of us," she said before turning to Reid. "Any sign of Baker yet?"

"Nope," he said, not looking up from the monitors. "But that's not a surprise. This place is big and there are lots of dark corners."

"Okay then," she said, not exactly heartened by that news. The time had come. She opened the office door and led them out.

The facility manager guided them to the kitchen, handing each of them a tray of hors d'oeuvres. Jessie took hers and followed a real server out the swinging doors.

She'd been so busy prepping for what they had to do that she hadn't bothered to take in her surroundings. But now, as she stepped out into

161

the mission courtyard, her breath was taken away. Even under such stress, she couldn't help but appreciate the place.

Everywhere she looked, she saw something impressive. The mission walls were decorated with murals, some of which may have been as old as the structure itself. The tops of the walls were partially carved out with ornate designs that seemed to tell biblical stories. The floor, both indoors and out, was a mix of different styles of tile, also clearly curated for maximum artistic effect.

Whole sections of the facility were cordoned off, likely because the tiles and walls were too delicate to survive extended interaction with humans. The fountain in the center of the main courtyard was defined by an elaborate ten-foot cross sculpture from which water gurgled out the top.

The hundreds of guests dressed like they belonged in the court of Louis XVI both added to and detracted from the majesty of the place. The outfits definitely created the sense that she had traveled back in time. But it also felt borderline disrespectful. This had once been a place of worship. That it was being used for such a vulgar, over-the-top event seemed somehow wrong. However, as she looked around, that wasn't Jessie's primary concern.

As beautiful as Ángel Montaña Misión was, it was also a potential deathtrap. The facility was massive, with long, poorly lit interior corridors and outdoor, covered walkways that were completely hidden in shadows. According to the site diagram the facility manager had shown them, there were multiple alcoves, sitting rooms, and gardens, all excellent places for someone to lie in wait.

Jessie tried not to think about that, and instead made her way through the throngs of people, looking for any sign of Sloane Baker. She especially kept an eye out for any flashes that might indicate a picture was being taken. Of course, it didn't take long to realize that was a useless endeavor. Cell phone pictures were being taken left and right. There were flashes everywhere.

She walked around as casually as she could, offering obligatory smiles to the guests who picked stuffed mushrooms off her tray. One woman tried to get her attention to ask for a drink, but she continued on, pretending that she hadn't heard her and ignoring the woman as she said something that sounded like "well, I never!"

She rounded the corner from the main courtyard to a long walkway that ran along the outside of one of the mission walls. Proceeding down the walkway, she navigated small pockets of revelers, looking for either

Sloane or the Goodsens. She was about to enter the main ballroom to search there when she noticed three people standing at the end of the walkway, where it dead-ended at an overlook next to the edge of a cliff. A couple with their back to her was speaking to a man by himself. She squinted at the man. He looked liked he might be Nicholas Goodsen.

She hurried over, speaking into her earpiece as she approached.

"I may have a visual on the husband," she muttered. "Back left corner of the venue. No sign of the wife. Going to engage now."

When she arrived, all three people looked over at her, surprised at how a mere server seemed to be inserting herself into their conversation.

"I think we're all fine for now," the solo man said. "You can take your mushrooms elsewhere.

"Mr. Goodsen?" she said, adopting what she hoped was a polite, subservient tone.

"Yes?"

"I'm terribly sorry to bother you but the facility manager had a question for Mrs. Goodsen. Is she available?"

"She's otherwise engaged at the moment," he said. "Can I help?"

"I'm afraid he specifically said that he needed Mrs. Goodsen. He was insistent that I find her."

"If it's that important, you can tell me," Goodsen said haughtily. "After all, I'm paying for this whole evening."

Jessie debated how best to handle this. Being honest with the guy would likely make things worse. If he freaked out and Sloane Baker was around to see it, who knows what she'd do? Ultimately, she motioned for Goodsen to step to the side with her, out of earshot of the couple he was with.

"I'm not positive but I believe this may be related to a surprise your wife has planned for you," she whispered conspiratorially. "That's why the manager needs her. If she's indisposed and you can direct me to her, I can let her know diplomatically."

That seemed to alleviate his concerns. He even smiled slightly.

"I see. She went to the ladies' room," he said, pointing back in the direction from which Jessie had just come.

"Thank you, sir. I'll go collect her. However, you may want to go to the security office just in case. The manager is there now. If he can use your assistance, he'll let you know. If he shoos you away, you'll know why."

"I'll do that," he said, now seemingly eager to go to the office.

Jessie waited for him to cut through the ballroom and disappear from sight before she headed to the ladies' room.

"Nicholas Goodsen is heading to the office," she said into her earpiece. "Once he arrives, he should be kept there for his own protection."

"Understood," Reid said in her ear. "Where are you headed?"

"Goodsen said his wife went to the restroom on the west side of the venue. I'm going there now. Any sign of Baker?"

"I'm in the ballroom," Chavez said. "She's not in here."

"Same in the central courtyard," Kat added. "It's crowded but there's no sign of her."

"I'm on the back veranda," Coyle said. "I just got here, but so far I don't see her."

Jessie could feel the apprehension rising in her chest. Time was running short. Sloane could act at any moment. She hurriedly pushed her way back through the endless crowd of guests until she could step off the walkway and move along the covered hallway that now ran parallel to it. The hall was in shadows and she was tempted to use her flashlight but worried it would draw unwanted attention.

She reached the ladies' room and was about to open the door when she decided to dump the stuffed mushrooms in the nearby trash can. As she yanked open the door, she held up the tray with her other hand, using it as a potential shield in case there was anyone inside with a bottle of acid spray.

The area near the sinks was empty. She was tempted to crouch down to look under the stalls but didn't want to put herself in a vulnerable position. Instead ,she called out.

"Is Janet Goodsen in here?" she asked in a loud whisper.

For a moment there was silence and she feared she'd missed Goodsen entirely. Then a peeved voice in the last stall replied.

"Who is that?" she demanded.

"I'm working with the venue ma'am," Jessie said vaguely, hiding the relief in her voice. "Can you please come out as soon as possible? The facility manager needs you in the security office."

"What is this all about?"

"I'll explain once you're out ma'am. But he told me it's quite time-sensitive."

"All right, hold on," Goodsen said, clearly frustrated.

The toilet flushed and Jessie used the noise to mask her voice as she updated the others.

"Located Janet Goodsen in the restroom. Will proceed to take her to the security office momentarily."

A few seconds later, Goodsen emerged, wearing a gold-embroidered gown with a wide hooped skirt and a gathered bodice. Her face was pinched, making the caked-on makeup crack slightly. She waddled over to the sink and washed her hands. When she was done, she turned to Jessie.

"Explain the situation, please," she instructed more than asked.

Jessie decided the time for diplomatic deception had come to an end. She needed to be straight with her.

"Mrs. Goodsen," she began. "I'm not actually a server for the venue. My name is Jessie Hunt. I'm a criminal profiler with the LAPD. We're investigating a series of murders over the last few nights that we suspect were committed by your photographer, Sloane Baker. We have reason to believe she may be targeting you or your husband next."

"What?" Goodsen said, clearly not processing it all. Her pinched face had gone slack.

"I'll explain more later, but right now, we need to get you to the security office. We haven't been able to find Baker and until we do, you're at risk. So I need you to come with me."

"Okay," Goodsen said vaguely, all traces of arrogance suddenly gone, now replaced by fear. Despite that, Jessie still wasn't convinced she understood the magnitude of the situation.

"Try to act normal," she ordered. "It's possible that Baker may have a spray bottle of some kind filled with acid. If she sees you, we don't want to give her reason to be suspicious or act rashly. Do you understand?"

Goodsen nodded.

"Okay," Jessie said, hoping she sounded confident. "Let's go."

She opened the door and poked her head out. The hallway looked deserted. She motioned for Goodsen to follow her. The woman stepped out into the hall and the door had just closed behind her when Jessie heard a voice she recognized.

"Ms. Hunt," Sloane Baker said, stepping out from an alcove Jessie hadn't noticed before. "What a pleasant surprise to see you."

165

CHAPTER THIRTY THREE

Jessie froze in place.

The woman had an unnatural, twisted smile on her face. She was wearing a bland floral dress with a gray sweater over it and holding something behind her back. In the darkened hallway, Jessie couldn't identify what it was, though she had her suspicions. Behind her, she could almost hear Janet Goodsen shaking. Swallowing hard, she made every effort to seem like nothing was out of the ordinary.

"Sloane, is it?" she said, impressed with how unflustered her voice was, "funny running into you out here. Are you working this event too?"

"I am," Baker replied, her eyes blazing with an intensity that had been nowhere in sight at the bakery. "Is the profiling business so bad that you have to take catering gigs?"

"No," Jessie said, forcing a chuckle. "I'm actually undercover. We arrested Jeanie Court as you know, but we also found some overlap between the murder victims and a few folks at this event. My captain thinks the killer might be one of the guests here tonight. I'm skeptical but I'm not the one in charge so I have to run it down. You know the drill, always beholden to the boss, right?"

"Right," Baker said, clearly not convinced. A long silence followed in which the only sounds Jessie heard were the distant chatter of guests and Janet Goodsen's heavy, shallow breathing only inches from her. She finally broke the quiet.

"You haven't seen anyone suspicious, have you?" she asked.

Baker's twisted smile turned into more of a malevolent grimace.

"To be honest, Ms. Hunt, you're the most suspicious person I've seen here tonight."

Jessie was still trying to think of a response when Baker yanked her arm from behind her back and raised it up. She was holding something in her hand, but it was hard to identify it in the dark. Jessie lifted the serving tray to protect her face, but before she could block her eyes, she heard a click. A flash of bright light illuminated the hallway, temporarily blinding her. She took a step back and shoved Janet Goodsen toward the restroom door.

"Get back inside!" she shouted.

When her vision cleared, she found that Baker had disappeared. She unholstered her weapon with one hand as she pushed Goodsen back into the bathroom.

"What was that?" the woman asked in a quavering voice.

"It was her camera," Jessie said quickly, scanning the hallway for movement. "Stay in the restroom. Lock the door from the inside. If that's not possible, check the maintenance closet for a broom to shove through the handle to block the door. Lock yourself in a stall. Don't come out until the police come for you."

"Please don't leave me," the woman begged.

"I have to," Jessie said, "People are in danger."

She shut the door and told herself to breathe slowly so she could hear any movement nearby. After a couple of seconds, a loud voice could be heard from the direction of the walkway where she'd found Nicholas Goodsen earlier.

"Hey," someone yelled, clearly put out. That voice was followed by several others who sounded similarly aggrieved. She headed in that direction.

"I located Baker outside the west side women's bathroom," she said into her earpiece as she moved. "She's on the move, headed toward the northwest corner. Janet Goodsen is hiding in the restroom."

"Converge on the area," Reid said in her ear. "Chavez, secure Janet Goodsen. Coyle and Kat, assist Hunt. Proceed with extreme caution."

Jessie emerged from the unlit hall onto the exterior walkway, where several people looked flustered, though not injured.

"Which way did she go?' she yelled.

One man in a silver tuxedo pointed to an opening in the walkway across from him. She ran over and discovered that the opening was actually the first step of a stone staircase that curled down and around the corner to what appeared to be a hiking trail below.

"She's gone down a staircase connected to the west walkway," she said. "It leads to a trail at the bottom."

"Wait for backup, Hunt," Reid ordered.

"The lights from the venue don't extend that far down. If I wait, she'll be able to get away in the dark. I'm going in."

"Wait," Reid shouted as she started down the steps. She yanked the earpiece out. The sound of his voice would be too distracting as she tried to listen for movement.

Quieting her own beating heart was another matter. With each step, she reminded herself to breathe long and slow. In one hand she had her gun, in the other the serving tray. After a few more steps, she came across Baker's camera, lying on the grass to the right of the steps.

Suspecting what the woman might be holding instead, she decided that light was more important than the minimal protection of the tray. It wouldn't do her much good if Baker snuck up on her with a spray bottle or syringe before she knew she was there.

She placed the tray gently on the step and pulled out her flashlight for the last few stairs. When she reached the bottom, where the stones gave way to the dirt trail, she shined her flashlight straight ahead. She could see that the path was about seven feet wide. On the other side of it, there was a narrow line of trees and bushes that ended abruptly at what looked to be a sheer drop-off.

She flashed the light to the left and right but saw no one. Pointing the light at the ground, she saw that the dirt to the right was undisturbed. To the left were footprints from what appeared to be heeled shoes.

She moved in that direction with her gun raised, shining the flashlight back and forth across the trail, intermittently checking for footprints. After about five paces she saw that the prints changed, indicating that Baker had removed her heels and was now barefoot.

Jessie could still hear Reid's voice shouting in her earpiece, even though it was now down by her shoulder. She wanted to shut it off entirely, concerned that Baker could hear it on the otherwise near-silent path. But doing so would require her to stash either her gun or flashlight and that wasn't going to happen.

She proceeded on. After another step, the flashlight caught a flicker from something shiny about ten feet ahead, under a bush. It took her a second to realize that it was one of Baker's shoes. She was just starting to move toward it when she heard a rustle behind her.

A shiver shot up from the base of her back to her neck and her fingers started to tingle. The sound had come from less than five feet away. She knew who it was. Sloane Baker was behind her and close enough to spray her, if not inject her. There was no way she could spin around, locate the woman, and shoot her before she was attacked. There was no way she could dive far enough away. With no other option, she began to speak.

"Don't do anything foolish, Sloane," she said slowly.

For a second there was no reply. When the woman did finally speak, her voice was unexpectedly calm. It was also very close.

"You haven't given me much choice, Ms. Hunt," she said. "My back's kind of up against the wall here."

Jessie allowed a second for her brain to catch up to her fast-beating heart.

"It doesn't have to be, Sloane," Jessie said, using the woman's name again, hoping to find some way to connect to her. "You can put down what you're holding and surrender. I know that whatever led you to this moment must have been very traumatic. You deserve the chance to explain how we got here. But that can only happen if I feel that I'm not in danger."

"But you *are* in danger," Baker said flatly. "You put yourself there. You didn't have to follow me. I was only doing what had to be done. These people *deserve* what they got. I was only rebalancing things. If you had let me be, I'd be halfway down the hill by now. But you didn't. And now here we are. And if I can't get away, I may have to do the next best thing."

"What's that?" Jessie asked.

But she knew the answer already. Baker had the emotionless affect of someone who had given up, who was no longer scared and just wanted to go out in a blaze of glory. So now Jessie was merely stalling, trying to find a way out of this that didn't involve being disfigured or worse.

"Take you with me," Baker said, just as Jessie suspected she would.

She stalled for time, fearing even before she spoke that the tactic wouldn't succeed.

"How about I put my gun down so you don't feel like your back is against the wall?" she offered.

"I think we both know it's too late for that."

Jessie could almost feel Baker's finger on the trigger of the spray bottle. She knew she was out of time. So she played the one last card that came to mind.

"Was it too late when you had to leave Temple University for a semester?" she asked quietly.

"What?"

"What happened that night?" Jessie demanded. "What was so bad that you had to drop out of school?"

169

"You don't know what your talki—!" Baker started to shout. But before she could finish the sentence, Jessie spun around, trying to simultaneously locate her with her gun and flashlight.

The distraction had provided her a moment's advantage, but too late, she realized it wouldn't be enough. As she pointed her gun in Baker's general direction, she heard the distinct sound of a liquid being sprayed from a bottle. At exactly the same time, she saw a burst of movement to her right, as something blasted out from the wooded hill and slammed into Baker.

CHAPTER THIRTY FOUR

Involuntarily, she snapped her eyes shut and stumbled backward, hoping to clear herself from the area where the spray had been dispersed. When she thought she was far enough away, she opened her eyes again.

She could see. And she felt no burning sensation on her face or hands. It seemed that she'd escaped the acid's reach. But Sloane Baker was no longer anywhere in sight on the path. In the darkness, she heard a loud grunting sound and aimed her gun and flashlight across the trail looking for any sign of the woman. That's when she saw it.

Baker was on the edge of the trail, with her back pressed up against a tree by someone that Jessie quickly identified. Baker's fingers were pressed tight against the trigger of the spray bottle by Kat, whose hand was clasped over them, trying to prevent her from squeezing again. Kat's body was blocking Jessie from getting a good shot at the other woman.

"Duck, Kat!" Jessie yelled, though it was apparent that any adjustment in her friend's position might allow Baker to free her hand and spray again. Suddenly, Baker snapped her mouth forward as if she was trying to take a bite out of Kat's face. Her friend yanked her head back. But in doing so, she lost her grip on Baker's fingers. She raised the bottle and aimed it Kat's face.

There was no time to yell "duck" again. Jessie didn't even try. Instead, she pulled the trigger. The gunshot exploded in the air. For a second nothing seemed to happen. The she saw the spray bottle drop from Baker's hand as she howled in pain. Her arm rested limply at her side. Blood poured down from a spot just below her shoulder.

She stumbled backward slightly and lost her balance. She tried to find solid footing, but she was too close to the edge of the trail, where the trees and bushes gave way to the cliff side. All at once she started sliding down the edge of the hill. She was almost out of sight when she reached out and grabbed Kat by the pant leg. Then she disappeared from sight.

Kat yelped as her feet came out from under her. She was being dragged to the edge. Jessie dropped the gun and flashlight and charged

171

after her. She dived toward her friend's outstretched hand. But before they made contact, Kat disappeared over the cliff side.

Jessie scrambled forward, hoping against hope. She peered over edge into the darkness. At first, she saw nothing. Then the moon emerged from behind a cloud and the scene below her cleared. Kat Gentry was just three feet below her, clinging to the narrow trunk of a tree growing out of the side of the hill. She groaned softly.

About forty feet below her was Sloane Baker. She had landed face-up on a boulder. Her right leg was twisted awkwardly beneath her body. Her neck was bent in an unnatural position. Blood was seeping out from under her head. She wasn't moving.

Jessie returned her attention to Kat and scooted out as far from the edge of the cliff as she could without losing leverage.

"Are you hurt?" she asked.

"I don't think so," Kat moaned more than said. "But I'm losing my grip on this tree."

Somewhere high above them, she heard Officer's Coyle's voice yelling, "Hunt, where are you?"

"At the bottom of the steps!" she yelled back before returning her attention to Kat. She extended her arm and gave an order. "Grab it. I'll hold you steady while you use me to pull yourself up."

"Are you sure you can do that?" Kat asked through gritted teeth. "I don't want you tumbling down past me."

Jessie looked her best friend square in the eyes, buoyed by adrenaline and certainty.

"Kat," she said without any hesitation. "Don't worry. I've got your back."

CHAPTER THIRTY FIVE

It took some cajoling, but eventually the EMTs let them leave Ángel Montaña Misión on their own.

Other than the cuts Kat had sustained when she tumbled over the side of the cliff, there were no injuries to speak of. Jessie had emerged completely unscathed. The same couldn't be said for Sloane Baker. The paramedic who treated Kat told them he thought Baker had likely died instantly upon impact, due to a broken neck.

On the drive back to the city, Jessie texted Ryan: *Case solved. Killer didn't make it. Heading home now. Can't wait to see you.*

The reply came quickly: *Same. Glad it's over. Will wait up. Hannah is too. She wants to say goodnight before bed. Seems to be making a real effort. I love you.*

She responded in kind: *I love you too.* With her most important communication taken care of, they called Decker. He sounded ecstatic, almost inappropriately so.

"The press is singing our praises," he said. "The online headlines all say things like 'LAPD gets justice for Jax.' Some of the reports specifically mention HSS. This is huge. Now if we can just nail the Night Hunter, the bigwigs at headquarters won't be able to touch us. They wouldn't dare shut down the unit that saved the city from two menaces threatening it at the same time."

"That's great, Captain," Reid said wearily. No one commented on his seeming outsized optimism.

"Oh, that reminds me," Decker said, oblivious to his detective's tone. "Hunt, we've got two units circling your block in ten minutes intervals. Until we catch this guy, you'll have round the clock protection, even at Trembley's funeral on Saturday."

"Thanks, Captain," she said, embarrassed to admit that she'd forgotten about the young detective who had been murdered only forty-eight hours prior. The thought of standing over his grave mere days from now was more than she could deal with in that moment. Reid glanced over at her, obviously sensing that she was on the edge of collapsing from fatigue.

"I'm going to drop these two off at home and come in to finish the paperwork, Captain," he said. "I'll see you in a few."

"Sounds good," Decker replied before adding, "Hold on, Winslow wanted to add something. I'm going to connect you to him now."

Jessie looked at the time. It was past 9 p.m. She was starting to wonder if Jamil ever slept.

"Hello," he said after just one ring.

"What are you still doing there?" she asked.

"Just wrapping a few things up before I go home," he said nonchalantly. "I'm expanding the surveillance camera range in my search for the Night Hunter's car. Detective Hernandez is certain the man's using an old clunker like he did before, one without GPS that he likely bought for cash. If I can get even one database hit in the area where Hallie Douglas was killed, I can start to extrapolate out from there."

"Do you think that will work?" Kat asked from the backseat.

"Not really," Jamil admitted. "But it can't hurt. That's not the reason I wanted to talk to you though. I guess it doesn't matter now but I did a little digging and found out why Sloane Baker left school for a semester."

"I won't ask what you mean by 'digging,'" Jessie said, sensing some of his tactics might have skirted the edge of legality. "What did you find?"

"She was arrested by campus police for stalking the girlfriend of a senior she'd become obsessed with. The cops thought she'd even broken into the girl's apartment to steal some personal items, though they couldn't prove it."

"I never saw any police report or court filings," Reid said.

"That's because she agreed to a deal," Jamil said. "She would leave school until the guy and his girlfriend graduated in the spring. If there were no additional incidents during that time, she could be re-admitted for her senior year and have the record of the incident sealed. That's what happened."

"It looks like she stayed on the straight and narrow for over a decade before she snapped again," Kat noted. "I wonder what pushed her to the breaking point."

Jessie thought back to the photo she'd found in the bedside table drawer at Baker's apartment. An unexpected pang of pity came over her. Sloane Baker may have gotten back into school, but she clearly didn't get the help she needed. Ultimately it took another decade for the

174

illness that had first flowered in college to re-emerge. Maybe if someone had reached out to her earlier it wouldn't have come to this.

"I suspect the breaking point has something to do with the guy with his arm around her and his face scratched out in that picture," she said. "But I suspect there were lots of smaller breaking points along the way. I doubt we'll ever know for sure."

"She didn't say anything on that trail with you?" Kat asked.

"She said the victims deserved it and that she was rebalancing things, but the situation escalated before we could really get into it."

They were approaching Jessie's house, so they said their goodbyes to Jamil. Reid drove up the block slowly so that they could look for anything out of the ordinary. But there was nothing obvious; no old men lurking in bushes, no thirty-year-old cars parked up the block. Everything looked like it usually did. He pulled up in front of her house.

"So will I see you in the office tomorrow?" he asked as she got out of the car.

"I'll have to stop by at some point to write a report on the weapon discharge but probably not until later in the day," she said. "The new semester started today, and I have my first lecture tomorrow. I told Decker that he had me until classes started up again and I meant it."

"Got it," Reid said, sounding slightly wounded. Jessie suddenly felt guilty at her harsh refusal.

"How about you call if you need anything? We'll do things virtually. You think you can handle that, old man?"

"Another reason I plan to retire soon," he muttered, "you kids and your new-fangled technology. I've decided—as soon as the Night Hunter is caught, and the department gives HSS a parade—I'm definitely turning in my shield."

Jessie smiled. As much as she would miss the guy's crusty professionalism, she thought he was making a wise move.

"We'll talk tomorrow," she told him. As she closed the door, Kat got out of the backseat.

"Just give us a minute," she said to Reid, before motioning for Jessie to join her on the sidewalk. Only when they were out of earshot did she continue. "I know that you and I aren't great, but are we at least better than we were?"

Jessie looked at her friend's pleading eyes and wanted so badly to say yes. They had broken the ice in the police station courtyard but there were still huge chunks they had to navigate.

175

"We're getting there," she finally said. "Let's get together later this week when we're not so rushed, maybe have lunch. We'll talk things through. That's all I can offer right now."

"I'll take it," Kat said, forcing a pained grin. "Stay safe, okay?"

Jessie nodded, then conceded slightly and gave her friend a hug. Kat returned it, gripping tightly. Then she got in the car and Reid pulled out. Jessie watched the taillights fade into the distance. As they rounded the corner, she saw a squad car heading toward her.

It must be time for the "every-ten-minutes" drive-by.

She waved and they did the same as they passed by. Then she heard the familiar sound of multiple locks on her front door sliding open. She turned to see Ryan open the door and ease down the first step.

He looked wiped out and was leaning more heavily than usual on his cane. Despite that, he had a broad, mischievous smile on his face, as if he was hiding some special secret. She was tempted to try uncover it, but decided tonight wasn't the night.

"Hello, stranger," she said walking up the white, stone path. The January winds had swept away the leaves and it looked unusually pristine. He met her halfway and they kissed. His lips were soft and warm.

"I've been waiting all day to do that," he whispered in her ear.

"There are other things I've been waiting to do," she whispered back.

His eyes widened in happy surprise.

"Then we should go in," he said, looking like a little boy who'd just been promised extra candy.

They were just reaching the front step when Jessie heard a bark. She turned around to find the retired professor, Delia Morris, walking her dog, Grant. She was walking more briskly than usual.

"Hi Delia," she called out, "Everything okay?"

But she could tell immediately that it was not. The woman's white hair, always a bit of a bird's nest, spilled down in front of her face. She was clutching her coat tightly around her with gloved hands and kept looking nervously back at the hedge that separated Jessie's yard from the next-door neighbor's. Grant looked agitated too and wouldn't stop barking.

"What's wrong?" Jessie asked, motioning for the old woman to come over, even as she undid the holster clasp on her gun.

"I saw someone on the other side of those bushes," Delia whispered hoarsely, too frantic to even make eye contact. "He looked very suspicious."

Under normal circumstances, Jessie might be inclined to assume that this was related to the woman's slipping cognitive function. But Delia's issues were memory related. When it came to moment-to-moment acuity, she was still pretty sharp.

"What did he look like?" Ryan asked, taking it seriously too.

"I couldn't see him clearly," Delia admitted, her voice choked with fear. "It's dark. He looks older and he was hunched over. But what really worried me was that he seemed to have some kind of binoculars or something. He was looking at your house, dear."

Jessie and Ryan exchanged looks.

"Do you have your gun?" she asked him.

"It's in the bedroom," he said.

"Okay," she replied, her mind revving up from its state of hibernation, "the squad car just went by. The next one won't cycle by for ten minutes so you should call this in. I'll go check it out."

"No," he protested. "You look exhausted. I'll do it. You go in and watch Hannah."

Jessie looked at him, unsure how to say what she needed to, especially with Delia right there. She could see how determined he was to catch the Night Hunter, to redeem himself. And she didn't want to embarrass him. But he was in no condition to go searching around in the dark. Before she could reply, she caught the look in his eye and knew she didn't have to say any of it. He got it even if he hated it.

"Never mind," he said quickly. "Just come inside. I'll call for backup."

"He could be gone by then," she told him. "This might be our only chance. I won't get close. I'll cross the street to get a good angle."

"Who could be gone?" Delia asked in a panicked voice that was partially drowned out by Grant's continued barking. "What's going on?"

Jessie looked at Ryan and could tell he was thinking the same thing as her.

"Everything's going to be okay, Delia," she said soothingly before turning to Ryan. "Take her in with you. We don't need him using innocent bystanders as bait."

"What is happening?" Delia pleaded.

177

"Come with me," Ryan told her, taking her arm and leading her back up the path to the house. "There's nothing to worry about. We're just going to have you stay at our place for a few minutes until we have everything under control."

"Can Grant come?" she asked meekly, apparently unaware that she was already dragging the little guy along by the leash.

"Of course," Ryan said. "Maybe if you picked him up, he wouldn't be so scared?"

Delia nodded and bent over to grab him. As she did, Ryan mouthed the words "be careful" to Jessie. She nodded that she would.

"Make sure to call for that backup," she instructed.

"Yes, ma'am," he said, saluting her before accompanying Delia to the house.

Jessie waited until they were inside, and she heard the door locks slide shut before turning her attention back to the hedge. Only then did she unholster her weapon. Without ever taking her eyes off the area that Delia had pointed to, she walked slowly across the street to the opposing sidewalk. She reminded herself to breathe, even as did her best to ignore the creeping sensation that started to grip her.

Even though she was young, in good shape, alert, and armed, she felt like this was the Night Hunter's game and she was just a pawn.

CHAPTER THIRTY SIX

Ryan made sure the security system was activated before turning his attention to Delia and her barking dog.

"Can I get you some water?' he asked.

"That would be lovely," she said, her eyes downcast and hesitant as she moved forward. "And perhaps something for Grant to nibble on- maybe a piece of cheese or two?"

"Of course," he said, starting for the kitchen.

"What's going on?"

He turned around to see Hannah standing in her bedroom doorway with a concerned look. He looked back at Delia. With her face covered in hair, he couldn't see her expression, but he didn't want to upset her any more than necessary.

"Why don't you go have a seat at the breakfast table?" he said. "I'll be right back to get that stuff for you and Grant."

Delia nodded and Ryan limped over to Hannah.

"Delia saw someone suspicious outside," he said quietly. "I'm about to call it in. We brought her inside just to be safe."

"*We?*" Hannah repeated.

Again, the sense of shame and helplessness welled up in him. His girlfriend was outside facing down a threat while he was reduced to getting treats for little dog. He couldn't decide if he was more consumed by fury or disgust at himself for putting them all in this position. But there was no point in sugar-coating any of it for Hannah. She deserved the truth, devoid of his attempts to protect his pride.

"Jessie just got home. She insisted on checking it out, which is why I want to call for backup. Why don't you come out here with us for now, just until this is resolved?"

"Okay," Hannah said without objection. "Just let me get my phone really quick."

She returned to her room and Ryan reached into his pocket for his phone. Then he remembered he'd left it on the coffee table. He started in that direction when he heard a growl.

He looked to see that Delia hadn't yet moved into the kitchen. She was still standing in the foyer. Grant was looking up at her with his teeth bared. That's when he noticed the syringe in her right hand.

He stared at her. Through the tangled hair, he could see a pair of cold, malevolent eyes gazing back at him. He recognized them instantly. They were the same eyes that had looked at him impassively on the street outside the Santa Monica hostel where Alan Trembley had been murdered. They were the eyes of the Night Hunter.

Ryan's heart turned cold and his mouth went dry at the same time. He felt like his feet were made of stone.

"I see the charade is up, dear," the man said, dropping the hoarse, high-pitched whisper and moving the hair out of his face, "excuse me, I suppose I should address you as detective."

It was only then that Ryan noticed blood dripping down the man's forehead from little strands of what looked like skin. In that moment he realized the Night Hunter wasn't wearing a wig. He was wearing Delia's hair, complete with her scalp.

"Where's Delia?" Ryan croaked, though he already knew enough to guess. He didn't really care what the man said. He was just hoping for an extra second to will his mind and body to unfreeze, to come up with a plan.

Ryan had no weapon. He had no phone. He was shaky on his feet. The Night Hunter was only ten feet away and though he might be old, that didn't mean he was weak. And from the video footage Ryan had seen of Hallie Douglas's murder, all it would take was a prick from that needle to incapacitate him.

Besides, there was Hannah to think of. He was responsible for her and based on the man's most recent victim—her lookalike—she was in more danger than anyone. This wasn't a time to fight. It was a time to run. But where?

"Um," Hannah said from behind him, having just left her room.

"That's him," Ryan said slowly. Even before he finished speaking, the Night Hunter had started advancing toward them. Ryan watched him approach, but just like the night that Alan Trembley died, he felt panic overtake him. He couldn't move.

Out of the corner of his eye he saw Hannah dart behind him to the left. She grabbed the closest thing of size she could find, a lamp on the table outside her room, yanked it out of the wall, and threw it.

The Night Hunter turned away, less out of fear of injury than to protect the syringe. As the base hit him in the back and smashed to the floor, Ryan's brain seemed to click on again and an idea burst to the front of it. "Get to the panic room."

Hannah understood immediately and dashed in that direction. Ryan ordered his feet to move as well, and he scuffled after her as fast as he could. By the time he got to the bookshelf opening, Hannah was already inside. Her eyes told him that the Night Hunter was right behind him.

Without aiming, he turned and swung his cane wildly behind him. The man was less than five feet away, almost close enough to inject him. But seeing the cane coming at him, the Night Hunter rocked back. He barely avoided getting hit and stumbled slightly as he tried to maintain his balance. That was all Ryan needed.

"Push the button," he yelled at Hannah as he dived through the narrow opening. Even before he hit the ground, he heard the bookshelf sliding shut. He rolled over just in time to see the Night Hunter's contorted, furious grimace right before the door closed.

The panic room lights flickered on. As Hannah helped him to his feet, they could hear the man outside, taunting them.

"You're only delaying the inevitable," he called out over the barking dog. "I've looked at the plans for this house too. I know its weaknesses. I know, for example, that the wall below this bookshelf is made of drywall, and that a small drill will penetrate it easily."

He stopped speaking and moments later they heard a yelp of pain. Grant stopped barking. Ryan and Hannah looked at each other. Neither wanted to acknowledge what had just happened.

"Can he get in here?" she asked, moving on quickly.

"Eventually, yes, but we'll be ready for him," Ryan said, sounding more confident than he felt.

He made no mention of his moment of frozen indecision seconds earlier and neither did she. He didn't even know if she'd picked up on it. Pushing the thought out of his head, he hurried over to the back wall and opened the middle of the three boxes attached to it. He pulled out the phone and handed it to her.

"Call the pre-programmed number," he instructed.

"Shouldn't you do that?" she asked.

"I'm busy right now," he said as he opened the weapons locker, took out one of the handguns, and began loading the clip. Hannah seemed satisfied with that answer and dialed the number. Within seconds, the duty officer at Central Station answered. Hannah held up the phone to Ryan's face. He identified himself and was just starting to explain their status when he heard a drill begin to penetrate the drywall. He cut his account short.

"Just send everyone. He's in the house."

"Responding now," the duty officer said. "Please stay on the line, Detective Hernandez."

"Can't do that," he said as he handed Hannah the weapon and began loading another. "Jessie Hunt is outside the house right now and she has no idea what's going on. I have to warn her."

"But Detective—,"

"Hang up," Ryan told Hannah, who cut the officer off immediately.

He was about to have her call Jessie when the Night Hunter shouted out again.

"I know your colleagues and your better half will be joining us soon," he yelled. "Unfortunately, by the time they arrive, I'll be long gone, and it will be far too late for you. I'm sorry we weren't able to have a proper jamboree, Detective, but this will have to do. By the way, have you ever heard of hydrogen cyanide?"

Ryan heard something being jammed into the drywall, followed by a loud hissing noise. His whole body went into overdrive.

"What's that?" Hannah demanded.

"Move to the back wall and hold your breath," he ordered, as he scurried to the cabinet in the back right of the room, where the gas masks were stored. He started to reach for the key on his keychain but decided there wasn't enough time.

"Step to the left," he told Hannah, then took a quick gulp of air and held his own breath. When she was clear, he raised his weapon, pointed it at the cabinet lock, and fired.

*

There was no one there.

Within seconds of crossing the street, Jessie had a direct line of sight to the hedge between her yard and her neighbor's. With the overhead street ight, it actually wasn't as dark as Delia had made it out to be. Plus, the hedge was so thin that there was no real place for anyone to hide.

Worried that the Night Hunter might have already abandoned that location and moved closer to the house, she crossed the street again back to her sidewalk. She considered walking around the side of the house but that seemed risky. In close quarters, he would have the advantage.

She started up the white, stone path to the front door when she noticed something she'd missed before. There were little smudges on the path that had seemed so pristine earlier. She bent down and touched one. It was wet and sticky. Holding her finger up to the streetlight, she thought it looked like blood. She smelled it and was even more certain.

A sudden shiver passed through her as she stood up again. Something was very wrong. She squinted at the smudges on the path more closely. They continued for several more paces toward the front door before disappearing completely. Then she realized what she was looking at: paw prints.

An image of Delia picking up Grant just before entering the house flashed through her memory. In that moment, she knew the truth and her blood ran cold. Terror rose in her chest. But even before she could attempt to contain it, the feeling dissipated on its own, as if her body knew she didn't have time for the fear.

She was just pulling out her phone to warn Ryan when she heard the sound of something shattering just inside the house. She put the phone back in her pocket, certain that the noise meant events were underway inside that would prevent him from checking texts.

She started toward the front door, and then stopped. If the Night Hunter was just inside, he'd hear the bolts unlocking and have the edge against her. Instead, she dashed over to the garage.

This alternative plan would take longer but she had no choice. The front door entry would make her a sitting duck, which wouldn't help anyone. At least this route gave her a chance.

As she entered the code on the panel on the wall adjoining the garage, she reassured herself that the people she loved were smart and resourceful and that choosing this course of action didn't mean she'd consigned them to certain death. She had to believe they were still alive in there.

After the code was accepted, another panel opened and she placed her palm on it. It took an interminable three seconds for her handprint to be approved. The garage door opened and she moved to the interior door that connected to the house.

Once that was open and she was inside the house, she pushed a different code on the panel just inside the door. That gave her ten seconds until the countermeasures activated. While she waited,

183

crouched low to the ground, a gunshot rang out. It took everything in her not to run down the hall right then. But she waited.

All the lights shut off just as an ear-splitting alarm began to sound. She rushed forward right as a red, flashing light began pulsing throughout the house. She moved quickly down the hall and poked her head into the kitchen. It was empty. She shimmied along the wall, past the sink and the dishwasher, then glanced into the living room. A shattered lamp lay in dozens of pieces on the floor. Just beyond that, in front of the bookcase in the hallway that doubled as the panic room door, was the lifeless body of Grant the poodle.

There was no one in sight. As she approached the bookcase, she heard a hissing sound. Then she noticed that just below it was a white canister that seemed to be jammed into the drywall. She bent down and saw words on the side that read: *hydrogen cyanide (2000 ppm).* The Night Hunter was poisoning her family.

She sensed movement out of the corner of her eye and looked up. An elderly man scurried from the laundry room at the end of the hall out the back door, disappearing from sight before she could fire. She stood up, using the bookcase as a shield in case he shot at her.

"Tough choice, Jessie," the man called out, barely audible over the echoing siren. "You can come after me and put me down, but if you do, that won't leave time to save your sister and your boyfriend. With the concentration of that gas, I'd say they have less than thirty seconds left. What'll it be, Jessie—love or vengeance?"

She knew this could be a trick to get her to expose herself so he could shoot her. And yet, she was still overwhelmed with rage. Everything inside her screamed that she should leap out and fire a barrage of bullets in the spot where she suspected he was hiding. She wanted to put him down. She wanted to make him pay.

But not at the price of her loved ones' lives. She wanted to believe that Ryan remembered the gas masks in the filing cabinet and that he had the key to it on him. But she couldn't take the risk. Fighting the urge to act rashly, she stayed put.

"What do you recommend?" she shouted back. But after five seconds of silence, she realized he'd only given her the ultimatum to stall her so he could escape. He knew what choice she'd make even before he asked her. Besides, she was certain that he didn't want their conflict to end with something as mundane as a gunshot.

She bent back down near the canister, trying to stay focused and ignore the ticking clock in her head. Her first instinct was to simply rip it out of the wall, but that would only expose her to the gas.

Leaning closer, she saw that there was a small knob on the back of the canister. After glancing down the hallway one more time, she put her gun on the floor and turned the knob to the right. The hissing stopped.

In the distance, she could hear the voices of officers shouting as they entered the house from the garage.

"We're in the main hallway," she called out before turning her attention to the people behind the bookshelf. "Ryan, Hannah—it's Jessie. The hallway is clear. You can come out."

There was no answer. She tried again, even louder this time.

"Are you okay?" she shouted, praying that Ryan had remembered about the gas masks in the small cabinet. Still there was no response. Her heart began to sink.

Then, quickly and silently, the bookshelf door opened.

EPILOGUE

They were both okay.

Only when they emerged unharmed and wearing gas masks did Jessie started breathing again.

It was actually Hannah who pulled *her* away from the door as Ryan closed it, reminding her that she was more at risk now than them without a mask of her own. They all rushed to the backyard, which had already been secured by several of the nearly dozen officers who had swarmed the house.

Once outside, Jessie saw that two panels of their backyard wooden fencing had been smashed, creating a section big enough to wriggle through. On the ground next to the broken wood was a shovel. Beside that was what looked to be the wig that the man had used to impersonate Delia. But as she looked closer and saw the blood, Jessie realized that it wasn't a wig at all.

Cops were now jumping over the fence to search the surrounding area. One looked like he was about to go through the hole that the Night Hunter had used to escape.

"No!" she shouted. "Seal that section of fence off. There's always the chance that he scraped himself on the way out, leaving DNA."

"The shovel too?" the officer asked.

"Sure," she told him, though she was less optimistic about that. She flashed back to the gloves that "Delia" had worn and knew she knew there wouldn't be any fingerprints. Then she turned Ryan and Hannah, who were removing their masks.

"Are you two okay?" she asked.

Hannah nodded silently. Ryan, who was still catching his breath, gave her thumbs up, though he looked less certain. She pulled them both into a hug, which lasted forever but not long enough. When they separated, Ryan offered a wry smile.

"Glad you chose love over vengeance," he said mildly.

"Yeah," Hannah agreed. "We were on pins and needles."

Jessie shook her head.

"I'm not ready for jokes just yet," she chastised.

An officer jogged over to them.

"There's no sign of any old man nearby," he said, "Any suggestions?"

Jessie closed her eyes, trying to get herself back into the right headspace. Her family was safe for the moment. She had to focus on her prey now. When she opened her eyes again, she called for several other officers to draw close. Once she had the attention of four of them, she launched in.

"With all the squad cars, sirens and alarms, there has to be a crowd gathering on the street," she said, talking as fast as her brain would allow. "He might be trying to hide among them. Look for anyone older, at least seventy, about 5'7 to 5'10, between 150 to 170 pounds, man or woman. He likes disguises."

Several of the officers had pulled out notebooks to take notes. She continued, not waiting for them to catch up.

"Have someone check the home of Delia Morris," she said, refusing to linger on the fate of the old woman. There would be time for guilt over that later. "She lives down the block. You'll find her body there. There's an outside chance he might be hiding in the house as well. More likely, he's using her car to escape the area. Have it flagged. He'll know we're looking for it. so he won't use it for long, just to get to whatever other vehicle he has stashed nearby. Once you have the make, model, and license on Morris's car, reach out to Jamil Winslow at Central Station. He's probably headed home but he'll want to go back to start searching the city camera database. Got all that?"

She watched the men furiously scribbling and hoped they had.

"Got it," one of them said and within seconds, they dispersed, leaving her alone with Hannah and Ryan, who both looked spent.

Suddenly, and all at once, the weight of everything hit her. She sat down on the steps of the back porch, silently watching an army of LAPD officers bustling about. Ryan sat down on one side of her and Hannah on the other. None of them spoke.

Jessie ran over it all in her mind. Her sister had almost died tonight, along with the man she loved. And had it happened, it would have been her fault. She had invited the wolf into their house, oblivious to his sheep's clothing.

The worst part was that if could he do it once, she was certain he could do it again. And she had no doubt that he'd try. There would be no escape from this nightmare until the Night Hunter was either in prison or dead. The realization was terrifying, but in a weird way, also clarifying.

187

This was no longer about hunkering down and defending what she had. The days of trying to turn their home into a fortress and hoping for the best were over. Until now, she had stood by as Ryan, Jamil, and the Central Station crew pursued this monster.

No longer. She was taking point. She was bringing the fight to him. He might be the Night Hunter but now Jessie was the one hunting him.

NOW AVAILABLE!

THE PERFECT MISTRESS
(A Jessie Hunt Psychological Suspense Thriller—Book Fifteen)

"A masterpiece of thriller and mystery. Blake Pierce did a magnificent job developing characters with a psychological side so well described that we feel inside their minds, follow their fears and cheer for their success. Full of twists, this book will keep you awake until the turn of the last page."
--Books and Movie Reviews, Roberto Mattos (re *Once Gone*)

THE PERFECT MISTRESS is book #15 in a new psychological suspense series by bestselling author Blake Pierce, which begins with *The Perfect Wife*, a #1 bestseller (and free download) with over 600 five-star reviews.

When wealthy suburban women are found murdered in their small town without rhyme or reason, Jessie soon realizes she is up against no ordinary killer. He is an unpredictable psychopath, beyond anyone she's ever been up against—and she will have to enter the dark canals of his twisted mind if she has any chance of saving the next woman on his list.

A fast-paced psychological suspense thriller with unforgettable characters and heart-pounding suspense, THE JESSIE HUNT series is a riveting new series that will leave you turning pages late into the night.

Book #16 (THE PERFECT IMAGE) will be available soon.

Blake Pierce

Blake Pierce is the USA Today bestselling author of the RILEY PAGE mystery series, which includes seventeen books. Blake Pierce is also the author of the MACKENZIE WHITE mystery series, comprising fourteen books; of the AVERY BLACK mystery series, comprising six books; of the KERI LOCKE mystery series, comprising five books; of the MAKING OF RILEY PAIGE mystery series, comprising six books; of the KATE WISE mystery series, comprising seven books; of the CHLOE FINE psychological suspense mystery, comprising six books; of the JESSE HUNT psychological suspense thriller series, comprising nineteen books; of the AU PAIR psychological suspense thriller series, comprising three books; of the ZOE PRIME mystery series, comprising six books; of the ADELE SHARP mystery series, comprising thirteen books, of the EUROPEAN VOYAGE cozy mystery series, comprising six books (and counting); of the new LAURA FROST FBI suspense thriller, comprising three books (and counting); of the new ELLA DARK FBI suspense thriller, comprising six books (and counting); of the A YEAR IN EUROPE cozy mystery series, comprising nine books, of the AVA GOLD mystery series, comprising three books (and counting); and of the RACHEL GIFT mystery series, comprising three books (and counting).

An avid reader and lifelong fan of the mystery and thriller genres, Blake loves to hear from you, so please feel free to visit www.blakepierceauthor.com to learn more and stay in touch.

BOOKS BY BLAKE PIERCE

RACHEL GIFT MYSTERY SERIES
HER LAST WISH (Book #1)
HER LAST CHANCE (Book #2)
HER LAST HOPE (Book #3)

AVA GOLD MYSTERY SERIES
CITY OF PREY (Book #1)
CITY OF FEAR (Book #2)
CITY OF BONES (Book #3)

A YEAR IN EUROPE
A MURDER IN PARIS (Book #1)
DEATH IN FLORENCE (Book #2)
VENGEANCE IN VIENNA (Book #3)
A FATALITY IN SPAIN (Book #4)
SCANDAL IN LONDON (Book #5)
AN IMPOSTOR IN DUBLIN (Book #6)
SEDUCTION IN BORDEAUX (Book #7)
JEALOUSY IN SWITZERLAND (Book #8)
A DEBACLE IN PRAGUE (Book #9)

ELLA DARK FBI SUSPENSE THRILLER
GIRL, ALONE (Book #1)
GIRL, TAKEN (Book #2)
GIRL, HUNTED (Book #3)
GIRL, SILENCED (Book #4)
GIRL, VANISHED (Book 5)
GIRL ERASED (Book #6)

LAURA FROST FBI SUSPENSE THRILLER
ALREADY GONE (Book #1)
ALREADY SEEN (Book #2)
ALREADY TRAPPED (Book #3)

EUROPEAN VOYAGE COZY MYSTERY SERIES
MURDER (AND BAKLAVA) (Book #1)
DEATH (AND APPLE STRUDEL) (Book #2)
CRIME (AND LAGER) (Book #3)

MISFORTUNE (AND GOUDA) (Book #4)
CALAMITY (AND A DANISH) (Book #5)
MAYHEM (AND HERRING) (Book #6)

ADELE SHARP MYSTERY SERIES
LEFT TO DIE (Book #1)
LEFT TO RUN (Book #2)
LEFT TO HIDE (Book #3)
LEFT TO KILL (Book #4)
LEFT TO MURDER (Book #5)
LEFT TO ENVY (Book #6)
LEFT TO LAPSE (Book #7)
LEFT TO VANISH (Book #8)
LEFT TO HUNT (Book #9)
LEFT TO FEAR (Book #10)
LEFT TO PREY (Book #11)
LEFT TO LURE (Book #12)
LEFT TO CRAVE (Book #13)

THE AU PAIR SERIES
ALMOST GONE (Book#1)
ALMOST LOST (Book #2)
ALMOST DEAD (Book #3)

ZOE PRIME MYSTERY SERIES
FACE OF DEATH (Book#1)
FACE OF MURDER (Book #2)
FACE OF FEAR (Book #3)
FACE OF MADNESS (Book #4)
FACE OF FURY (Book #5)
FACE OF DARKNESS (Book #6)

A JESSIE HUNT PSYCHOLOGICAL SUSPENSE SERIES
THE PERFECT WIFE (Book #1)
THE PERFECT BLOCK (Book #2)
THE PERFECT HOUSE (Book #3)
THE PERFECT SMILE (Book #4)
THE PERFECT LIE (Book #5)
THE PERFECT LOOK (Book #6)
THE PERFECT AFFAIR (Book #7)

THE PERFECT ALIBI (Book #8)
THE PERFECT NEIGHBOR (Book #9)
THE PERFECT DISGUISE (Book #10)
THE PERFECT SECRET (Book #11)
THE PERFECT FAÇADE (Book #12)
THE PERFECT IMPRESSION (Book #13)
THE PERFECT DECEIT (Book #14)
THE PERFECT MISTRESS (Book #15)
THE PERFECT IMAGE (Book #16)
THE PERFECT VEIL (Book #17)
THE PERFECT INDISCRETION (Book #18)
THE PERFECT RUMOR (Book #19)

CHLOE FINE PSYCHOLOGICAL SUSPENSE SERIES
NEXT DOOR (Book #1)
A NEIGHBOR'S LIE (Book #2)
CUL DE SAC (Book #3)
SILENT NEIGHBOR (Book #4)
HOMECOMING (Book #5)
TINTED WINDOWS (Book #6)

KATE WISE MYSTERY SERIES
IF SHE KNEW (Book #1)
IF SHE SAW (Book #2)
IF SHE RAN (Book #3)
IF SHE HID (Book #4)
IF SHE FLED (Book #5)
IF SHE FEARED (Book #6)
IF SHE HEARD (Book #7)

THE MAKING OF RILEY PAIGE SERIES
WATCHING (Book #1)
WAITING (Book #2)
LURING (Book #3)
TAKING (Book #4)
STALKING (Book #5)
KILLING (Book #6)

RILEY PAIGE MYSTERY SERIES
ONCE GONE (Book #1)